EVERLASTING EMBRACE

AMANDA ASHLEY

Everlasting Embrace

This book is published on behalf of the author by the Ethan Ellenberg Literary Agency.

You can reach the author at:
Email: darkwritr@aol.com
Website: www.amandaashley.net OR www.madelinebaker.net

EVERLASTING EMBRACE

Love comes in many guises. Little does Rylee Wagner realize that her chance encounter with a stranger on the beach will turn her whole life upside down. Her heart goes out to Alex when she learns he's mourning the deaths of his wife and unborn child. Still, there's no denying the instant attraction between them.

Alex O'Donnell is immediately drawn to Rylee. She's young and beautiful. Her compassion for his loss is a balm to his wounded soul. But there are things he can't share with her. Like the fact the he's a vampire hunter, or that a vindictive vampire is responsible for the deaths of his wife and child.

Alex knows he should stop seeing Rylee. Every minute he spends with her puts her life in danger. But once he holds her in his arms, he prays that it will be an everlasting embrace.

BOOKS BY AMANDA ASHLEY

"Born of the Night" in Stroke of Midnight
"Midnight Pleasures" in Darkfest
"Music of the Night" in Mammoth Book of Vampire Romance
A Darker Dream
A Fire in the Blood
A Whisper of Eternity
After Sundown
As Twilight Falls
Beauty's Beast
Beneath a Midnight Moon
Bound by Blood
Bound by Night
Dead Perfect
Dead Sexy
Deeper Than the Night
Desire After Dark
Desire the Night
Donovan's Woman
Embrace the Night
Everlasting Desire
Everlasting Embrace
Everlasting Kiss
His Dark Embrace
Immortal Sins
Jessie's Girl
Maiden's Song
Masquerade
Midnight and Moonlight
Midnight Embrace
Night's Kiss
Night's Master
Night's Mistress
Night's Pleasure
Night's Promise
Night's Surrender

Night's Touch
Quinn's Lady
Quinn's Revenge
Sandy's Angel
Seasons of the Night
Shades of Gray
Sunlight Moonlight
The Captive
The Music of the Night
Twilight Desires
Twilight Dreams

Dedication

*For my readers, who, like me,
can't get enough of Rhys.*

TABLE OF CONTENTS

Chapter 1

Alex O'Donnell stared at the headstone, his lips moving silently as he read the words hand-carved into the stone by his father.

Paula Jane O'Donnell
Beloved Wife and Daughter
Taken from us too soon

"Too soon," Alex murmured.

Unbidden, came the memory of the night just over four months ago when he had come home and found Paula dead. Guilt ate at his soul. Had he been home where he belonged, she would be alive today. But no, he had been determined to go out and make one last kill.

And it had cost him everything.

He remembered that night as if it had happened yesterday. Coming home, entering the kitchen through the garage door, knowing immediately that something was wrong…

He had stood there for several moments, letting his eyes adjust to the darkness, while he listened for any sound that would indicate an intruder was still in the house.

It hit him when he left the kitchen and stepped into the living room.

The scent of blood.

Fresh blood.

Adrenaline pumping, heart pounding, he ran down the hall toward the master bedroom and switched on the light.

Paula lay on the bed, her eyes wide and staring, a gaping hole in her throat. Splashes of bright-red blood stained the sheets, the pillow case beneath her head, the bodice of her nightgown, the bedroom walls.

Taking a deep breath, he moved woodenly toward the bed and dipped his fingers in her blood.

"They won't get away with this," he said hoarsely. "By your life's blood, I swear I'll find whoever did this and make them pay."

Turning away, he dropped to his knees and emptied the contents of his stomach on the floor. He had seen death before. Hell, he had caused a lot of it, although he wasn't sure you could kill a vampire since, technically, they were already dead. He had seen his brother, Brandon's, body after a female blood-sucker killed him. But this…

Alex closed his eyes and retched again.

When he could manage it, he regained his feet and covered her body with the bedspread.

It wasn't until he turned away from the ghastly scene that he saw the message scrawled in blood on the wall.

You killed my mate
I have killed yours
Rot in hell

Alex had stared at the words, his mind reeling. How had the vampire's lover found him? He had taken all the necessary precautions to ensure that he couldn't be traced. There was no license plate on his car to identify him. His home phone number was unlisted, his mailing address was a P.O. Box. He never carried any identification when he was on the hunt. He'd sprayed himself with Scent-B-Gone…

He swore a vile oath as he recalled that night. The bottle had been nearly empty. He should have gone home for more, but he had been so gung-ho to take one last head, he had used what little he'd had on hand and hoped it would be enough.

And Paula and his unborn child had paid the price for his impatience.

He glanced at the bed, seeing the blood-stained walls and sheets in his mind. This was the reason hunters rarely married. Family members made easy targets for blackmail and revenge. He had promised Paula he would give up hunting the Undead. If he had kept that promise, his wife would still be alive and his child with her...

"They won't get away with it," he said, reaffirming the vow of vengeance he had made the night she died. "By your life's blood, I swear I'll find whoever did this and make them pay." And then, as guilt and regret knifed through him, he whispered, "Forgive me, Paula."

The funeral had been surreal, the days that followed a nightmare from which he couldn't awake. The police had come by the house with follow-up questions. He had received numerous sympathy cards from friends that only served to emphasize his loss.

Day after day, he wandered through the empty house like a lost soul.

And maybe that's what he was.

What he always would be.

Chapter 2

Late the next night, his father stopped by. "How are you doing, son?" Noah O'Donnell asked.

Alex shrugged. Although he had been avoiding friends and family like the plague, he was suddenly glad to see his old man.

Noah followed him into the living room and sank into his favorite easy chair. Alex dropped down on the sofa, his hands shoved in the pockets of his jeans.

"Mom sends her love."

Alex nodded.

Silence fell between them. They hadn't talked about Paula or much of anything else since the funeral. Alex supposed his father's next words had been inevitable sooner or later.

"Do you have any idea who did it?"

Alex shook his head. The O'Donnells were descended from a long line of hunters. There wasn't much his old man didn't know about vampires. Noah had been hunting the creatures for over thirty-five years. In that time, he had acquired a vast store of knowledge about the current Undead community.

"What was the name of that vampire you destroyed a while back?" Noah asked.

"He was going by the name of Eduardo Tietjen. My informant said the vamp had been on a killing spree that covered three states. All his victims were young girls. The parents of the deceased kids got together and came up with a sizeable reward."

Noah grunted softly. "I've heard of Tietjen. He was one of the old ones."

"Yeah. He turned to ash as soon as I staked him." Only very old vampires did that. The rest just sort of shriveled up.

"I'll see what I can find out," Noah said. "In the meantime, try to get some rest. You look like hell."

Alex nodded. That pretty much summed up the way he felt, too.

They made small talk for another few minutes before Noah stood. "Call your mother. She's worried about you."

"I will."

Noah regarded his son for several moments, then wrapped him in a bear hug. "It's only been a few months, my boy. It will get easier with time. I'll let you know if I get a lead on Tietjen's mate."

"Thanks." He followed his dad outside and watched him drive away.

"Vampires." Alex spat the word as he went inside and closed the door. He had hunted them all his adult life, hated them for the blood-sucking monsters they were, for the people they thoughtlessly killed, the innocent lives they ruined. His own brother had been murdered by a vampire. And in a cruel twist of fate, his sister, Daisy, had fallen in love with one of the creatures.

Of course, now that Alex had met a few vampires up close and personal, and since Daisy had recently joined the ranks of the Undead, he tended to view them in a whole new light. Not long ago, he had condemned them all as wholly evil, soulless monsters that were beyond any hope of redemption. But Daisy wasn't some mindless killing machine who preyed on the lives of innocents, and neither was her husband, Erik Delacourt. Even the feared Master of the West Coast vampires, Rhys Costain, had proved to have an unexpected streak of humanity.

Alex blew out a sigh. His sweet little sister, a vampire. Maybe it was ironic justice, since she had once been a Blood Thief, stealing blood from vampires while they slept and then selling it on the Internet. It was a lucrative business for those brave enough to attempt it.

Muttering an oath, Alex filled a glass with Jack Daniels. Carrying the bottle with him, he slumped into the easy chair beside the fireplace and stretched his legs out in front of him.

He drained the glass in his hand in a single swallow, then poured himself another shot. He had never been much of a drinker, but the way he felt tonight, he knew all the whiskey in the world wouldn't be enough to ease the pain or erase his guilt. Still, it didn't stop him from filling his glass a third time.

And then a fourth.

He had thought about calling his sister after his father left until he remembered she was bound for some remote island with her vampire husband.

Even if she'd been home, Daisy wouldn't be able to help him. But Rhys Costain…ah, Rhys Costain, venerable Master of the West Coast vampires, might be just the answer. If anyone could help him find the bloodsucker who had killed Paula and the baby, it was good ole Rhys.

Alex stared into his glass, his thoughts going back in time. He and his sister had been hunting vampires the first time they encountered The Master of the West Coast vampires. Of course, they hadn't known it was Costain's lair when they found it.

Alex grinned wryly at the memory. He had gone inside to take the vampire's head and come darn close to losing his own instead.

He and Costain had a hell of a history, first fighting each other and then teaming up to defeat Tomás Villagrande, a murdering bloodsucker who'd had his eye on destroying Costain and taking over as Master of the West Coast vampires. It had taken Daisy, Erik, Costain, Costain's lady love, Megan, and Alex to corner the ancient vampire. It had been Costain who had delivered the final, killing blow.

Downing another shot, Alex grinned. "Hell of a battle," he muttered.

It wasn't a fight he was likely to forget. He had suffered a couple of broken ribs, a sprained ankle and a broken arm in the brief, bloody battle.

During the fight, he had let Costain feed on him. Which meant the Master of the West Coast vampires owed him a favor.

"You're indebted to me, ole buddy," he mumbled as he staggered down the hall to the guest room. "Yep, you owe me big, and it's time to pay up."

Late the following night, Alex stood in the middle of the master bedroom and knew he couldn't stay in the house any longer. Sure, he could buy a new bed. He could paint the walls and replace the carpet, but he would never forget what had happened here.

After packing a few things, he called his parents and asked them to put the house up for sale.

"Are you sure that's for the best, son?" his father asked. "You probably shouldn't be making any important decisions just now."

"I'm sure."

"What about the furniture?"

Fighting back tears, Alex said, "Sell it. Give it away. I don't care. Put Paula's stuff and mine in storage for now. I don't know when I'll be back."

"Where are you going?"

"I'm leaving for Los Angeles first thing in the morning."

Looking concerned, Noah said, "Keep in touch, son. We're here if you need us."

"I know. Thanks, Dad. Give my love to mom. And tell her not to worry. I'll call her soon."

After disconnecting the call, Alex took one last look around, then walked out the front door.

He didn't look back.

Chapter 3

Alex felt like hell when he reached Los Angeles. It was close to 3 p.m. by the time the plane landed and he claimed his luggage. After renting a car, he drove to Hollywood, checked into the first hotel he saw, and hit the sheets.

He felt a little better when he woke four-and-a-half hours later. He took a quick shower, decided to skip dinner, and drove out to Costain's night club, *La Mort Rouge.*

The Red Death, located on a deserted stretch of highway outside the city, catered to an elite clientele. According to Daisy, only vampires—and mortals who got their kicks from nourishing the Undead—were allowed entrance.

After parking the car, Alex sprinted across the parking lot and knocked on the door. A tall man clad in a black suit, an impeccable white shirt, and a long black cloak opened the door.

"May I help you, sir?" He had a voice reminiscent of Lurch from the Addams Family.

"I'm looking for Costain."

"Is he expecting you?"

"No, but I think he'll see me."

"Who shall I say is calling?"

"Alex O'Donnell."

The man's face remained impassive, but a slight twitch of one brow made Alex suspect the doorman had heard his name before.

Taking a step back, Lurch said, "This way."

A narrow hallway illuminated by candlelight opened onto the club's main room. A bar stretched along the far wall. High-backed booths lined one side of the room. A grand piano stood on a raised platform in the far corner. Not surprisingly, the lighting was subdued. Music with a dark, sensual beat filtered through the sound system. A handful of couples sat at the half-dozen small, damask-covered tables located at intervals around the room. An ebony vase containing a single blood-red rose sat in the center of each table. The walls were covered with dark red paper, the floor was polished oak.

Alex noted several women, all beautiful, all wearing tags bearing French names, as he followed the Lurch sound-alike up a short flight of stairs.

The man nodded at the door located to the right of the stairs, then took his leave.

Alex was about to knock when the door opened and Rhys Costain stood there.

Tall and slim, the vampire had short, dark-blond hair and inscrutable brown eyes. Although Costain was over five hundred years old, he didn't look a day over twenty-one.

Costain stared at him, one brow raised. "What the hell are you doing here?"

"I need a favor."

"As long as you're not here to try to take my head. *Again*." Costain retreated into his office, calling, "Come in," over his shoulder.

Alex shivered as he crossed the threshold and felt the vampire's inherent preternatural power wash over him. A quick glance showed walls papered in a dark red-and-gold stripe that made Alex think of Old West brothels. Plush gold carpeting covered the floor. A pair of antique oak filing cabinets stood against one wall. The chair behind the chrome-and-glass desk was rich black leather. There were no windows in the room.

Standing hipshot against a corner of his desk, Costain gestured at a red velvet chair.

Alex hesitated a moment, then took a seat.

Rhys crossed his arms over his chest as he regarded Daisy's brother. He wasn't sure he liked O'Donnell, but he respected him. "What kind of favor are you looking for?"

Alex cleared his throat. "I killed a vampire name of Eduardo Tietjen a few months back. The night after I took his head, someone murdered my wife. They left me a note, written in Paula's blood, saying I'd killed their mate and they had killed mine." Alex took a deep breath. "They killed more than my wife. They killed our unborn child."

"I see. So, you want me to hunt this vampire down and take her out?"

"No. I want you to tell me where I can find her so I can do it."

"That might cause some trouble for you with the Master of the East Coast vampires."

"But I thought…" Alex frowned. "When you destroyed Villagrande, didn't that make you Master of the East Coast?"

"As soon as word got out that Villagrande had been destroyed, a vampire by the name of Morag declared she was taking over the East Coast." Costain lifted one shoulder in a negligent shrug. "More power to her if she can hold it and the Southern states, too."

"You didn't want to take Villagrande's place?"

"Hell, no. I've got enough to look after here." A slow grin spread over Costain's face. "Besides, I'd rather spend my time with my woman."

"How is Megan?"

"Never better. She's gone to England and Scotland with her parents."

"Why didn't you go?"

Rhys shrugged. "They asked me, but they didn't really want me along. Anyway, I thought it would be good for Megan to spend some time alone with her folks."

"So they're okay with her new lifestyle?"

"I'm not sure *okay* is the word I would use, but they've accepted it. Not that I gave them any choice."

"You forced the change on Megan?"

"In a way. She got hit by a car and was in a coma. After a few weeks, the doctor informed her parents there wasn't much hope for recovery."

"So you took things into your own hands."

"Damn right. I carried her to my lair. Turning her was the biggest risk I've ever taken. Thankfully, the change brought her back to me."

"I guess accepting the change was their only option if they wanted to see their daughter again."

"Exactly," Rhys said.

Alex rested his elbows on the arms of the chair and leaned forward. "Do you know who Tietjen's mate is?"

"No. All I know about him is that he spent most of his time back east. But I'll ask around and see what I can find out."

"Thanks."

"Where are you staying?"

"At the Roosevelt over on Hollywood Boulevard." Ironically, he'd been given Room 212, the same room Carl Kolchak had used back in 1974 in an episode of the *Night Stalker* titled "The Vampire."

"Nice place. I spent a few nights there shortly after it was built back in 1927. Lots of big time movie stars stayed there back in the thirties and forties—Fairbanks, Pickford, Gable and Lombard."

"Yeah?"

Rhys nodded. "They say Marilyn Monroe's ghost still haunts the place. Montgomery Clift's, too, if you believe in that sort of thing."

"Do you? Believe in ghosts?"

"I've never seen one, but what the hell, I've seen a lot of other strange things. What about you?"

Alex shrugged. "I've never given it any thought."

Rhys regarded O'Donnell curiously for a moment. "Tell me something. Have you changed your mind about what we talked about last year?"

"No." Alex shuddered, remembering that Costain had offered him the Dark Gift at the time. It's bad enough having a sister and a brother-in-law who are vampires."

"From what I hear, Daisy's got no complaints."

Alex shrugged. "Maybe not right now. It's all still new to her. Hell, it might even be exciting. But it ain't natural, and it ain't right."

"Who's to say what's right?" Rhys asked, his voice harsh.

"Well, I guess a man who's killed as many people as you have wouldn't see anything wrong with it."

"Sounds like the pot calling the kettle black to me, hunter," he said, emphasizing the last word. "Isn't that what hunters do? Kill?"

"Big difference. Your kind are already dead. And I don't prey on people to survive." Alex raked his fingers through his hair.

Rhys crossed his arms over his chest. "You're right. I've killed in my time, and enjoyed doing it. But that was then, and this is now."

"What happened?" Alex asked, his voice thick with sarcasm. "Did you suddenly find religion?"

"No," Rhys said, smiling. "I found Megan."

Alex snorted disdainfully. "Don't tell me. You were saved by the love of a good woman."

"Scoff if you must, but it's the truth. She changed my life."

"And now she's like you."

"Megan will never be like me," Rhys said quietly. "Turning her into a vampire didn't make her a monster. She's still the same warm, sweet, caring woman she's always been."

"Uh-huh. From what I hear, things didn't work out so well for her best friend."

"As I told Megan, becoming a vampire brings out the best— or the worst—in people. It brought out the worst in Shirl. And in myself, in the beginning." Rhys looked thoughtful for a moment. "If Shirl hadn't thrown in with Villagrande, she might still be alive."

"Yeah? Well, this little stroll down memory lane isn't getting me any closer to finding out who killed my wife."

Rhys pushed away from the desk. "If I hear anything about Tietjen, I'll let you know."

"I'd appreciate it," Alex said, rising. "Give my best to Megan when you see her."

Rhys closed the door behind Alex, his brow furrowed thoughtfully. Once a hunter, always a hunter, he mused. But then, it was bred into the boy's genes. His father, brother, and sister had all been hunters of one kind or another.

Still, he owed the kid a favor and he always paid his debts.

A thought took Rhys to the new council headquarters down by the beach. Since Tomás Villagrande had burned the old house to the ground last year, Rhys had bought a new place. It was a small, single-story house, the wood siding weathered and gray. A white picket fence surrounded the yard. The scent of the ocean was strong, accented by the whooshing of waves endlessly rushing to the shore.

Since the house was rarely used except for occasional meetings, only the living room was furnished. Two butter-soft brown leather sofas faced each other in the middle of the room. A pair of over-stuffed leather chairs flanked a recently acquired walnut coffee table. There were no carpets in the house, and no other furnishings.

He had summoned the Vampire Council earlier that evening, instructing them to convene at midnight. When he opened the door, an indrawn breath told him they were all waiting inside. The council had shrunk considerably since Tomás Villagrande's visit to the city. Of the six former members, only Rupert Moss, Julius Romano and Nicholas remained.

Villagrande had destroyed the others.

Since then, Rhys had brought another member on board. Randolph Morris was a recently-turned vampire who kept his primary lair in Bozeman, Montana. He was a short, rotund man in his mid-thirties, with frizzy red hair, pale-blue eyes, and a liberal sprinkling of freckles across his too-large nose. He was, Rhys thought, the most unlikely looking vampire he had ever known.

The members of the council all looked at him expectantly when he entered the room. Rupert occupied one sofa. Dressed in unrelieved black from head to foot, he sported a pencil-thin mustache and wore his black hair slicked back, which only added to his resemblance to a 1930s matinee idol.

Gray-haired, tall, angular and wrinkled, Nicholas slouched in one of the chairs. He wore a natty, gray pin-striped suit over a crisp white shirt and tie. He had been turned when he was in his mid-seventies. Rhys knew very little about the man, since Nick rarely talked about what he had done before being turned. He spent most of his time in Arizona.

Julius stood with one shoulder propped against the mantel, idly paring his fingernails with a switchblade. In his former life, he had been a drug dealer on the mean streets of East Los Angeles, and he looked the part. He had dark brown hair and close-set brown eyes that were constantly moving. A red-and-black snake tattoo ran the length of his left arm from wrist to shoulder.

Morris sat on the other sofa, one foot tapping nervously on the floor, his expression uncertain.

"So," Rupert drawled, "what are we here for?"

"It isn't another rogue vampire, is it?" Nicholas asked, grimacing. "We haven't recovered from the last one."

"An acquaintance of mine is looking for information on a recently deceased vampire who went by the name of Tietjen," Rhys said. "Any of you ever heard of him?"

"Eduardo Tietjen?" Julius asked.

"You know him?"

Julius caressed the head of the snake on his arm. "I met him in Tijuana when I was a fledgling. He's the one who created my tattoo."

"He was a tattoo artist?" Rupert asked. "Seems like an odd occupation for a vampire."

Julius shrugged. "He was good at it. Who killed him?"

"It doesn't matter." Rhys dropped into the vacant chair. "What else do you know about him?"

"Not much," Julius said. "He was a little over four hundred years old, used to like to hang out in Tijuana and Cabo San Lucas."

"Ah, the good life," Nicholas said with a wistful smile. "I honeymooned in Cabo many years ago. Of course, it wasn't the popular place it is today when Miriam and I stayed there…"

"You can reminisce later," Rhys said, his voice sharp. "Go on, Julius, did Tietjen have a girlfriend? A wife? A significant other?"

"Not that I know of."

"Do you know who turned him?"

"He claimed it was Sandoval, but I don't know if that's true. I always thought Tietjen said it just to make himself seem important."

Rhys swore softly. Sandoval was a six-hundred-year-old vampire who kept his permanent lair in Spain. A vampire's powers grew stronger as he aged. Those under a hundred were considered young; those over five hundred—like himself - were considered ancient.

"I'll get in touch with Sandoval," Rhys said. "In the meantime, if any of you hear anything, let me know."

Moments later, Rhys was alone in the house. He had no desire to play nursemaid to Daisy's brother, but he owed the man a life debt, and it had to be paid.

Chapter 4

Strolling along the shore at Seal Beach, Alex kicked a clump of seaweed out of his path. He had little hope that Costain would learn anything helpful, but he'd had no one else to turn to.

Hands clenched at his sides, Alex dropped down on the sand and stared out at the ocean. The moon's light danced over the surface of the waves as they rushed toward the shore and then receded. Millions of stars lit the sky. Paula had loved the beach.

He swore a vile oath. What the hell was he doing here?

Destroying the vampire who killed his wife and unborn child wouldn't bring either one of them back. Most likely, it would only lead to more killing, perhaps even his own destruction. And what the hell did it matter? His brother was dead. Paula and the baby were dead. Daisy was a vampire. Sure, his parents would miss him, but they had each other. And what did he have? Nothing but a shit load of guilt and remorse.

He rubbed his fingers together as he remembered the warm sticky feeling of Paula's blood on his hands. He wouldn't rest—couldn't rest—until he had fulfilled his vow to avenge her death and that of their unborn child. And if he died in the attempt, so be it.

He stared into the distance. Catalina Island was out there somewhere. Paula had mentioned wanting to take a trip to the island to see the flying fish and ride on a glass-bottom boat after the baby was born.

Muttering an oath, he pulled his cell phone out of his pocket and connected to the Internet. Once online, he found the hunter website on the Dark Web, clicked on Vampires Wanted, then refined his search to those residing in Southern California. There were half a dozen—four male and two female.

He was mapping the location of the nearest male when Costain hunkered down beside him.

"Dammit, man, don't do that!" Alex exclaimed.

"Sorry," Rhys said with a wry grin. "Want me to ring a warning bell next time?"

Alex glared at the vampire.

Rhys jerked his chin at Alex's cell phone. "Looking for anyone in particular?"

"No." Alex slid the phone into his back pocket.

"You aren't thinking of hunting in my territory, are you?" The vampire's tone was mild enough but his eyes were hard as flint.

"What if I was?"

"I wouldn't advise it, but you do what you want."

"Is that a threat?"

"Consider it a warning. Any vampires in my territory are here under my protection. It would be considered a breach of etiquette if they were destroyed."

"Breach of etiquette?" Alex said, grimacing. "Give me a break."

"You have a lot to learn."

"How'd you find me? Oh, right!" Alex said, with a snap of his fingers. "I gave you my blood." It was an experience he wasn't likely to forget.

"That was a hell of a night." Rhys remarked. "And a hell of a fight. We were damn lucky."

More than lucky, Alex thought. Their encounter with Tomás Villagrande, the Mast of the East Coast Vampires, had been epic. Villagrande had been the world's oldest vampire. Not long ago, he had decided he wanted a change of scene and made his way to the West Coast, leaving one body after another in his wake. Once he arrived, he had decided to challenge Costain for the city. It was a battle Alex wasn't likely to forget.

It had taken Alex, Erik, Daisy, Megan, and Rhys to defeat Villagrande In the heat of battle, with Rhys down and almost out, Alex had dragged himself across the floor and offered Rhys his blood. Rhys hadn't taken much, but it had given the vampire the strength he needed to stay in the fight. In the end, Rhys had driven a stake into Villagrande's heart. In moments, the ancient vampire's body began to shrink in on itself, the flesh melting away, the bones disintegrating, until there was nothing left but dust.

Alex grinned inwardly. In days gone by, minstrels would have written songs about the battle, elegies would have been written. It had been strange, fighting alongside Costain instead of against him. No doubt about it—love, war, and politics made for strange bedfellows or, in Alex's case, drinking partners.

It hadn't been the first time Alex had let a vampire feed off him. He had fed Daisy's husband, too. And Daisy's husband had shared blood with him, although Alex had no memory of that. It had happened the day they had stumbled onto Costain's lair, although they hadn't known it was his at the time. Rhys had awakened before Alex could take his head. He didn't remember much after that. Daisy had told him she'd gotten worried because he'd been gone so long, rushed into the house and found him on the floor—covered in his own blood—trying to fight off the Costain. She'd thrown holy water in the vampire's face and managed to drag Alex out of there. With nowhere else to turn, Daisy had taken him to Erik.

Alex glanced at Costain. "What are you doing here?" he asked, shoving the memory aside.

Costain shrugged. "Nothing better to do with Megan out of town."

"Did you find out anything about Tietjen?"

"Nothing concrete."

"I knew it was a long shot," Alex said. "To tell you the truth, I didn't really expect to learn anything here. I just needed to get away." Away from the pity in his parents' eyes, the sadness and accusation in the eyes of Paula's family. Away from the house where she had been murdered.

"I'm sorry for your loss," Rhys said quietly.

"Thanks. I don't suppose death means much to you."

"It's a part of life." Rhys stared out at the water, his expression pensive. "I've watched a lot people die."

"I guess it's something you get used to when you've lived as long as you have."

"Yeah."

Alex picked up a handful of sand and watched the grains trickle through his fingers.

"Like sands through the hour glass," Rhys muttered with a wry grin.

Alex dusted off his hands. "Very funny."

"My offer to bring you across still stands."

"No, thanks, I like being human." But he couldn't help remembering the picture Costain had once painted in his mind. *You're judging a way of life for which you have no experience,* the vampire had told him. *You have no idea what it's like to have the strength of twenty men, to be able to transform into mist, to move faster than the human eye can follow, to scale a building or leap a barrier with no effort at all, to cross the country with a thought, to see and hear and touch the world in ways that mortals can never know. You wouldn't believe how addicting that power can be.*

"Well," Rhys said, "if you change your mind, you know where to find me."

"Yeah."

Alex watched Costain rise effortlessly to his feet and then, between one heartbeat and the next, the vampire was gone.

Costain sounded like a recruiter for the Undead, Alex mused, spouting all that crap about how great it was to be a vampire. What was so terrific about drinking blood and living only at night? Sure, it might be fun to have all those paranormal abilities, but he liked barbequing on summer days, feeling the warmth of the sun on his face, savoring his mother's devil's food cake. He liked cooking and even more than cooking, he liked eating. He wondered if Daisy ever regretted her decision to become a vampire. Their parents had been shocked when they learned Erik had turned their daughter, but when your parents were hunters, their initial horror was to be expected.

Alex shook his head. One vampire in the family was more than enough.

He was on his way back to his car when something that looked like a small horse plowed into him, knocking him flat on his back.

A moment later, he heard a voice calling, "Max! Max! Come back here!"

Alex was trying to dislodge the slobbering beast from his chest when a woman ran up and snapped a leash on the St. Bernard's collar.

"I'm so sorry," she said. "He's not very well-trained. Are you all right?"

"Yeah, fine." Rising, he wiped his face on his shirt sleeve.

"Are you sure?"

"Positive." She looked like an angel in the moon's pale light. Her long, golden hair was pulled back in a tail. Her eyes were light—blue or gray—he couldn't be sure. The top of her head just reached his shoulder. She wore a pair of cut-off blue jeans and a red t-shirt that said *Photographers do it in the dark.*

"Well, as long as you're all right, I'll be going." She dug into her pocket and handed him a crisp white business card edged in gold. "If you ever need your picture taken, give me a call."

"Will do."

"I'm really sorry," she said again. Taking a firm hold on the dog's leash, she turned and jogged back toward the pier.

Alex stared after her, then called, "Hey, wait up," and ran after her.

"Don't tell me," she said dryly, "all of sudden, your back is hurting and you know a good lawyer."

"What? No. No, nothing like that. I just thought, well, maybe I could buy you a cup of coffee."

"I don't think so."

"Then maybe you could buy me one? I mean, after all, it's the least you can do after that monster dog attacked me."

She laughed, a full-throated sound filled with merriment. "Do you know where the Java Hut is?"

"No."

"When you leave the parking lot, turn left. Go down two blocks. It's on the right side of the street. I'll meet you there in…" She glanced at her watch. "Twenty minutes."

"Twenty minutes," Alex said, then wondered what the hell he was doing. He was here to find out who killed his wife, not hook up with some curvy blond.

But fifteen minutes later, he was sitting at a front booth in the Java Hut Café.

After handing Max over to his owner, Rylee packed up her cameras and her tripod, grabbed her backpack, and jogged down the beach to the parking lot. After stowing her gear in the trunk, she slid behind the wheel and turned the car toward home.

Rylee slowed as she neared the traffic light at the corner. She never should have told that guy on the beach she would meet him at the Hut, but the pain in the depths of his eyes, the wistfulness in his smile, had touched her heart. Her invite had been impulsive and one she now regretted. With the recent killings in the city, a girl had to be out of her mind to meet a complete stranger at this time of night.

So, she was surprised to find herself making a U-turn at the next light and heading back toward the café.

She found him sitting at a table near the front, staring out the window, apparently so lost in thought he was unaware of her presence until she cleared her throat.

"I didn't think you'd come," he remarked, looking up at her.

"I wasn't going to." Rylee shook her head. "I really don't know why I'm here."

He gestured at the chair across from his. "Well, now that you are, you might as well take a load off."

Rylee hesitated a moment, then sat down.

"I'm Alex," he said, offering her a faint smile. Up close, he saw that her eyes were the clear, light blue of early morning. "Nice to meet you, Miss Wagner."

Her brows shot up in surprise. "How did you know my name?" she asked, her voice tinged with suspicion.

"I read your business card."

"Oh, of course. Call me Rylee." She hadn't paid much attention to his looks earlier but now, in the well-lit café, she couldn't help noticing that he was a tall, good-looking guy with an athletic build, a tan that spoke of hours spent in the sun, dark brown hair and brown eyes.

"Nice to meet you, Rylee. Where's the mutt?"

"Oh, Max isn't mine. I borrowed him for the shoot tonight."

Alex jerked his chin toward her t-shirt. "So, you really are a photographer?"

"Yes, free-lance. It doesn't pay much, but I love it. Do you live around here?"

"No, I'm here on…on business." He glanced at the menu as the waitress headed their way. Rylee opted for a bacon, lettuce and tomato sandwich and a Coke. Alex decided on a cheeseburger, fries, and coffee.

"So," Rylee said when the waitress left to turn in their order, "where are you from?"

"Oregon, originally. I live in Boston now."

She glanced pointedly at his wedding ring. "Is your wife here with you?"

Taking a deep breath, he released it in a long, slow sigh. "No."

Rylee bit down on her lower lip, wishing she hadn't said anything. Alex didn't have to say his wife was deceased. It explained the pain in his eyes. "I'm sorry."

He pushed away from the table. "This probably wasn't a good idea."

"Alex…"

"I'm afraid I'm not very good company." He dropped a twenty on the table. "It was nice meeting you," he murmured, and headed for the door.

Rylee stared after him, sorely tempted to follow him, to take him in her arms and comfort him. And how silly was that? She'd only spent a few minutes with the man and didn't really know anything about him—except that he was hurting deep inside. And yet she couldn't help feeling that he needed her.

She hurried outside, hoping to catch him, but she was too late.

He was already gone.

Chapter 5

Rhys gave Babette an affectionate pat on the rump, kissed her cheek, and left the room. She was a pretty young thing, with short curly black hair and the brightest green eyes he had ever seen. Like all the mortals who frequented *La Mort Rouge,* Babette got her kicks by letting vampires feed off her. There had been a time, before Megan, when he would have taken more than her blood, but he was a married man now, bound to one woman. He had a lot of faults, but infidelity wasn't one of them.

He paused on his way to the office. Was that Alex sitting at the end of the bar? What the devil was he doing back here?

Giving in to an uncharacteristic bout of curiosity, Rhys moved swiftly across the floor and took the seat beside O'Donnell's. He jerked his chin at the empty shot glass in front of the kid. "Can I buy you another?"

"Sure."

Rhys signaled for the bartender. "I'll have a glass of port," he said. "And bring my friend whatever he's drinking. And leave the bottle. He looks like he needs it."

With a nod, the bartender hurried away.

Rhys braced his elbow on the bar and studied the kid's face. "What brings you back here?"

"Didn't have any place else to go." Alex picked up his glass as soon as the bartender refilled it and downed the shot in a single swallow.

"You might want to go slow with that."

Alex shrugged as he poured himself another. "I got nowhere to go and nobody waiting for me when I get there."

"Instead of getting wasted, why don't you find Babette and go make use of room number three?"

Alex glared at him. "Are you crazy? My wife just died."

"I'm not telling you to fall in love with the girl. I just thought a little recreational sex might take your mind off your troubles for a while."

"Yeah, well, thanks for the offer, but I don't think so."

"Come on," Rhys said. "Let's get out of here. Bring the bottle, if you like."

"Where are we going?"

"My lair."

"Where's that?"

Taking hold of Alex's arm, Rhys said, "I have a little penthouse apartment in a high-rise in West Hollywood."

And the next thing Alex knew, they were there. Looking around, he couldn't help being impressed as his feet sank into plush blue-gray carpet that must have been two inches thick. Matching black leather sofas faced each other in front of a white marble fireplace veined in gold. A life-sized statue of a golden-haired Madonna stood in one corner.

Alex gestured at the figure, one brow raised in amusement. "A Madonna? Seriously?"

"Beautiful, isn't she?"

"Yeah. I just never thought of you as the religious type."

Rhys shrugged. He had stolen the statue from a Catholic church three centuries ago.

Alex looked at the painting over the fireplace. "Is that an original?"

"A Botticelli."

"Must be nice to be rich."

"Indeed. Sit down." Rhys gestured at the bottle of Jack Daniels clutched in O'Donnell's hand. "Can I get you a glass, or do you want to just drink it straight from the source?"

"I'll take a glass," Alex said, dropping down on a corner of the sofa nearest him. "Thanks."

Rhys splashed some port from a crystal decanter into a goblet, then handed the glass to Alex before taking a seat on the other sofa. "You can drink yourself into oblivion tonight," he remarked as the kid filled his glass. "But the pain will still be there tomorrow."

"I guess you know all about pain, having caused so much of it."

"You might want to choose your words with a little more care, hunter."

"Yeah. Sorry," Alex mumbled.

Leaning back, Rhys stretched his legs out in front of him. "I never understood why it was okay for your kind to kill mine, but not for my kind to kill yours."

"You don't just kill us," Alex said, his words slurring. "You feed on us. Whoever killed my wife drank her blood before they ripped out her throat. It ain't right." He slammed his hand on the arm of the sofa. "Drank her blood," he said again, his eyes haunted. "Killed my son. My son. Damn vampire," he mumbled, and toppled over sideways on the sofa.

Rhys caught the glass and the bottle before they hit the floor. Setting both on a nearby table, he lifted Alex's legs onto the sofa. "You poor stupid fool," he muttered, shoving a throw pillow under the kid's head. "You're gonna get yourself killed."

Alex woke with a groan. He'd had hangovers before, he mused, but this was the mother of them all. The last thing he remembered was passing out on one of the sofas in Costain's lair. He had no recollection of how he'd made it back to his hotel room. A glance at his watch told him it was a quarter-to-three.

He groaned again. His head throbbed relentlessly. The light hurt his eyes, the ticking of the clock echoed like thunder in his ears. Sitting up resulted in a wave of nausea that sent him sprinting for the bathroom. The whiskey that had tasted so great going down tasted a hell of a lot worse coming back up.

Standing on shaky legs, he brushed his teeth, rinsed his mouth, then staggered back to the bedroom. Picking up the hotel phone, he dialed room service. The last thing he felt like doing was eating, but his old man swore that a bacon, egg, and cheese omelet washed down by a cup of hot black coffee was a sure-fire cure for a hangover.

After putting in his order, he headed for the shower. He stood under the spray for ten minutes, his forehead resting on the cool tile. After drying off, he tugged on a pair of clean jeans and a t-shirt.

His order arrived a short time later.

He forced himself to eat, then sacked out on the sofa.

When he woke again, he felt marginally better, though his head still throbbed. He pulled on his boots, grabbed his jacket, then looked around for his keys. He found them on the dresser, along with a note from Rhys, that read:

I'm not your mother or your keeper. Either stay sober or stay home.

"Good advice," Alex muttered. Tearing up the note, he grabbed his keys and his wallet and left the hotel.

He drove around until dark, then headed back to the beach where he had met Rylee. He knew the odds were slim to none that she would be there again tonight, but there had been something about her that he couldn't forget. Something that made him almost desperate to see her again.

After parking the car, he strolled along the shore line, all the while telling himself it was a waste of time.

But sometimes, when a man's at the end of his rope, Fate takes pity on him.

He hadn't gone far when he saw Rylee walking barefooted along the shore. She smiled uncertainly when she saw him.

"I'm sorry about last night," Alex said. "I shouldn't have run out on you like that."

"It's all right."

"No, it's not. My mom always said there's no good excuse for bad manners."

"Don't worry about it. I could see you were upset about something."

"Yeah, well, my wife passed away some months ago. I'm still trying to cope with it."

"I'm so sorry."

"Can I walk with you for a while? I mean, unless you need to go?"

"Walking is good," she said.

They strolled in silence for several minutes before he said, "I came down here hoping to find you."

She smiled up at him. "What a coincidence. I came hoping to see you again."

Her smile, the warmth of her words, was like a balm to his troubled soul. "Tell me about yourself," he said. "What do you like to do for fun?"

"Everything! Surfing, beach parties, Disneyland, movies. And roller coasters—the higher and faster, the better."

"Favorite color?"

"Hot pink, of course," she said, pointing at her t-shirt. This one said, *Never play leapfrog with a unicorn*.

"Favorite movie?"

"Oh, too many to name. How about you?"

"The Lord of the Rings trilogy."

"Which character are you?"

"I always thought of myself as Sam, but Daisy—she's my sister— she thinks I'm Aragon."

Rylee studied him a minute, then nodded. "I can see that."

"Favorite song?"

She brushed a lock of wind-blown hair away from her cheek. "Anything by Toby Keith."

"Ah," he said with a smile. "Country girl."

"All the way. How about you?"

"Anything but rap and hip hop."

"How long are you going to be in town?"

He paused to gaze out at the ocean. Moonlight shimmered on the face of the water. Far off in the distance, he heard the lonely wail of a foghorn. He glanced sideways to find Rylee looking up at him. "I don't know. Probably longer than I first thought."

"I'm glad. Would you like to talk about what's bothering you? I'm a good listener."

Alex hesitated a moment. Then, staring out at the ocean again, he said, "My wife, Paula, was engaged to my brother before I married her. When he passed away, she and I spent a lot of time together. We both loved him and it eased the pain a little, sharing time together, talking about Brandon. She was lonely. I was lonely." He shrugged. "We never should have married. You can't build a lasting relationship on shared grief. I loved her, but I wasn't *in* love with her. Do you know what I mean? Once the newness wore off, we both realized we'd made a mistake. But by then she was pregnant. The baby made a difference, gave us a reason to stay together."

Rylee laid her hand on his arm and gave it a squeeze.

"The baby died with her."

"Oh, Alex, you really have been through hell, haven't you?" Wanting to comfort him, wondering if she would be rebuffed, Rylee took a deep breath and then slipped her arms around him. "I'm so sorry for your loss," she said, blinking back her tears. "I wish there was something I could say, something I could do, that would make it better."

"You are," he murmured. "Just by being here." He rested his forehead against hers. "This is crazy. I hardly know you, and yet..."

"It seems like we've known each other forever," she said, finishing his thought for him.

"Yeah. But it's..."

"Bad timing," she said glumly. "I know. You're still grieving and you live in Boston and..."

"And there's things about me that you don't know." He moved away from her, then stared at the waves lapping at his feet. Vampires had no civil rights. There were no regulations against hunting the

Undead, no laws against taking heads or selling vampire blood on the Internet. Law enforcement agencies, doctors, nurses, and people in similar occupations knew vampires existed, but, for the most part, no one mentioned the Undead community. For obvious reasons, both hunters and vampires kept a low profile.

Rylee crossed her arms under her breasts. "I understand. Like I said, bad timing."

"Rylee…"

"Don't. I'm a big girl. I can take a hint."

Alex dragged a hand over his jaw. He wasn't sure what he wanted to say, but whatever it was, he was going about it all wrong. "Listen…"

"No, it's all right," she said, her words coming out in a rush. "It's just that I'm a little confused. I mean, you said you came here hoping to find me and now…"

Not knowing how else to shut her up, Alex pulled her into his arms and kissed her. And for one brief moment, he forgot everything except the warmth of her lips, the certainty that she was what he had been looking for his whole life.

Taking a step back, he blew out a breath. What the hell was he doing, kissing a stranger while he was still grieving for Paula and his son? Shame engulfed him. What kind of monster was he, to want to be with another woman so soon?

He had told himself he had come here looking for Rylee so that he could apologize for last night. But that was a lie. He was here because he hadn't been able to think of anything but her since he'd run out of the café. There was something about her that soothed his pain, made him feel like life might be worth living again. And that, too, was just wrong.

"Alex, please don't feel guilty. It's normal to look for comfort when you're grieving. You're only human, after all. At times like this, people need each other more than ever."

"You don't understand…dammit, I shouldn't be feeling like this about you…about anyone…so damn soon." How was he to know if this was real or not? What if he was making the same mistake he'd made with Paula, confusing comfort and companionship for something deeper and more lasting?

"Good bye, Alex," she said quietly. "It was nice meeting you. I hope you find what you're looking for."

As Alex watched her turn and walk away, every instinct he possessed screamed at him to go after her, warning him that if he let her go this time, Fate might not be kind enough to let him find her again.

"Rylee!" he cried. "Wait!"

She didn't stop, but it didn't take him long to catch up with her. He passed her, then wheeled around to face her.

She came to an abrupt halt to avoid running into him. "Alex, leave me alone."

"I can't. I know it's wrong but I just don't care." He jammed his hands in his pockets to keep from reaching for her. "I don't know how to explain it, but I feel like…like…hell, I don't know. I mean, it sounds crazy, but being with you…I…it feels like I've come home."

"That *is* crazy," she agreed.

"Yeah, I was pretty sure you'd think so."

She laughed softly, her eyes crinkling at the corners. "I know it's crazy because I feel the same way about you."

Alex stared at her, dumbfounded. "You do?"

"I'm twenty-seven years old, and I've never felt this way in my whole life." She started walking again, and he fell into step beside her. "Life's funny, isn't it?"

"Yeah, funny," he muttered ruefully.

They walked in silence for a time. Alex wasn't sure how it happened, but after a while, his hand was holding hers. She didn't seem to mind.

When they came to a large flat-topped rock, Rylee stopped. "Let's rest for a while."

Alex sat beside her, his hand still holding hers. He gazed out at the ocean, thinking it wasn't big enough to hold his guilt, or deep enough to wash it away. And yet, sitting there beside Rylee, he knew an incredible sense of inner peace.

He sighed when she rested her head on his shoulder. Lifting his gaze toward heaven, he murmured a silent prayer of thanks for the woman at his side, hoping, pleading, that whatever it was between them would last.

Chapter 6

Sylvi looked at Magdalena and shook her head. "I still don't think killing the wife of a hunter was a wise thing to do. And not just any hunter, but a member of the notorious O'Donnell family."

"Wise?" Magdalena exclaimed. "Wise? He destroyed the love of my life! Eduardo and I were together for two hundred years. Two hundred years, Sylvi! Was I just supposed to let his killer go unavenged? Pretend it never happened? I don't think so!"

"What if he comes after you?"

Magdalena snorted. "He doesn't know who I am, or where I live."

"He didn't have any trouble finding Eduardo," Sylvi reminded her.

"And I didn't have any trouble finding him!"

"Too bad he wasn't home."

"I wouldn't have killed him even if he had been there," Magdalena said.

"Why not?"

"That would have been too quick, too easy. I want him to have time to grieve for his wife the way I'm grieving for my Eddie. I want that hunter to hurt the way I'm hurting, although that's probably impossible. There's no way he could have loved that puny mortal woman the way I loved my husband." A pair of crimson tears leaked from her eyes. "Two hundred years, Sylvi. And now he's gone." Magdalena slammed her fist on the table, cracking the wood. "When I feel that O'Donnell has suffered long enough, I'm going to hunt him down and kill him." She smiled, a hungry, predatory smile. "Not too quickly, of course."

CHAPTER 7

Rhys lifted his head as a familiar scent filled his nostrils. Glancing over his shoulder, he saw the O'Donnell kid striding toward him.

"Hey," Alex said by way of greeting.

"Hey, yourself. What are you doing here so late?"

"I didn't feel like going to bed."

Rhys nodded. "People are going to think you're one of us, considering the hours you've been keeping."

With a shrug, O'Donnell sat on the bar stool next to Costain's. "Day or night, it's all the same."

Rhys took a deep breath, one brow raising inquisitively. "You don't smell lonely."

"What the hell does that mean?"

"You've been with a woman. She has long blonde hair," Rhys said, plucking a strand from Alex's jacket. "She uses almond shampoo. Wears perfume by Yves Saint Laurent." He sniffed the air. "And likes peppermint toothpaste."

"Very funny," Alex muttered.

"Am I wrong?"

"I don't know her well enough to know if you're right or not. I just know she smells good." *And tastes better.* "Can I get a drink in here that's not warm and red?"

"Seems to me you killed a bottle of Jack Daniels the other night," Rhys said, grinning. "But I'm sure we have more. Gaston, bring my friend a whiskey."

Alex reached for the shot glass as soon as the bartender set if down, murmured, "Bottoms up," and downed it in a single swallow. Signaling the bartender, he gestured for another.

"I don't like drunks in my establishment," Rhys said, his voice mildly reproving.

"Yeah, yeah," Alex muttered.

"This girl, she seems to have you tied up in knots," Rhys said, crossing his arms over his chest. "All the booze in the world won't help."

"How do you know?" Alex tossed back the whiskey. "Hell, you probably don't even remember what it was like to be human."

"That may be true, but I've seen enough drunks to know alcohol isn't the answer to anything."

Alex nodded, his expression glum.

"So, what is it about this girl that has you so muddled?"

"What is it?" Alex exclaimed. "All I can think about is her."

"Men have been thinking about women since time began."

Alex glared at him. "I'm in mourning! My wife hasn't even been dead for six months yet, and all I can think about is another woman! That's what's wrong with it!"

Rhys made a vague gesture of dismissal. "Life goes on. You can mourn your wife and grieve for your unborn child for the rest of your life, but it won't bring them back."

Alex rolled the empty shot glass back and forth between his palms. "Have you ever lost anyone you cared for?"

"Once, long ago, when I was very young. And very stupid." He rarely let himself think of the woman he had killed for betraying his love. Beautiful, deceitful, Josette, dead by his own hand.

"Did you grieve for long?"

"No, but she put me off women for a good, long time."

"I guess Megan turned you back on," Alex said with a leer.

"You could say that. The first time I saw her, I knew I had to have her."

"Well, it's different for you. You're not human."

"I can fix it so you aren't human, if you think that will help."

"No, thanks." Alex slammed the shot glass down on the bar top. "No way! We've got enough vampires in the family already."

"So, why did you come here tonight?"

"Nowhere else to go. I came to L.A. hoping you could help me find whoever killed Paula, but…" He shrugged. "I guess I might as well go back home."

"Do you think that's a good idea?"

"I'm not learning anything here that can help me find Paula's killer."

"That's true, but in the meantime, she's not finding you, either."

Alex stared at Rhys. "What?"

"Which word didn't you understand?"

"You think she's hunting *me* now?"

"I'd bet your life on it. Are you willing to do the same?"

Alex swore under his breath. It had never occurred to him that the vampire who had killed his wife might want him dead, too. And then he frowned. "Why didn't she just wait until I came home that night and take me out?"

"Being a vampire myself, I'd say she wants you to suffer and worry for a while first."

Alex slumped back against the bar. Just when you thought things couldn't get any worse, they did.

It was early afternoon when Alex woke after a restless night. Lying there, one arm flung to the side, he stared up at the ceiling. Paula and his son were gone, and Costain was right. Grieving wouldn't bring them back. Was it wrong to find a few moments of forgetfulness in Rylee's company?

They hadn't made plans to meet again. Her business card didn't include an address, just her phone number and email. But he knew somehow that if he went back to the beach tonight, he would find her there, waiting for him.

Closing his eyes, he summoned her image—hair like fine, golden strands of silk, guileless blue eyes, skin as smooth and clear as a newborn baby's. He frowned. Yes, she was beautiful, but it was more than her appearance that made him feel at peace.

Turning onto his side, he stared out the window. Maybe she possessed some sort of supernatural power like the vampires and the werewolves. She didn't smell like a vampire, though. He didn't think she was a werewolf. Perhaps she was an angel fallen to earth, he mused with a smile. She certainly looked like one.

Shaking off his fanciful thoughts, he closed his eyes and drifted back to sleep.

It was hours later when he woke again. He lingered in bed for a few minutes, then, throwing the covers aside, he headed for the bathroom to shower and shave. Even though he wasn't really hungry, he took the elevator down to the hotel dining room and ordered a cheeseburger and fries, most of which he left on the plate.

Later, he took a long walk. Hands shoved deep in his pockets, he let his thoughts wander. It was no surprise that vampires rose to the front of his mind. They had killed his brother. Turned his sister. Killed his wife and child. And now one of them might be hunting him. And yet, when he needed someone to talk to, he had sought out a vampire. And not just any vampire, but the Master of the West Coast. A vampire Alex had once hunted.

Not long ago, he had hated all of them. But that was before his sister joined the ranks of the Undead. Before she married Erik. Before he got to know Rhys.

Damn, but life was strange, he thought as he crossed the street. Very strange indeed.

Returning to his hotel room, he changed his clothes and headed for the beach. He tried to tell himself he wasn't going there in hopes of seeing Rylee, but it wouldn't wash. A man could lie to his friends, but he couldn't lie to himself.

He parked the car, kicked off his sandals, and jogged toward the shoreline.

A woman sat on a blanket near the water. Moonlight danced in her hair, streaking the gold with silver.

She glanced over her shoulder and waved while he was still a good distance away.

He might have wondered how she had known he was there, but it was hard to think when she was watching him, her luscious pink lips curved in a smile of welcome.

"Hey, Rylee."

"Hi, Alex. I was hoping I'd see you tonight."

He dropped down on the blanket beside her—close, but not too close.

"How was your day?" she asked.

"Long and boring, until now," he said, his gaze resting on her face.

"Mine, too. Have you decided how long you'll be in California?"

"Not really. I should probably go home and get back to work." His first job would be hunting the vampire who had killed Paula and the baby.

"What kind of work do you do?" Rylee asked. "You never said."

"Let's not talk about that now."

She looked at him curiously for a moment, then shrugged. "Have you had dinner?"

"Not really," he said, thinking of the burger he'd left mostly uneaten earlier. "Have you?"

"Not yet."

"What are you in the mood for?"

"Anything you want is fine with me. If you like fish, there's a great little restaurant at the end of the pier."

"Sounds good to me." Rising, he offered her his hand. "Shall we?"

The restaurant wasn't crowded. There were tables at one end, a bar at the other. The lighting was subdued, the ambience suited more for couples than families. Framed photos of tall ships and sailboats and schooners adorned the walls, along with a pair of crossed oars, and a net littered with colorful starfish.

When they were seated, Rylee ordered a shrimp dinner, Alex ordered lobster and a bottle of wine.

After placing their order, Alex sat back, at a loss for words. He didn't usually have trouble making small talk, but tonight he felt as tongue-tied as a teenager on his first date.

Rylee stared out the window and he studied her profile, thinking again how lovely she was and then feeling guilty for noticing.

"You're very quiet," she remarked, turning to face him.

He grinned self-consciously. "I haven't done a lot of dating in my time. I guess I'm a little rusty."

"Why don't you tell me about yourself? You really haven't said very much."

"If I told you about my life, my family, you'd probably get up and leave."

"You don't come from a long line of ax murderers, do you?"

"Not exactly."

Her face paled a little. "What does *that* mean?"

He should tell her the truth, he thought, and maybe he would, once he knew her better. "I'm kidding. I've got a place in Boston. The requisite number of parents. A married sister, Daisy. We're all pretty ordinary. My dad's retired, my mom's the world's best cook. I'm sort of between jobs at the moment. What about your family?"

"My parents live in San Francisco. I'm an only child. Mom runs a day-care center. My Dad is a police officer, well, a detective." She shrugged. "I guess we're all pretty ordinary, too."

"There's nothing ordinary about you, Rylee. Trust me."

"I'm going out of town for a few days," she said after the waitress dropped off their order.

"Oh?"

"It's my Mom and Dad's twenty-fifth wedding anniversary."

"When are you leaving?"

"In the morning. The party is this Friday night. I probably won't be back until next Wednesday. Will you still be in town when I get back?"

"I don't know." He hated to see her go, Alex thought glumly, although a few days apart might be a good thing. It would give him a chance to sort out his feelings. He had intended to give up hunting, but that wasn't an option now, not until he'd avenged Paula's death. And maybe not then. It was the only thing he knew.

If what Rhys had said was true, and the vampire who killed Paula would likely come after him, then spending time with Rylee might very well put her life in danger. And if there was one thing he didn't want, it was another woman's blood on his hands.

"Do you need a ride to the airport?" he asked.

"No, I'm going to drive. I hate flying, and I want to take some photos of the ocean on the way back."

After dinner, Alex paid the check, then walked Rylee to her car.

"I'll miss you," she said as she unlocked the door.

"I'll miss you, too." More than you can imagine, he thought, as he watched her slide behind the wheel. "Have a safe trip."

"I hope things get better for you," she said with a wistful smile. "Goodbye, Alex."

Bending down, he kissed her lightly on the cheek, then closed her door, wondering if he would ever see her again.

CHAPTER 8

Alex lay in bed, his fingers laced behind his head. He wasn't accomplishing anything here in LA. Maybe he should just go back to Boston. He'd had a text from his dad saying they had an offer on the house. He could move in with his folks for a while, although he wasn't sure he could bear seeing the pity in their eyes. Still, he had nowhere else to go, no one else who gave a damn what happened to him.

He grimaced. That wasn't entirely true. Daisy loved him. And her blood-sucker husband was a pretty decent guy, all things considered. And not a bad artist.

And then there was Rylee…if he returned to Boston, he'd probably never see her again.

Unable to sleep, he climbed out of bed, tugged on his jeans, tucked in his t-shirt, and pulled on his jacket. It was second nature to shove a stake into the waistband of his pants and make sure there were a few bottles of holy water in his jacket pockets before he left the hotel.

Exiting the lobby, he stood on the sidewalk for a moment, then turned left and started walking. The streets were pretty much deserted at this time of the night, with only a few winos huddled in doorways here and there. A cop car cruised by, slowing while the two officers inside looked him over.

Lost in thought, it took Alex a minute to realize he was being followed. In a strictly reflex action, he whirled around, his right hand curling around the stake hidden under his jacket. A flash of hell-red eyes stared back at him as the vampire rushed toward him. Instinct took over. In a swift move that had become second nature, Alex drove the stake into the vampire's heart and gave it a quick twist.

The vampire had been young. Had he been one of the old ones, he would have turned to dust. As it was, he dropped like a rock, a look of astonishment on his face.

Alex stared at the body. Had the vampire been hunting him in particular, or just looking for any mortal stupid enough to be out prowling the streets alone, late at night?

"Dammit." Dropping to his knees, Alex quickly searched the vampire's pockets and came up with an expired driver's license that identified the deceased as Jack Giordano, of Boston, Massachusetts.

"Boston," Alex muttered. Eduardo Tietjen had lived in Boston. Alex lived in Boston. Of course, it could be just a coincidence that this vampire was from the same place, but Alex didn't believe in coincidence.

He shoved the license into his pants pocket, then stood there, debating what to do. Ordinarily, he would have taken the vamp's head, but he had left his blade in the car. Not that it mattered. Beheading a corpse on the street would leave a hell of a mess behind.

Hoisting the body over his shoulder, he walked quickly down the sidewalk. He made a sharp left onto a side street and dumped the body, with the stake still lodged in its chest, under a hedge, and hoped the sun would find the corpse before the cops did.

He was about a block away from the Roosevelt when Rhys fell into step beside him.

"Dammit, man!" Alex exclaimed. "Don't do that!"

"You're out late," Rhys said. His voice was mild, but Alex didn't miss the layer of steel underneath.

"Yeah. Couldn't sleep."

Rhys lifted his head and sniffed the air. "There's blood on your hands, and it isn't yours."

Keeping his face impassive, Alex wiped his palms on his jeans.

"You killed one of us."

"How the hell do you know that?"

"How the hell do you think?"

"Oh." There was no hiding his thoughts or his actions from the Master of the City, not since they had shared blood. "Was he one of yours?"

"No, fortunately for you."

There was no anger in Costain's voice, no threat, but fear twisted Alex's gut.

"Who was it?" Rhys asked.

"I don't know." Alex pulled the vamp's driver's license from his pocket and offered it to Rhys.

"Giordano," Rhys murmured. "Whoever's looking for you has a long reach."

Alex nodded.

"You might want to find another hotel," Rhys suggested. "And sign in under another name."

"What aren't you telling me?"

Rhys twitched one shoulder. "I've heard of Giordano. He was turned five or ten years ago. Before that, he was a hit man for the mob in New York."

Alex came to an abrupt stop. "The mob!" Good Lord, what had he gotten himself mixed up in now?

"He's not connected anymore," Rhys said. "He faked his death when he was turned."

"So, what's his connection to Tietjen?"

"Maybe there isn't one."

"Yeah, that's why you told me to find a new place to stay."

"Better safe than sorry. Maybe you should move in with me for a while."

"Out of the frying pan," Alex muttered as they reached his hotel.

"I can stay at the club if that'll help you sleep better."

"Thanks, I think I'll take you up on that."

Alex left Rhys waiting outside while he returned to his room to pack. He wasn't sure moving into the vampire's lair was such a great idea, but he'd be safe as houses there.

After checking to make sure he hadn't left anything behind, Alex took the elevator to the lobby, paid his bill, then headed for the garage to get his car.

Rhys was waiting by the curb when Alex pulled up in front of the Roosevelt. The vampire snorted contemptuously when he opened the door to a rather run-down Chevy and slid into the passenger seat. "Maybe you should drive my car, too."

"Hey, this was the only rental they had."

"Do you want to drive this, or my Jag?"

"Are you serious? You'd let me drive your Jag?"

"Only if you're insured."

Alex pulled away from the curb, then glanced at Rhys. "All right, why are you being so generous?"

"You gave me your blood when I needed it. Your sister is married to my best friend. And a vampire I don't know attacked you in my city." Rhys slid him an amused glance. "I can throw you out of L.A. if it'll make you feel better."

Rhys gave Alex directions to his lair, and a short time later, Alex pulled up in front of a tall, glass-fronted building.

"Park this heap in the garage," Rhys said. "It's an embarrassment to the neighborhood."

With a grimace, Alex drove down the ramp to the underground garage.

"Pull in there," Rhys said, jerking his thumb at an empty space adjacent to the stall where his smoke-gray Jag was parked.

Getting out of the car, Alex grabbed his suitcase from the back seat, then followed Rhys to an iron-barred door located across from the Jag. Rhys unlocked the door and stepped inside. Overhead lights came on when he crossed the threshold.

Alex glanced around as they walked down a wide corridor inlaid with black and white tiles to a bank of elevators. It was, he thought morbidly, quiet as a tomb.

He knew a moment of uneasiness when he followed Rhys onto the elevator. What the hell was he doing here, in the middle of the night, with the Master of the City?

Beside him, Rhys chuckled. "Too late to turn back now."

"Very funny."

When they reached the tenth floor, they took a private elevator up to the eleventh. Moments later, the elevator opened, revealing yet another door, this one made of what looked like solid steel.

"Here we are," Rhys announced, sliding his key into the lock. "Home, sweet home."

"You're a regular laugh riot," Alex said.

Entering behind him, Rhys flicked on the lights. "Bedroom's in there," he said, gesturing toward a door to Alex's right.

With a nod, Alex stepped into biggest, most outlandish bedroom he had ever seen, and that included the orange horror of the guest room in Erik's house. The walls here were papered in a dark red similar to that in Costain's bar. The carpets and the heavy drapes over the windows were the same shade. A thick black quilt covered an enormous bed; a black stone fireplace took up one entire wall; a floor-to-ceiling TV screen took up another. There were more paintings in here. Alex figured they were probably originals, like the Botticelli in the living room. A curio cabinet held a number of figurines in varying sizes—all depicting demons, dragons, or vampires stalking their prey.

"What are you running here?" Alex asked with a wry grin. "A brothel?"

"I guess it is a little over the top," Rhys said, coming up behind him. "But I don't spend much time here since I met Megan. Still, she's anxious to redecorate."

"Gee, I can't imagine why," Alex remarked, dropping his suitcase on the foot of the bed. "Are you still living at her place?"

"For another month or so. We bought a house up the coast in Granite Hills just outside Frisco. It needs some major renovations, if you know what I mean."

Major renovations undoubtedly included installing state-of-the-art vampire security, Alex thought.

"Well, make yourself at home," Rhys said. "I'll be at the club if you need me. The keys to the Jag are on the mantel."

"All right." Alex took a deep breath. "Thanks for everything."

"Yeah, yeah," Rhys muttered, and then, in the blink of an eye, he vanished in a swirl of sparkling silver motes.

Alex shook his head, amused to find himself holed up in the lair of a vampire he had once sought to destroy.

Life didn't get any weirder than that.

It was a little after four in the afternoon the following day when Alex pulled out of the penthouse garage. He had to admit, the vampire's apartment had every creature comfort you could ask for—the TV was the best money could buy, the furniture and carpets were top of the line. Alex had enjoyed the best night's sleep he'd ever had in that big bed. The shower was large enough for two. Or three. The only thing missing was a well-stocked kitchen.

Driving down Hollywood Boulevard, Alex's thoughts turned toward Rylee. He wasn't sure what to make of their friendship, or where it was headed. It was tenuous at best. They'd made no plans to meet when she got back from Frisco, he mused as he pulled into the parking lot of the first restaurant he saw.

Inside, he took a seat in the back. There were only a handful of customers in the place, but then, he'd missed the lunch crowd and it was still a little early for dinner. After the waitress took his order—steak and eggs and coffee—he pulled out his cell phone and did a search of known vampires in the area. There weren't many, and there were no addresses for those who were listed.

It was just as well, he thought, as he tucked into his meal a few minutes later. Rhys had warned him, not too subtly, not to hunt in his territory.

Thinking of vampires brought Giordano to mind. Had he been sent by the vampire who killed Paula? Looking back on what had happened in the clear light of day, it seemed unlikely.

No one but his parents knew where he was. He had no ties to the bloodsucker who had killed his wife. And even if she—or he—had his scent, it was impossible to track him across thousands of miles. Wasn't it?

He frowned, thinking it wouldn't surprise him if Rhys could manage it. But then, the Master of the West Coast Vampires was a law unto himself.

Alex signed the check, added a hefty tip for the waitress, and left the restaurant. With nothing better to do, he hopped in the Jag and drove along the coastline.

It surprised him how much he missed Rylee. He hardly knew her, yet she was constantly in his thoughts. What would she think if he told her about his past, about his vow to avenge Paula? Would she be horrified to know how he earned his living? Intrigued? Repulsed? Would she even believe him? What would she think if he introduced her to Daisy and Erik? Most people didn't believe in vampires.

He drove from Hollywood down to San Diego, stopped to buy a cup of coffee and a hamburger, then turned around and headed back.

It was a little after ten when he reached West Hollywood. He pulled up in front of Costain's lair, then pulled away from the curb and drove to *La Mort Rouge*.

Rhys glanced over his shoulder when Alex entered the club. "Where the hell have you been? I thought you'd stolen my Jag and left town."

Alex frowned as he took his customary stool beside Costain. "How'd you know I was gone? Weren't you lost in the dark sleep of your kind?"

"Awake or asleep, I will always know where you are."

Alex stared at Costain. That was a disconcerting thought if he'd ever heard one.

Chapter 9

Alex woke early Tuesday afternoon, his first thought, as always, for Rylee. He hadn't seen her since last Wednesday. Six days ago, he thought glumly. They been the longest six days of his life.

Throwing back the covers, he headed for the bathroom where he took a quick shower, then pulled on jeans and a shirt and stomped into his boots. He was sleeping later every day, he mused as he ran a comb through his hair. Not surprising, since he'd been hanging out at *La Mort Rouge* with Rhys until the wee small hours of the morning.

Alex dragged a hand across his jaw. He was living like a vampire. Maybe it was time to go home. He glanced around the bedroom, thinking he'd miss hanging out in Costain's lair. The place was decadent and he loved it.

Grabbing the keys to the Jag, he made his way down to the garage. He was going to miss driving the Jag if he left L.A., he thought as he slid behind the wheel and listened to the engine purr to life. But more than the car, he was going to miss Rylee.

He'd had no destination in mind when he pulled out of the garage, but, somehow, he found himself pulling into the Java Hut's parking lot.

After taking a table near the window, he ordered ham and eggs and pancakes for breakfast even though it was way past time for lunch, then leaned back, coffee cup in hand, and chided himself for being a fool.

He had finished the ham and eggs and was halfway through the stack of pancakes when Rylee walked in looking cute as hell in a pair of cut-off jeans, sneakers, and a blue t-shirt. The shirt had a picture of a Milky Way candy bar on it and beneath the graphic were the words, *Save the Earth—It's the Only Planet With Chocolate.*

She started toward an empty table near where he was sitting, smiled uncertainly when she saw him.

And he knew in that moment that there was no sense in fighting it. He was crazy about her. He waved her over, felt a warm rush of relief when her smile grew wider. Hurrying toward him, she sank into the chair across from his.

"You're back early," he said. "What happened?"

"I missed you."

They were, he thought, the sweetest words he'd ever heard.

Alex couldn't stop looking at her, couldn't ignore how her presence made the day brighter, warmer, happier. Damn, he felt like some horny kid in love for the first time. And in light of his current situation, that was just wrong. But, wrong or not, he couldn't deny how he felt.

He sat back in his chair as the waitress came to take Rylee's order. "Are you finished, sir?" she asked, gesturing at his plate.

"Yes. Could I get another cup of coffee?" He smiled at Rylee as the waitress left to turn in her order. "Do you have any plans for the day?"

"I'm going to drive up the coast to see if I can find some sea lions."

"Are they lost?"

She made a face at him. "No, silly. I'm doing some shots for a Greenpeace calendar."

"Oh. Well, you've got a nice day for it."

"I got some great shots of a couple of bottlenose dolphins on my way home on Sunday."

Alex nodded. Now that she was here, he'd hoped to spend some time with her, but she obviously had other plans for the day.

"If you're not doing anything, you're welcome to come along."

"I'd like that."

"Great."

Funny how just being with Rylee made everything seem possible.

They made small talk while they ate. Alex overrode her objections when he insisted on paying for her lunch.

As they left the restaurant, he suggested they take his car.

"But my camera gear is in mine," Rylee pointed out.

"Yeah, but my car's a smoke-gray Jag XKR that can do zero to sixty in less than six seconds, and I'm dyin' to drive it again."

"All right," Rylee said with a good-natured grin. "You win!"

After they transferred her gear and an old blanket to the Jag, they were on their way.

"This is really nice," Rylee said, running her hands over the leather upholstery. "I've never ridden in a Jag before."

"It's a beaut," he agreed. "I wish it was mine."

"Whose is it?" she asked as she fastened her seatbelt.

"Belongs to a guy I know."

"He must be a heck of a good friend to let your borrow it. And rich, too."

Alex shrugged. He wasn't sure he'd call The Master of the City a friend, but he wasn't about to tell her the truth about Costain.

"And a trusting one," Rylee remarked. "If I had a car like this, I'm not sure I'd lend it to my best friend or anyone else."

"If anything happens to this one, he'll just buy another."

"He must be *really* rich. What does a car like this cost?"

"I don't know. Somewhere around a hundred grand, I'm guessing."

"Wow. Must be nice," she muttered.

"Yeah." Not that he was poor, Alex thought. He made good money as a hunter, but he would have to live a long time and take a lot of heads before he could come close to having the amount of money Costain had accumulated in the last five hundred years.

He switched on the radio, found a station that played mostly oldies, and grinned when Rylee started singing along to "Walking on Sunshine." She had a nice, clear voice. She seemed to be having such a good time, Alex decided to join in.

They both burst out laughing when the song ended.

"We make a nice duo," she remarked.

"Yeah, as long as the radio is loud and no one else is listening."

She punched him on the arm. "Come on, we weren't that bad."

"Well, *you* weren't. How far up the coast are we going?"

"Hobson Beach."

"Never heard of it."

"Well, it's not really much of a beach. It's off the highway and you have to climb over a lot of rocks to get to the sand. And that's pretty much under water when the tide comes in."

"And you like it why?"

"We used to go camping there every summer when I was a kid. A dead whale washed up on the beach a few years ago. That was really something to see. There was a little girl on the beach with her dad. She was only four or five years old and she started crying when some of the whale's blood got on her tennis shoes." Rylee laughed at the memory. "She didn't like the smell, either. Can't say as I blamed her. It was nasty. I got some great pictures, though. A couple of them appeared in the local paper."

Alex glanced at her, one brow raised. "I hope you're not gonna use the dead whale photos in the calendar."

"Of course not! Still, it was an awesome sight. You see whales in movies and aquariums, but until you stand next to one, you don't realize just how big they really are. The one that washed ashore was a blue whale about seventy feet long."

"What killed it?"

"They think it was hit by a ship."

"I guess it happens." He could see the ocean now, a vast expanse of quiet blue-green water that stretched away to the horizon.

"We're here," Rylee said, pointing at the upcoming off-ramp. "Turn there."

It wasn't much of a campsite—a small store, a couple of restrooms, an outdoor shower where you could rinse off your feet, a small grassy area near the end of the road. Huge boulders separated the campsites from the ocean below. Alex saw several squirrels scurrying around in the rocky crevasses.

He parked the Jag, helped Rylee with her camera cases, then locked the car.

He followed her up a set of stone steps and down the other side. The tide was out and they walked along the shore. Beach houses lined the street above the campground.

Rylee found a place she liked and Alex spread the blanket on the sand, then sat down, wishing he'd brought a pair of trunks and a surfboard. Rylee sat beside him with her knees drawn up as she gazed out at the water.

"So," he asked. "Do you think we'll see anything?"

She shrugged. "I don't know, but it doesn't matter. If I don't get any shots today, there's always tomorrow."

"I'm beginning to think you're just using your work as an excuse to spend the day at the beach."

"Found me out, did you?" she asked, grinning.

He laughed. "Whatever your reasons, I'm glad to be here with you."

"Me, too, you."

An errant breeze lifted a few strands of her hair. Alex curled his hands into fists, surprised by the sudden need to smooth her hair back, to touch her and taste her. "Rylee, would I be out of line if I kissed you?"

"No." She leaned toward him. "And even if you were, I wouldn't care."

He slipped his hand around her nape, drawing her closer, and then he kissed her, ever so gently, his mouth moving over hers in gentle exploration. "This is wrong," he said, abruptly drawing away. "I shouldn't…"

"I know," she agreed. "Very wrong." They hardly knew each other. He was still in mourning. But it didn't seem to matter. Leaning forward, she cupped his face in her palms and then paused.

"Hey," he said, "don't stop now."

She smiled, then claimed his lips with hers.

Alex combed his fingers through the wealth of her hair. It slid through his fingers like fine silk. Her lips were warm and pliable, sweeter than anything he had ever known. "We should probably stop," he said when Rylee lifted her head, but there was no conviction in his tone.

"You're right," she agreed, even as she kissed him again.

His arm curled around her waist to draw her down on the blanket. Her body molded itself to his if she had been made for him. He had often heard the expression "sparks flew." Now, as his tongue stroked hers, Alex knew, for the first time in his life, what it meant.

He might have made love to her right then, right there, if the sound of amused laughter hadn't cooled his ardor. Looking up, he saw two teenage girls clad in brightly-colored bikinis staring down at them.

"Geez, mister," one of them exclaimed with a grin. "Get a room!"

Laughing uproariously, the two girls ran down the beach.

"Not a bad idea," Alex muttered, sitting up.

"I guess we got a little carried away there," Rylee said, smoothing a hand over her hair. "I—oh! Look!" Scrambling to her feet, she pulled one of her cameras from the case and ran down to the water's edge, snapping wildly as a blue whale surfaced.

Rising, Alex ran after her. "Hey," he called, pointing, "is that another one?"

"Yes! A young one."

It was an awesome sight, Alex thought as he watched the behemoth and her calf move gracefully through the water. And even better because he was sharing it with Rylee.

Standing there, watching her eyes glow with excitement, Alex admitted he was in real trouble. Not from the Master of the West Coast Vampires. Not from Eduardo Tietjen's vengeful mate.

No, the real trouble was standing right beside him.

They stayed at the beach until the sun dipped below the horizon, then he took her out to dinner at Red Lobster. It was late when he pulled into the Java Hut parking lot. "Can I see you again tomorrow?" he asked, pulling up next to her Mazda.

"Gee, I don't know. I have appointments throughout the day, and then I'm meeting a new client for dinner at seven. I'm not sure how long it will last. I'd blow it off, but it's a deal that's too good to pass up."

"How about Thursday?"

"That would be great." Digging a slip of paper out of her handbag, she wrote down her address. "I had a wonderful time today."

"Me, too." When their gazes met, he leaned toward her. She met him halfway, her eyelids fluttering down as he kissed her.

Feeling ten feet tall, he got out of the Jag and opened her door. When she stepped out, he gathered her gear and carried it to her car.

"Until next time," she said, after he'd stowed her cameras in the trunk.

Alex smiled, then kissed her one more time. He waited until she was drove out of the parking lot before climbing into the Jag.

"Day after tomorrow," he murmured, and wondered how he could wait that long.

CHAPTER 10

Alex was surprised to find Costain sitting on the sofa, a glass of wine in hand, when he returned to the vampire's lair. He didn't know why he was surprised. The place belonged to Costain, after all.

"Been to the beach again, have you?" Rhys asked.

"Yeah, how'd you know?"

"I can smell it on you for one thing." Rhys inhaled deeply. "I can smell the woman, too. You've been with her before."

With a shake of his head, Alex dropped onto the sofa across from the vampire. "You know, it really sucks—you should pardon the pun—not having any secrets from you."

Rhys chuckled. "Yeah, that's what Megan says, too."

"Have you found out any more about Tietjen's mate?"

"No. She's an elusive creature. None of my contacts even knew Tietjen had a woman. I'm not sure how they managed to keep their relationship under the radar unless they never went anywhere together. It's notoriously difficult to keep secrets in my world."

"Great."

"I'd rather talk about you and this woman. Rylee. Odd name for a female."

"I'd rather *not* talk about her."

"Does she know what you do for a living?"

"No." Hunting vampires was the only thing he had ever wanted to do. He loved the hunt. The way his mouth went dry, the way his heart raced with excitement as he pitted his cunning and strength against those of a supernatural creature.

Alex plowed his fingers through his hair. If he intended to pursue his relationship with Rylee—he still wasn't sure if that was a good idea—he would have to tell her the truth before things got serious. If they did. He blew out a breath. He was supposed to be searching for the monster who had killed his wife, not mooning over some beautiful, blue-eyed photographer.

"I think you've got it bad," Rhys said, with a wry grin.

"Dammit, stay out of my head!"

Rhys drained his glass and set it on the end table. "Well, I'll leave you to brood. I just came by for a change of clothes."

Rising, Alex stretched his back and shoulders. "Listen, thanks for letting me stay here, and for the use of the Jag."

Rhys dismissed his thanks with a wave of his hand. "I'd stay off the streets after dark if I were you."

"Yeah, well, maybe my best chance of catching this killer is to make myself a target."

"It's your life. If you need me, holler," Rhys said. "Mentally, of course."

"Of course," Alex said dryly.

A shimmer in the air, and the vampire was gone.

"Damn," Alex murmured. "I wish I could do that."

Unable to sleep, Alex rolled out of bed. Thinking a drive might relax him, he pulled on his jeans and a sweatshirt, grabbed the keys to the Jag and left the Penthouse.

Driving down Hollywood Boulevard, his thoughts drifted toward Rylee. He couldn't remember when he'd had such a good time, or felt so carefree. Just thinking about it made him feel guilty as hell, as if he was somehow cheating on Paula.

Dammit. He should stop seeing Rylee, not just because he was supposed to be in mourning, but because every minute he spent with her put her life in danger.

He was in a foul mood when he pulled up in front of *La Mort Rouge*. He didn't want company. He didn't want conversation. All he wanted was to forget the wife he had lost and the woman he had found.

The man at the door didn't ask Alex for his name this time, just took one look at his face and waved him inside.

It was after midnight and the club was crowded. Customers—mostly dressed in black - lined the bar. A few couples danced to the slow, sensual music drifting through the sound system.

Edging around the dance floor toward the bar, Alex glanced at the numbered doors as he passed by. Even as he watched, he saw a voluptuous brunette wearing a low-cut black dress, three-inch heels, and black lipstick knock on door number three and then duck inside.

Alex frowned, wondering if she was vampire or prey.

He spotted Costain sitting at his usual place at the end of the bar, a crystal goblet in one hand, his arm around the waist of a tall redhead.

Rhys nodded at Alex. "Thought I told you to stay inside after dark."

"When I need mothering, I'll call home."

"Suit yourself. Monique, this is Alex. Alex, this is Monique. Her date for tonight didn't show up and she's hungry. I don't suppose you'd like to take his place?"

Alex glared at Costain. "That's not remotely funny."

"You might enjoy it," Rhys said.

Monique smiled at Alex. "I can guarantee that," she promised in a voice dripping with honey.

"Yeah, well, thanks," Alex said. "But no thanks."

Monique ran one long, blood-red fingernail down the side of Alex's neck. "If you won't give me a drink, how about a taste?"

"Dammit, Costain, call her off!"

"Okay, Monique, that's enough." Rhys jerked his chin toward a man sitting alone at the far end of the bar. "Go see Laurant. He's always ready and willing."

"Oh, all right," Monique said with a pout. "But he's not as pretty as this one."

Laughing, Rhys swatted her on the backside as she sashayed toward the other man. "It wouldn't have hurt you to give her a taste."

"If you're so worried about her, why didn't you give her some of what you're drinking?"

"This?" Rhys held up his glass. Dark red liquid swirled inside. "It's just remarkably expensive port sweetened with a splash of O-negative."

Alex grimaced. Turning away, he signaled the bartender and ordered a whiskey straight up.

Rhys scowled at him. "I don't want to have to carry you out of here again."

"Yeah, yeah, I remember what you said."

"So, what brings you here?"

Alex shrugged. "Too late to go out. Too early for bed."

"What happened to the blonde?"

"I took her home. I'm not going to see her anymore."

"That's probably wise."

"Yeah, that's me, Alex O'Donnell, filled with the wisdom of the ages."

"Stop feeling sorry for yourself," Rhys said. "You needed a drink, you've got one. You need some physical relief, this place is crawling with beautiful, willing women. You need to forget the woman, I can help you there, too."

Alex considered it a moment, then shook his head. In spite of everything, he didn't want Costain to wipe Rylee from his memory.

"Just want to drown yourself in misery, huh?"

"You're not real big in the sympathy department, are you?"

"Not one damn bit," Rhys admitted gruffly. "If you're looking for sympathy, you'll find it in the dictionary after 'sucks.' Or you can go see a priest. I'm a realist. Every hunter bags the wrong prey once in a while. It was your turn. And son, you really bagged the wrong game this time."

"You've heard something," Alex said. "Spit it out."

"Randolph called me a while ago. It seems you pissed off a big fish. Eduardo Tietjen's mate is Magdalena. We all thought she was dead, destroyed in a fire three centuries ago. Apparently Tietjen found her in what was left of the building just before the sun did. He carried her off—Randolph didn't know to where. Anyway, Tietjen hid her away, took care of her, brought her nourishment. It took a long time for her to recover and when she did, they became lovers."

Alex tossed off his drink and called for another. Just his luck that Tietjen's mate considered Eduardo both savior and lover. He rubbed a hand across his jaw, thinking that if it wasn't for bad luck, he wouldn't have any luck at all. "Is Magdalena in L.A.?"

"Randolph's informant wasn't sure."

Alex shook off his disappointment. "Thanks for the update." He pulled a twenty out of his pocket and slapped it on the bar. "I'm outta here."

He needed time to think. He needed a good night's sleep. And then he needed to see Rylee one more time so he could tell her goodbye.

Rylee stepped out of the shower and dried off. With her hair wrapped in a towel, she sorted through her closet, looking for something to wear—something casual, but not too casual. She decided on a modest blue knit dress that had always been a favorite. She laid it out on the bed, then rummaged in the closet for the dyed-to-match heels.

Funny, how life turned out, she mused as she ate a quick breakfast of tea and toast. Just when you thought you'd never meet Mr. Right and you were ready to stop looking, he showed up where you least expected to find him. It must have been Fate that had her accept the shoot at the beach the night she met Alex, she thought, as she brushed her teeth. The job had come up at the last-minute, and she had almost turned it down. True, the two of them hadn't gotten off to the best of starts, but after last night, there was no denying that there was something there. Something she wanted to explore further.

After leaving Hobson, they had gone to dinner, sharing jokes and laughter as if they had known each other for years instead of days. There had been a moment when their eyes met and it seemed as if everything else faded away and there was no one else in the restaurant but the two of them. It had been a magical moment. Of course, they would have to take it slow. He was mourning the loss of his wife and child and he needed time to grieve. However long it took, she could wait. They had plenty of time. Heck, she thought with a grin, she didn't even know his last name.

In the bedroom, she brushed out her hair and applied her make-up. Slipping the blue knit over her head, she smoothed it over her hips, stepped into her heels and grabbed her keys, already late for her first appointment.

Rylee smiled at Mr. Dean Alger, pleased with the way their meeting had gone. "I'm sure I can do a good job for you, Mr. Alger," she said, gathering her handbag.

"I've no doubt of that, Miss Wagner. You come highly recommended."

"Thank you, sir. I look forward to working with you."

"And I, you. We'll be in touch."

Rylee was humming as she left the restaurant. Mr. Alger and his partner were opening a new sporting goods store at the beginning of the year and they had hired her to supply photographs for their catalogue, which would be both print and digital. The best part was, she already had some great wildlife stills she had never used that would be perfect for what Alger had in mind.

It had been a been a most productive day, she thought as she drove home. A former client had called with a new contract, she had made several calls to confirm dates and times, and now she was looking forward to her dinner appointment with Clyde Summerville—a well-known Hollywood agent who was interested in having her shoot candid photographs of some of his more famous movie star clients for his new office. If it panned out, it would be a lucrative gig, and might lead to more work from other Hollywood agents, actors or actresses.

But it was Alex who occupied the majority of her thoughts. He had been on her mind all day, whether she was sitting at her desk filling out paperwork, answering her mail, having a late lunch with her best friend, Connie, or discussing business with Mr. Alger. If her last appointment tonight had been with Alex instead of a Hollywood agent, her day would have been perfect. But she would see Alex tomorrow. Just thinking about it made her smile.

Now, spraying on a bit of cologne, Rylee found herself thinking of him once again. She'd had a couple of crushes in her life, but nothing epic, no break-ups that had left her broken-hearted for more than a day or two.

She was just about to sit down and relax with a cup of tea before her meeting with Summerville when the doorbell rang. Wondering who it could be, she padded into the living room to see who had come calling.

And felt her heart skip a beat when she opened the door and saw the man she'd been thinking about only moments ago. "Alex! What are you doing here?"

"I'm sorry. I forgot you had a late appointment."

"It's all right, I have a few minutes," she said, taking a step back. "Come on in."

He hesitated before crossing the threshold.

"I was just having a cup of tea. Would you like one?"

"No, thanks." Too much booze and too little sleep the night before had left him hung-over and out of sorts.

"Would you rather have coffee? I made a fresh pot a few minutes ago, but decided to have tea instead."

"Yeah, that sounds good. Thanks."

He followed her into the kitchen, sat at the small round table in front of the window while she filled a large blue mug.

Rylee carried her tea cup and his mug to the table, then sat down across from him. "I didn't expect to see you tonight. Is something wrong?"

"We need to talk."

"Oh?" Those four words never preceded anything good.

Alex leaned back in his chair, suddenly at a loss for words. Now that he was here, he wasn't sure how to begin or how much to tell her. Stalling, he sipped his coffee. He could feel Rylee's gaze on his bowed head, knew she was waiting for him to tell her what was on his mind.

"Rylee, I don't know any easy way to say this, so I'll just spit it out. It isn't safe for us to be together. I killed a vampire named Eduardo Tietjen not long ago and now his mate is hunting me. She's the one who killed my wife. If she finds the two of us together…I don't know what she'd do to you, but I can't put your life in danger any more than I already have."

"Vampires?" Rylee glared at him. "If you don't want to see me anymore, just say so. You don't have to make up some preposterous story."

"I wish that's what it was, but it's true. All of it."

"I don't believe you," she said, her voice laced with anger and confusion. "There's no such thing as vampires and everybody knows it." How could she have been so wrong about him? The guy was a lunatic. Monsters, indeed!

Alex wasn't surprised by her reaction. Most people didn't believe bloodsuckers existed. Sure, stories about the Undead made headlines every now and then, but most people dismissed them out of hand. Rhys and his ilk did their best to stay under the radar and it had been Alex's experience that mankind was a lot happier thinking such tales were just bogus headlines to sell more papers or spike TV ratings.

"Rylee…"

"Okay, say I believe you, which I don't. Why did you kill the vampire?" Stupid question, she thought. What else would you do with them?

"I'm a hunter. It's what I do for a living."

He really *was* crazy. "I think you'd better go."

"Dammit, Rylee, it's true! Why the hell would I make up something like that?"

"I'm sure I have no idea!"

"Those stories about a serial killer in the newspaper and on TV, they're vampire kills. Dammit, Rylee, you have to believe me," he said fervently. "Your life might depend on it."

His voice, sharp with the ring of truth, sent a sudden chill down her spine. What if he wasn't crazy? What if it *was* all true? Oh, but how could that be? And yet he didn't look like he was kidding. He looked deadly serious. She frowned. It would explain all those bodies drained of blood. Puncture wounds in their necks. Was it possible he was telling the truth?

She closed her eyes a moment, her thoughts chaotic as she thought about what he'd said. Why would be make up such an outrageous lie? If he didn't want to see her any more, he could have ended it with a phone call. Or come up with a more plausible story.

Taking a deep breath, she met his gaze across the table. "So, let me get this straight. You hunt vampires for a living? And you kill them?"

He didn't blink. Didn't look away. Just nodded, his expression solemn.

Rylee felt the blood drain from her face. "And that's why you came to L.A.? To find the…the vampire who killed your wife."

"Yes."

"I don't know what to say."

His gaze searched hers. "Do you believe me?"

"I don't want to. It all sounds so outlandish. So…so *Twilight Zone*." But what if it *was* true? What if her life really was in danger?

"I wanted to tell you what I did for a living soon after we met, but I thought I'd wait until we knew each other better." He stared out the kitchen window. "If Magdalena's in town, I can't put your life in danger."

Rylee glanced around her kitchen. Everything looked just as it had a short time ago, and yet, if what Alex said was true, it changed everything, and life as she knew it would never be the same again. Maybe there really were monsters in the closet and under the bed. And stalking Alex…

Everything he'd said was incredible. Inconceivable. And yet she knew deep in her heart that it was probably true whether she wanted to believe him or not. Just as she knew that her feelings for him hadn't changed, which might be the most bizarre thing of all.

Deciding to believe him, at least for the moment, she asked, "How long have you been a hunter?"

"Since I was seventeen. It's what my family does." Or did, he thought as he pushed away from the table. "Listen, thanks for the coffee. I'm sorry it had to end like this. I wish…" Oh, hell, there was no point in wishing for what could never be. "I just wanted you to understand why we shouldn't see each other anymore."

Rising, he skirted the table and brushed a kiss across the top of her head. Then, needing to hold her close one last time, he lifted her to her feet. "I'll never forget you," he whispered, as he drew her into his arms. "Never." He kissed her then, long and slow, as if he had all the time in the world to memorize the sweetness of her lips, the way her body molded so willingly to his.

He released her reluctantly. "Please understand, Rylee," he said, his voice thick with regret. "I can't have your blood on my hands, too." His gaze moved over her, filled with such longing it made her heart ache.

And then he headed for the door.

Rylee stared after him, listening to the sound of his footsteps as he walked out of the kitchen and out of her life. She stood there for several minutes, then dropped back down on her chair as the numbness that had cushioned his parting words gave way to a flood of tears.

CHAPTER 11

A lex stood on the sidewalk outside Rylee's house for several moments. Resisting the urge to go back and tell her that he had made a mistake, he slid behind the wheel of the Jag and then just sat there with the engine idling.

The evening stretched ahead of him, long and empty. Going back to Boston seemed like the best thing to do. He had several loose ends to tie up at home.

He needed to decide what to do with Paula's things. Find a new place to live.

He needed to decide what to do with the rest of his life. Being a hunter no longer seemed as exciting as it once had. He had spent half of his life tracking and destroying creatures like Costain and what did he have to show for it? A dead wife and child, and a heart filled with guilt and grief.

Alex stared wistfully at Rylee's house. If he didn't have a spiteful vampire breathing down his neck, he would go home and settle his affairs in Boston, then come back to L.A. and pursue a relationship with her.

He grinned faintly, wondering what she would think of his family. Would she be able to accept Erik and Daisy, or be horrified by the thought of having in-laws who were vampires? If he quit hunting, what would he do for a living? Sure, he had some money stashed away, but it wouldn't last forever. He had considered becoming a chef not long ago. The idea still held some appeal. He was a helluva good cook. He loved experimenting in the kitchen. He knew how to wield a big knife, he thought with a wry grin. And cooking was nice, safe work compared to what he was used to.

Heaving a sigh, Alex pulled away from the curb and headed for *La Mort Rouge.* Lost in thought, he paid little attention to the truck behind him until he turned onto the narrow road that led to the club, and the truck followed him. He knew a moment of concern, then blew it off. The club was a popular hang-out for a certain clientele, after all.

It wasn't until he parked the Jag and the truck pulled up behind him, blocking his escape, that he realized he should have listened to that little warning voice in his head, but by then, it was too late.

The thing that crawled out of the driver's side of the truck was about seven inches over six feet and built like a Mack truck. The two that emerged from the back seat were a few inches shorter but just as wide. They were human on the outside but their eyes were dead. Alex had seen their kind before and knew they were under some kind of supernatural control. Revenants, perhaps, raised by a vampire.

For all his bulk, the first revenant moved like lightning, hauling Alex out of the Jag before he had time to reach for his kit under the seat or make a run for it. Alex tried to break free of the hulk's hold as he was dragged across the blacktop, but it was like trying to wrestle a mountain.

The creature tossed him into the bed of the truck, then climbed in after him, one ham-sized fist grabbing hold of Alex's ankle and yanking him backward when he tried to scramble over the side. Alex grunted in pain as his head slammed against the truck bed. The second revenant hopped into the truck's passenger seat, the third slid behind the wheel and pulled out of the parking lot.

The hulk grinned as he pulled Alex closer, enfolding him in a one-armed bear hug from which there was no hope of escape.

Alex grimaced when he saw the rag in the monster's hand. Soaked in chloroform, no doubt. *Dammit!* he thought as the hulk slapped the cloth over his nose and mouth. *Costain's been shadowing me for days. Where the hell is he now, when I need him?*

It was his last conscious thought before everything faded to black.

Awareness returned gradually—sound, feeling, sight. Alex groaned softly as he opened his eyes. And wished that he was still safely unconscious when he realized he was in a basement, his wrists secured to an iron pipe over his head, his feet dangling a foot above the cement slab.

A glance to the left made his stomach clench. The three revenants stood against the wall, unmoving, their eyes closed.

Alex stared at them. They didn't seem to be breathing. Were they even alive?

The door across from him creaked open and Alex's interest in the revenants disappeared when he saw the woman framed in the doorway. She was of medium height, with dark brown hair and a figure that was shapely, if a trifle plump. She stood there a moment, just staring at him. Had he been able, he would have fled from the hatred emanating from those cold, gray eyes. He knew in his gut that this was Tietjen's mate, just as he knew that he would never leave this place alive.

The knot of dread in his stomach grew even tighter when the vampire reached behind her and dragged Rylee into the room.

"No!" The word hissed from Alex's lips. "Let her go! She has nothing to do with this!"

Magdalena put her hand in the middle of Rylee's back and pushed, hard. Rylee stumbled and fell forward. With her hands bound behind her back, she had no way to break her fall. She landed heavily, the air whooshing out of her lungs. She turned her head at the last minute and Alex heard the dull thud as she hit the floor.

"Dammit!" He tugged against the ropes that bound him. "Let her go!"

In a blur too quick to follow, Magdalena crossed the room to stand in front of him. "How long have you known her?" she demanded, eyes flashing. "A few days? A month? I spent *centuries* with Eduardo!"

"She's nothing to me. We just met."

"Liar!" She dragged a long, sharp nail down his left cheek, laying it open to the bone.

Alex inhaled sharply, then bit down on his lower lip, determined not to cry out. He grimaced with revulsion when she wiped a bit of blood away with her fingertips and brought them to her lips.

"Don't worry, hunter," she purred. "I'm not going to kill her." She smiled, showing her fangs. "But you might."

He swallowed hard, the warm blood trickling from his cheek and down his neck forgotten as her eyes went red. "No!" he cried, his voice hoarse with terror and revulsion. "Just kill me!"

Her laughter echoed off the walls, cold and brittle, like dead leaves blown by the wind. He recoiled when she bit into her wrist, but his struggles were in vain as she grabbed a handful of his hair in one hand, forced his mouth open with the other and let her blood drip onto his tongue.

Gagging, he spit it out.

And then she grasped his shoulders in both hands, her fingers digging into his flesh like talons as she buried her fangs in his throat.

Alex was vaguely aware of Rylee screaming, of his body growing weaker as the vampire drank.

And drank.

The world went red.

And then gray.

And then blessedly black as he spiraled headlong into a cold, endless abyss.

Rylee huddled in one corner, shivering. Her back and shoulders ached from being forced into the same uncomfortable position for so long, but at least that dreadful woman had gone, taking those scary creatures with her.

Time and again, her gaze was drawn back to Alex. He hung suspended from an overhead pipe, his body slowly turning one way and then the other. He was deathly pale save for the dark ribbons of drying blood on his left cheek and along the side of his neck. She couldn't tell if he was still breathing.

Choking back her tears, she tried to fight off the sense of hopelessness that was eating away at her sanity, but it was impossible. She didn't know where she was, and neither did anyone else. But even more disquieting was the fear that, in some way, the woman's bite had turned Alex into a vampire and that when he woke, she would be his first meal.

She had screamed earlier, screamed until her throat was raw, but there was no one to hear her cries. Minutes ticked by like hours. She was shivering and uncomfortable and frightened out of her mind. And just when she thought things couldn't get any worse, there was a peculiar ripple in the air and a man appeared in the center of the room— seemingly out of nowhere. A tall man dressed all in black, with dark-blond hair. When he looked at her, his eyes were cold and calculating.

She cringed when he approached her.

He didn't seem to notice.

"I'm not going to hurt you." Leaning down, he untied her hands, then turned away.

Rylee massaged her wrists, all the while keeping a wary eye on the stranger, but he seemed to have forgotten she was there as he released Alex from his bonds, then lowered him gently onto the floor and squatted beside him.

Summoning her courage, Rylee asked, "Is he dead?"

"Not yet." He answered without looking at her.

"She bit him."

He nodded. "Did he drink from her?"

"She…she made him drink some but he spit it out. Is he going to turn into a vampire?"

"If he survives the night," he replied, his voice coolly dispassionate. "I haven't yet decided."

"Can't you do anything to help him?"

He shrugged. "I can leave him alone and see if he survives, in which case he'll be bound to whoever turned him. Or I can give him my blood, and he'll be bound to me instead."

Scrambling to her feet, Rylee stared at him in horror. "You… you're a…?"

"A vampire. Yes."

She backed as far away from him as she could get. A fresh wave of terror chilled her to the bone with the realization that the man bending over Alex hadn't come to save them.

Rhys studied Alex, the frightened woman forgotten as he listened to the ever-slowing, erratic beat of the boy's heart. Only minutes left to decide his fate.

"Dammit," Rhys murmured. He had been a vampire long enough to know when a man was at death's door. Apparently the other vampire—Magdalena, he assumed—hadn't given Alex enough of her blood to turn him. But she'd taken enough to kill him. Would Alex hate him if he saved his life? And what about Daisy? Would she thank him for turning her brother or despise him for letting him die? But there was no time to discuss it with Daisy or her husband or with his own wife. The decision had to be made now.

Shit! Life had been so much easier when he'd had no entanglements with other vampires and their human kin. He swore again, then bit into his left wrist. He stared at the dark-red blood oozing from the wound. He was going to have a hell of a time explaining to the Vampire Council why he had chosen to save the life of a hunter. But what the hell, he was the Master of the West Coast Vampires. He could do whatever the hell he pleased.

"Alex." Parting the boy's lips, Rhys held his bleeding wrist over the kid's mouth. "You must drink."

Behind him, the woman made a strangled sound.

And fainted dead away.

Rhys swore softly. He would worry about what to do with her later.

He watched his blood trickle onto Alex's tongue, smiled faintly when the kid swallowed once, twice, then grabbed hold of his arm and drank as if he would never let go.

He let the kid drink until the color returned to his cheeks and his heart was again beating slow and steady. When he pulled his arm away, Alex made a soft sound of protest, then went limp.

Rising, Costain lifted Alex and slung him over his shoulder, then transported the two of them to the bedroom in his penthouse lair. Alex didn't stir as Rhys undressed him and tucked him into bed.

"Damn," Rhys muttered irritably as he returned for the woman. "No good deed ever goes unpunished."

Chapter 12

Rylee was shaking so badly she couldn't get her house key in the lock. She kept telling herself this couldn't be happening, that in spite of everything Alex had told her—in spite of what she had seen with her own eyes—vampires didn't exist, that she was having the mother of all nightmares. But there was no denying the fact that the blond vampire standing behind her was very real. After somehow whisking Alex away, he had returned to the basement, swept her into his arms, and brought her home, though she had no recollection of how they had arrived or how he knew where she lived. A million questions and fears warred within her.

She practically jumped out of her skin when he reached around her.

A touch of his hand unlocked the door and it swung open. He arched one brow at her stunned expression, then gestured for her to go inside.

"Don't open your door for anyone after dark," he advised as she stepped inside. "And I mean *anyone*, whether you know them or not."

She made a scoffing noise. "If they're vampires, won't they just unlock the door like you did and walk in?"

"I can't go inside."

"Why not?"

"Vampires can't enter a home uninvited. Something about the power of the threshold keeps us out." He smiled at her.

It didn't make Rylee feel any better. Or any safer.

"I'd advise you to study up on vampire lore, Miss Wagner. Most of it's wrong, but some of it's right."

She wondered, briefly, how he knew her name. "I don't believe you can't come in."

Rhys blew out a sigh, then took a step forward. Trying to cross the threshold was like slamming into a block wall.

Rylee's eyes widened as the air whipped around her. "You really can't cross the threshold?"

"Not without an invitation. So, like I said, don't invite strangers into your house. If you're smart, you won't go out after dark." He paused, his gaze running over her. "How did Magdalena find you?"

Magdalena. The vampire who had killed Alex's wife. Rylee shuddered. "I'm not sure. The last thing I remember is getting into my car." She had missed her meeting with Summerville, but somehow that didn't seem important now.

"She probably mesmerized you. If she tries again, she'll likely send someone else in her place—perhaps even someone you know—which is why you have to be careful."

"You mean like those…those…whatever they were?"

"Exactly. She's an old and powerful vampire. And she's mad as hell."

Rylee shivered. She had felt that power. It had crawled over her skin like some alien infection. "Is Alex going to be all right?"

"I don't know. Tomorrow night will tell the tale. But he's still in the land of the living, so to speak. If you're smart, you'll forget everything that happened tonight. And you'll forget about Alex. I don't think he'll be fit company for you or anyone else for quite a while."

Rylee swallowed hard. She knew everything he said was true, but putting Alex out of her mind was going to be impossible. Just as she was never going to forget this man or the female vampire who had kidnapped her.

Alex opened his eyes slowly, surprised to find himself in bed. He didn't recall driving back to Costain's lair…

He bolted upright, his heart hammering in his chest as he glanced around. What was he doing here? The last thing he remembered was hanging in a basement like a side of beef, with Magdalena chowing down on the side of his neck. And Rylee! Oh, Lord, where was she?

"Relax, kid."

"Rhys?" Alex turned toward the sound of the vampire's voice. "What happened? How did I get here? Where's Rylee?" He swallowed, then grimaced. His mouth felt desert-dry, his tongue thick.

"All in good time. How do you feel?"

"Like hell." Suddenly overcome by gut-wrenching pain, he sat up and wrapped his arms around his stomach. Magdalena had sliced his cheek open. Maybe it was infected. He lifted a hand to his cheek, wondering if he'd be horribly scarred. His skin was caked with dried blood but there was no wound. So why did he hurt so bad? "Did she poison me or something?"

"Not exactly."

Alex took a deep breath, confused by the abrupt onslaught on his senses. It was pitch black in the room, yet he saw everything clearly—Costain standing at the foot of the bed, arms crossed over his chest, each figure in the curio cabinet, the paintings on the wall.

He frowned when he heard the sound of a truck backfiring, the barking of a dog, footsteps from the street below. How was that even possible? They were eleven floors up in an apartment that was virtually soundproof.

An indrawn breath carried myriad scents—from the outside.

"What's happening to me?" he asked as another wave of pain knifed through him. He stared at Costain, who stood there watching him like he was a rare bug in a science experiment. It was the look in the vampire's eyes that answered his question. An expression that bordered on pity.

"I think you know," Rhys answered quietly.

"She turned me, didn't she?" he asked, his voice flat, as the events of the night before flashed before him.

"No."

"No? I don't believe you." His hands clenched into tight fists. "I can see everything clearly, even though it's pitch black in here. I can hear things I shouldn't be able to hear."

"She didn't bring you across," Rhys said, then paused before, adding, "I did."

Alex stared at him. "Why?" he asked, his voice little more than a hoarse whisper. "Why would you do that?"

"It seemed like the right thing to do, at the time."

"Shouldn't it have been *my* decision?"

"If you'd been conscious, I might have asked first, but there wasn't time. She didn't give you enough of her blood to turn you. I suspect she's never made another vampire. But she took enough to kill you. So I made the decision on my own."

"You had no right!"

In the blink of an eye, Rhys was beside the bed, one hand clamped around Alex's throat. "Fledglings are a lot of trouble," he growled, his eyes blazing red. "You want to be dead? Just say the word."

Alex stared up into the vampire's face and knew Costain wasn't bluffing.

"So, what'll it be?" Rhys asked, his hand tightening around Alex's throat. "Life or death?"

Scarcely able to draw a breath, he croaked, "Life, dammit!"

"Are you sure?" Rhys asked, displaying his fangs. "I haven't eaten tonight."

"Dammit," Alex gasped. "Let go of me, you bloody monster."

Rhys grinned as he released his hold on Alex's throat. "Welcome to the wonderful world of the Undead."

Alex scowled at him. "You've got a lousy sense of humor, you know that?"

Rhys shrugged. "Vampire or human, life is what you make it. You can accept what you've become, or you can spend the rest of your existence fighting against it. It's up to you."

"How did Megan react?"

"She was upset at first, angry with me for what I'd done, a little afraid of what she'd become. But she took to it readily enough once she accepted it."

"What about you? Was this something you chose?"

"Hell no. But I knew there was no going back, so I decided to embrace it."

"Would you be human again, if you could?"

"No." Rhys grabbed a pair of pants from the foot of the bed and tossed them to Alex. "Get dressed. You need to feed."

Alex caught the jeans in one hand, only then noticing he was naked beneath the sheet.

"You might want to shower first," Rhys suggested.

"Wait. Where's Rylee? Is she all right? Magdalena didn't... didn't...?"

"The girl's fine. I took her home."

"She knows? About you? About me?"

"Yeah. If you're smart, you'll stay away from her for your own good. And hers. It isn't wise to be around people you care for until you have all your hungers under control."

Costain was right, Alex thought. The last thing he wanted to do was hurt her.

Turning on his heel, Costain left the room and closed the door behind him.

Just as the vampire had closed the door on his old life, Alex thought bitterly.

He sat there for several minutes, trying to comprehend what had happened to him, even as he tried to decide how he felt about this unexpected life-style change. He snorted. Life-style. More like Undead-style.

Rising, he paced the floor, his mind reeling. He felt like himself and yet he felt different. All of his senses were heightened. His vision was remarkable. He could see each individual fiber in the carpet, each grain of wood in the bedside table, details that he had never seen with his mortal eyes.

His body felt lighter, as if he was no longer subject to gravity. He was able to process a dozen things at the same time—he could hear a fly crawling across the ceiling, knew a man was jogging on the sidewalk below, knew it was a tall man in a hurry by the length of his stride. A diesel truck fired up three blocks away. Somewhere in the distance, a man and a woman were quarreling over what to watch on TV.

Cursing softly, Alex padded into the bathroom and stepped into the shower. What would Daisy think? What would his parents think? What did *he* think?

Vampire.

He raked his fingers though his hair. He had to be having a nightmare, he thought as he washed the dried blood from his face and neck. That's all it was. A bad dream.

He clung to that hope while he dressed, then followed Costain into the elevator and down to the street below. It wasn't until Alex looked in a store window and didn't see his reflection staring back at him that the truth hit home.

The hunter had become the hunted.

He was a vampire.

Nosferatu.

Undead.

And nothing would ever be the same again.

<h1 style="text-align:center">CHAPTER 13</h1>

Rhys slid a glance at his companion as they strolled down a nearly deserted side street. "Didn't it ever occur to you that one day you might piss off a vampire who would turn you out of spite?"

"Not really," Alex said with a shrug. "Maybe. I can't say I spent a lot of time worrying about it."

"And now it's happened."

"Yeah."

"Well, look on the bright side," Rhys remarked. "Being a vampire should come easy to you."

"Easy!" Alex exclaimed bitterly. "What are you? Nuts?"

"You know pretty much everything there is to know about us," Rhys said with a shrug. "What we can do, what we can't. How to destroy us. You used to be a hunter. You're still a hunter. Only your prey has changed."

"Dammit, Costain, I can't hunt people!"

"Sure you can. It's a hell of a lot easier than hunting vampires."

Alex snorted. He had no doubt of that.

"Okay," Rhys said. "We're not here to discuss the pros and cons of being Nosferatu. What are you in the mood for?"

Alex glared at him. "You need to work on your sense of humor, you know that?"

"Pay attention. Up ahead, there's a young couple. Do you want the male or the female?"

"Is there a difference?"

"Other than the obvious?" Rhys asked with a grin, then turned serious. "As a rule, male vampires are attracted to mortal females and female vampires tend to hunt males. There's not much difference in the taste of male or female, but there are subtle differences in blood types. You'll have to taste a few to decide which you prefer."

Alex stared at him. "You're putting me on, right? Blood is blood."

"Not really, but you'll find that out sooner or later. You don't have to worry about tainted blood. If you drink from someone who's high on booze or drugs or has a fatal disease, it won't affect you."

"Yeah, okay."

"So? The male or the female?"

"The female. I can't imagine nibbling on some guy's neck."

Laughing, Rhys quickened his stride. He caught up with the couple as they reached their car, hypnotized them both with a look, then waited for Alex to catch up.

"Okay, the first step is usually calling your prey to you. Once that's done, you can mesmerize them so they don't struggle, unless you're in the mood for a fight."

Alex stared at the woman. She was young, in her mid-twenties, with short, curly, black hair and dark-brown eyes. She stared at him blankly. Muttering, "I can't do this.," he backed away.

"Yes, you can." Leaning forward, Rhys bit the woman's neck, just enough to draw blood.

The coppery scent of it quickly filled the air. Alex felt an ache in his gums, the brush of his fangs against his tongue.

"Forget your human ideas of right and wrong," Rhys said, "and just do what comes naturally."

Alex started to refuse, but the scent of the woman's blood sang to him, making him forget everything but the sudden, overwhelming desire to sink his fangs into her throat, to taste the rich red nectar that flowed just beneath her skin, to hear her heart beating in time with his own.

Hardly aware that he was moving, he wrapped his arms around her and bent his head to her throat.

"Careful," Rhys admonished. "Mortals are fragile creatures. If you don't want to kill her, you need to listen to the sound of her heartbeat. It will tell you when it's time to stop."

Alex's head jerked up. "Kill her? Dammit! Of course I don't want to kill her." But even as he said the words, his newborn instincts were urging him to drink again, to drink until he was intoxicated with it. Nothing had ever tasted so good or so sweet.

Or so right.

Horrified, he let her go and backed away.

With a word, Costain released the couple from his thrall. Before they were fully aware of their surroundings, he grabbed Alex by the arm and transported the two of them back to his lair.

"So," Rhys drawled, "was it as bad as you expected?"

Alex stared at him. "You know darn well that it wasn't." Feeling guilty, he dragged a hand across his jaw. "I wanted to take all of it."

"That's normal, for fledglings. You can control that urge, if you want to. It helps that the desperation to feed wears off after a while. Just remember, I don't allow any killing in my territory."

"Have you told Megan about me?" Alex asked.

Rhys nodded.

"What did she say?"

Rhys grinned. "She said welcome to the family."

Alex snorted. "I wonder what Daisy will think."

"I reckon you'll find out soon enough."

"Yeah." Alex frowned. "I was attacked outside the club. Where the hell were you? You've known every move I've made since I got here and when I need you, you're nowhere."

"I was fighting a battle of my own at the time," Costain said.

"Yeah?"

"A pair of hunters ganged up on me, to their regret. I got to you as soon as I could. Now, I need to meet with the Council and let them know about Magdalena. And about you. Come on."

"You go ahead."

"Sorry, sonny boy, but I'm not leaving you alone. And I'll be spending my nights in the penthouse for a while."

"I don't need a babysitter," Alex snapped.

Rhys arched one brow. "I'm responsible for you now, *fledgling*, and I intend to be here to see you through these first difficult days of transition."

They stopped by *La Mort Rouge* to pick up the Jag, since Costain felt like driving. Alex sat back, staring out the window as he tried to come to terms with what he'd become. For once, Rhys had nothing to say, no sardonic remarks, for which he was grateful. His senses were so overloaded, he wasn't sure he could concentrate on anything. It was disconcerting, being bombarded with myriad sights and scents—the purr of the car's engine, the odors of oil and gasoline, the music drifting from the radio, the smell of trees and grass, smoke from a barbeque.

Long before they reached their destination, he caught the scent of sand and sea, heard the roar of the waves endlessly rushing to the shore.

He caught the distinctive scent of vampires when Costain pulled up in front of a weathered, gray house surrounded by a white picket fence. Even though he was now one of the Undead, Alex knew a moment of disquiet as he followed Rhys through the front door. Save for two brown leather sofas, a coffee table and a couple of chairs, the room was empty of furniture.

Four male vampires waited inside.

"This is Alex," Rhys said. "He's my fledgling and as such, under my protection, the same as the rest of you."

The men nodded their understanding, though Alex could see they were all curious about the details. None were forthcoming.

"Alex, the dark-haired Valentino look-alike is Rupert Moss," Costain said. "The old man is Nicholas. Randolph Morris is the redhead. And the dude with the snake tattoo is Julius Romano."

The vampires each acknowledged Alex in turn.

"So, what are we doing here?" Nicholas asked.

"Alex is being hunted by a vampire named Magdalena. I don't know anything about her except that she's old and vindictive. I don't want any of you to do anything, I just wanted you to be aware of her presence."

"She can't be worse than Villagrande," Romano remarked.

"That's for sure," Nicholas muttered. Alex had to agree.

Rhys glanced around the room. "Any questions?"

"Where's your pretty bride?" Romano asked with a leer.

"None of your business," Rhys snapped, eyes flashing fire. "We're done here." Pivoting on his heels, he stalked out of the house.

"A little touchy there, aren't you?" Alex said, following Rhys outside.

"Yeah. I get that way when Megan's been away too long."

"When's she coming home?"

"I'm not sure. I paid for the trip, told her parents to stay as long as they wanted." He swore under his breath. "I'm beginning to think that was a mistake."

Alex chuckled softly. It was still hard to believe that the notorious Rhys Costain had lost his heart to a woman.

During the next few nights, Rhys was constantly at Alex's side. When he protested yet again that he didn't need a babysitter, Rhys snickered.

"You know a lot *about* vampires," the Master of the City remarked as they strolled down Sunset Boulevard, "but you don't know how to *be* one."

"So, what do I need to know?"

"How to turn into mist, for one thing. It comes in handy, now and then."

"Okay, Master, how is it done?"

"Mostly, it's mind over matter. If you concentrate hard enough, it will happen."

Alex remembered watching Costain shimmer and disappear and wishing he could do the same. Be careful what you wish for he thought, with a wry grin. "Okay, Teach, what do I do first?"

"You need to think of yourself as weightless, without form or substance. Don't try to force it. And when it happens, whatever the hell you do, don't panic." He looked around. "It's too crowded here."

Costain chose a football field in a school yard in another city for Alex's first attempt.

Alex shifted from one foot to the other, suddenly uncertain. What if he turned into mist and couldn't turn back? Or if he floated over the fence and never found his way home? Had it been anyone but Costain standing beside him on the fifty yard line, he would have chickened out. *Shit!*

Taking a deep breath, he closed his eyes and imagined he was a ghost, no longer subject to gravity, no longer with a physical body. Feeling suddenly weightless, he opened his eyes and realized he was floating six feet above the ground. His physical body was gone, yet he could see Rhys, hear the distant sounds of traffic, but he couldn't speak.

It was scary as hell and yet, exhilarating at the same time.

He floated through the air, then panicked when a gust of wind carried him further than he wanted to go.

"Remember what I said," Rhys called. "Stay calm and concentrate."

Body, body, body, Alex thought desperately, and sighed with relief when he felt solid ground beneath his feet.

Rhys chuckled. "It gets easier and less scary after a time or two. Other things come without conscious thought—increased strength and speed, enhanced senses, the ability to heal almost instantly, to read minds, to bend mortal wills to yours."

Alex scrubbed a hand over his jaw. Those were powers he'd known about from being a hunter. But now the shoe was on the other foot, so to speak.

Costain's head snapped up. "I smell prey. Come on."

Prey, Alex thought, and wondered if the day would come when he no longer thought of humans as anything but a means to ease his thirst.

CHAPTER 14

Rylee sat in front of her computer, unable to concentrate on the paperwork at hand. A week had passed since that dreadful night when she had learned that vampires were real. It had changed her life dramatically. She had taken to sleeping with a light on, made sure to be home before dark, kept her curtains drawn and the doors and windows closed and locked day and night.

Being unable to work after dark was cutting into her profits, since she'd had to turn down several evening weddings and a twenty-fifth anniversary party at Huntington Beach.

The headline in the morning paper had screamed *"Bodies Found Drained of Blood in L.A."* Once, she would have scoffed at such stories, certain the morbid headlines were merely a ploy to tease viewers and increase ratings. But no more. Vampires were no longer a myth, but a stark, terrifying reality. She had seen them with her own eyes.

She remembered fainting when that scary blond vampire had fed Alex his blood. Had Alex survived the night? If so, he would be one of the Undead now. Were the two of them responsible for the reported deaths in the city? She couldn't imagine Alex doing such a thing, but she had no trouble believing the other one capable of it. No trouble at all.

Alex. She sighed as she saved her latest additions to QuickBooks. She missed him dreadfully. It hurt, knowing he was forever lost to her now. She told herself it shouldn't matter. They had only seen each other a few times. She hardly knew him.

But her heart ached just the same.

Feeling trapped in Costain's apartment, Alex paced the living room floor back and forth. Back and forth. Rhys had forbidden him to go out alone, but he thought he might go mad if he had to spend one more night cooped up in this place with nothing to do.

He didn't know where Costain had gone or when he planned to return. His master's parting words had been, *Stay put until I get here.* And that had been hours ago.

Alex swore under his breath. He missed his old life. Missed being awake during the day, able to come and go as he pleased. He told himself he was hungry for his favorite foods, but that was a lie. He loved the taste of blood. The idea sickened him even as thinking about it aroused his thirst.

He missed Rylee. Her smile. The sound of her laughter. The way she made anything seem possible. He had felt a sense of peace when he was with her. A week since he'd seen her and every day worse than the last.

As much as he longed to see her again, he knew Costain was right. He was no fit company for anyone right now, not even himself.

He swore again. He had to get out of here. Somewhere quiet that didn't smell like vampire.

Almost before he realized what he was doing, he found himself at the beach where he had first met Rylee. He didn't know what surprised him more, the fact that he had actually transported himself across the miles, or the fact that Rylee was there, asleep on a blanket.

For a moment, he just stood there, drinking in the sight of her and thinking how much he missed her. And then he frowned. What the hell was she doing out here alone, after dark?

"Rylee," he called softly. "Rylee, wake up." When she didn't stir, he bent down and gently shook her shoulder. "Rylee."

Rylee woke with a start, then jackknifed into a sitting position. The shiver that ran down her spine had nothing to do with the cold and everything to do with the man standing beside her.. The image of the blond vampire dribbling blood into Alex's mouth flashed before her eyes. He was one of them now. Undead. She sensed the change in him, that same not-quite-human vibe she had felt from the other two vampires.

She didn't waste time screaming or asking questions.

Scrambling to her feet, Rylee turned and ran down the beach as fast as her legs could carry her. And all the while, the word *vampire* whispered in the back of her mind.

She risked a glance behind her, but he wasn't there. Lightheaded with relief, she kept running. Until she slammed into something unyielding.

Rylee did scream then, or at least tried to. Fear trapped the cry in the back of her throat and she could only stand there, trembling in Alex's arms. Arms that felt like solid steel, yet held her lightly, until she tried to wriggle free and found there was no escape.

"It's all right, I'm not going to hurt you," Alex said quietly. And hoped it was true.

"Then let me go!" Her voice came out in a breathless rush.

"Later."

She stared up at him, her eyes wide. "How did you find me?"

"I wasn't looking for you, at least not consciously."

"Please," she said, speaking slowly and distinctly, as if he were some wild animal who needed soothing. "Just let me go."

"You're not going to run away again, are you? There's not much point in it, since you can't outrun me."

"Then I won't run."

He looked at her dubiously, but let her go.

It took all the willpower Rylee possessed not to bolt. But he was right, there was no way she could hope to outrun him. Hadn't he just proved that? "So, what now?"

"I don't know," he murmured, with a rueful shake of his head. "This is all new to me. And scary as hell, believe it or not."

"Oh, I believe it." Her gaze slid away from his. "Well, goodnight."

"Rylee, please, don't go. I swear I won't hurt you," he said again. It wouldn't be easy, keeping his hands off of her. A shift in the breeze carried her scent to his nostrils. He heard the blood flowing warm and sweet through her veins, the rapid beating of her heart, the scent of fear that danced over her skin. He clenched his hands at his sides to keep from reaching for her. "Will you sit with me for a few minutes?"

"Do I have a choice?"

Alex frowned as he recalled how Costain had mesmerized the young couple. Did he have that same power? Could he impose his will on Rylee, make her do whatever he wanted? Concentrating, he reached out with his mind, felt his thoughts brush hers, and knew he could easily bend her will to his. It was a heady, frightening sensation and he immediately backed off. What the hell was he thinking? Did he want to force her to stay with him? Did he want to be alone?

He knew what Rhys would do, but what would Daisy do? Once he asked himself that question, the answer was easy. Taking a step back, he said, "I won't force you to stay if you really want to go."

Rylee stared at him. Strange, she thought, but now that the choice was hers, she didn't want to leave. Hoping she wasn't making a huge, perhaps fatal, mistake, she sat on a nearby deadfall.

Alex gestured at the place beside her. "May I?"

"I guess so." She hadn't quite wrapped her mind around the fact that he was a vampire hunter and now he was a vampire. It was unbelievable.

Moving slowly so as not to startle her, he sat down, though he left a good distance between them. "You shouldn't be out here alone, after dark."

"I know. I fell asleep."

"You're lucky I'm the one who found you."

"Yes," she murmured, although she didn't feel lucky. Only frightened. And sad.

Now that she was willing to abide his company, Alex didn't know what to say.

Only a few feet separated them, but it might as well have been the Pacific Ocean, he thought bleakly. Because they were leagues apart.

"That horrible woman," Rylee said, "She was the mate of that vampire you killed, wasn't she?"

"Yeah."

"And the man who rescued us? He's a friend of yours?"

"His name's Rhys Costain. I guess you could say we're friends. He's the Master of the West Coast Vampires."

"What does that mean?"

"Mainly that he's very old and very powerful. The master vampires here in the United States have divided the country into territories, with each one ruling a particular area."

Rylee shuddered. The thought of more creatures like Costain was a frightening possibility to contemplate. "Sounds like the Mafia."

"Yeah, in a way. Vampires are territorial creatures. Very jealous of their hunting grounds. The ones who live here have all sworn allegiance to Rhys. In return, he protects them."

"And now you're one of them?"

Alex shrugged. "He's not just the Master of the West Coast. He's my master now." Seeing the question in her eyes, he said, "When a vampire turns a human, he becomes their sire—their master. He's supposed to teach them what they need to know to survive."

She nodded. "So, he's like your boss?"

"You could say that." Alex frowned. He hadn't really thought about the implications of that until now. Costain would be his master for as long as the two of them lived. Only Costain's death—or his own—could free him.

"What are you going to do now?"

Gazing out at the ocean, he murmured, "I don't know." All he knew was hunting. Of course, his physical needs were few these days. His future expenses, save for clothes and a secure place to spend the day, would be negligent. He no longer needed health or dental insurance. His grocery bills would be non-existent except for an occasional bottle of wine.

Fighting the urge to reach out to him, Rylee folded her hands in her lap. "I'm so sorry, Alex." Pity welled within her when he turned to face her. He looked so lost and alone, his eyes haunted. "What about your family? Will they stand by you?"

"Yeah. My sister, Daisy, is a vampire. She's married to the one who turned her." He laughed bitterly. "You wouldn't think a family of hunters would have so many blood-suckers."

Not knowing what to say, Rylee gathered her courage and reached for his hand.

Alex stared at her fingers, entwined with his, and wondered how she could bear to touch him. "I guess you just never know what life has in store for you."

"Is it awful, being what you are?"

"I don't know. I haven't been one long enough to find out. I always thought vampires were monsters until my sister became one. It didn't really change her. She's still the same, sweet kid she always was."

"Do you *feel* different?"

Alex frowned as he considered her question. Different? Sure, he felt different, but he didn't feel like a monster. He slid a glance at Rylee. Her blood called to him. His instincts urged him to pull her into his embrace and take what he so desperately needed. Wanted.

Afraid of hurting her, he eased his hand from hers and gained his feet.

"Alex?"

He gazed down at her, wondering what she wanted. And then he remembered he hadn't answered her question. Shrugging, he said, "To tell you the truth, I don't know how the hell I feel. I guess only time will tell."

"Yes," she murmured. "Time."

The wind shifted, carrying her scent to him again. He stared at the pulse throbbing in the hollow of her throat, closed his eyes as he listened to the siren call of her heartbeat.

With a strangled cry, he turned and ran down the beach, his feet pounding the sand as he fled the almost overpowering urge to bury his fangs in her slender throat and never let her go.

Rylee huffed a sigh of regret, certain she'd seen the last of him, even though it was probably for the best. He was a vampire now, no longer human, even though he looked the same, sounded the same.

To her surprise, he reappeared moments later.

Keeping his distance, he said, "You shouldn't be out here alone. I'll take you home."

She started to object. Then, remembering Magdalena, she said, "I have my car."

"Right. Let's go." Afraid to get too close, Alex trailed her from a distance. When she unlocked the Mazda, he climbed into the back seat.

Rylee looked at him askance, but didn't say anything.

When they reached her house, he got out of the car and waited at the end of the driveway until she was safely inside, looking out at him. "I'm sorry, Rylee," he called. "I won't bother you again."

His gaze moved over her for stretched seconds, as if to burn her image into his mind. And then, with a wave, he turned and strolled down the sidewalk.

Rylee stared after him while hot tears trickled down her cheeks. She wept for what he'd become, for what he'd lost that could never be regained. Sobbed for the ache in her heart because he had changed—changed in ways that made just being with him more dangerous than she had ever imagined.

Costain was waiting for Alex when he materialized in the penthouse living room.

"What the hell were you doing at the beach?" Rhys inhaled sharply, then frowned. "With that woman?"

"I had to get out of here," Alex retorted. "I was going stir crazy. I needed to spend some time alone, without you hovering over me like some hungry vulture, watching my every move."

Rhys grunted softly. "Been that bad, huh?"

Alex shrugged.

"I just don't want you to do anything you'll spend the rest of your existence regretting," Rhys said quietly, and there was a wealth of remorse in his tone. "How's the girl?"

"Rylee." Alex sank down in the chair across from Costain. "Beautiful."

"Sounds like you were falling for her."

"I could have," he admitted. If it hadn't been for his guilt over Paula's death. If Rhys hadn't turned him into a monster.

"Feeling sorry for yourself, O'Donnell?"

"Why shouldn't I?"

"You're alive," Rhys said, grinning. "More or less."

Alex glared at him.

"Stop whining. You were turned by a powerful vampire. That power passes to you. You've got a place to stay for as long as you need it. You're pretty well off, near as I can tell. Your family won't have any trouble accepting you. As for Rylee, she won't be the first woman—or the last—to fall for a vampire. Granted, relationships between our kind and mortals don't always end well, but..." Rhys lifted one shoulder and let it fall. "It worked out all right for Daisy and for me. Why not you?"

"You finished?" Alex muttered irritably.

"All right. End of lecture." Costain cuffed him on the arm. "Let's go get a drink."

Alex had expected to go hunting, so he was surprised when Rhys transported the two of them to *La Mort Rouge*. "What are we doing here?" he asked, glancing around the club.

"No need to hunt when there are a dozen beautiful women here who are more than eager to satisfy our thirst."

Taking a seat at the bar, Alex looked at the numbered doors.

Rhys moved behind the bar and filled two glasses with wine. Handing one to Alex, he jerked his chin toward the leggy blonde striding toward them, hips swaying provocatively. "Ah, Jean Marie," he murmured.

She smiled at Alex. "Who might this be?"

"This is Alex. Alex, this lovely creature is Jean Marie. Why don't you take her to one of the empty rooms? She'll be happy to satisfy your appetites," he said with a leer. "All of them."

"Thanks, but I don't think so."

"Not to your taste? Perhaps you would prefer Juliette or Monique? Perhaps Angelique?"

"Do you not find me pleasing?" Jean Marie asked with a pretty pout.

"What? No, no, you're beautiful."

With a smile, she reached for his hand and tugged him to his feet.

Staring daggers at Costain, Alex reluctantly followed the blonde into room number seven.

"What is your pleasure, *mon ami vampire?*" she crooned as she closed the door and leaned back against it.

Alex muttered an oath. She was a beautiful girl, perhaps in her early twenties, although the worldly-wise expression in her eyes made her seem older. She wore a dark-red gown with slits in the sides that showed off her legs, while the low-cut bodice revealed a generous amount of creamy white cleavage.

Taking his hand, she moved to the bed and tugged him down beside her. "Don't be afraid, Alex," she said, her voice husky. "I won't bite." She laughed softly as she brushed her hair away from her neck. "I'll leave that to you."

Alex stared at her. Jean Marie was a beautiful girl, there was no doubt about that. And more than willing. Her blood smelled like ambrosia and his hunger quickly stirred to life, demanding to be fed. Drawing her into his embrace, he buried his fangs in her sweet flesh and wished, fleetingly, that it was Rylee moaning softly in his arms.

Sitting at the bar, Rhys chuckled as the scent of blood drifted from room number seven.

CHAPTER 15

Rylee reclined in a tub full of lavender-scented bubbles, willing herself to relax and trying not to cry. She didn't know why she was so upset. Sure, it was terrible, what had happened to Alex, but they hardly knew each other. Still, she had felt a kinship with him, a kindred soul. Deep in her heart, she had hoped that, when his mourning period was over, they might pursue their mutual attraction and see where it led.

But that would never happen now.

If she lived to be a hundred, she would never forget him, or the way he'd made her feel.

Over the next few days, Rylee threw herself into her work. She took every day-time job that came along in an effort to keep from thinking about Alex. She took photos of a half-dozen movie stars for Summerville, sent a portfolio of wildlife shots to Alger.

When she wasn't working, she wrote new copy for her web page, balanced her checking account, rearranged her kitchen cupboards, rummaged through her closet and threw out the shirts, skirts, and pants she hadn't worn in over a year.

None of those tasks kept her from thinking about Alex. What did vampires do with *their* time? Granted, they slept all day. Did they spend their nights hunting? She shuddered to think of him preying on helpless men and women, stealing their blood. In movies, vampires always killed their prey—or turned them into other vampires. Was that fact or fiction? Was being Undead as awful as she thought it would be? What did his family think?

Sitting at her computer, she looked up vampires on Google, amazed by the number of links that came up. It would take years to sort through them all, she thought, as she clicked on the first one, then scrolled through the information. To her surprise, every country in the world had its own vampire myths and traditions. She closed the link, thinking perhaps Amazon would be more help. But, there again, the number of books on the subject was mind-boggling. She checked the table of contents on one volume—*How to Become a Vampire, How to Destroy a Vampire, How to Identify a Vampire, Preternatural Powers, Myths and Legends*. More info than she ever wanted to know.

She paid strict heed to what Rhys had told her. Each night, she walked through the house, making sure all the windows and doors were securely locked, the curtains drawn. Except for the night she'd fallen asleep on the beach, she made sure to be home before nightfall.

And it was starting to get to her. In the past, she had enjoyed jogging in the evening, doing night shoots, going out to dinner or a movie with her college friend, Connie. But no more. She had seen what lurked in the shadows of the night and it scared the crap out of her.

With an oath, Rhys crumpled the newspaper and tossed it into the trash can behind the bar. Damn Magdalena! Every night, she left more bodies in her wake. Damn her hide! The last thing he needed was a rogue vampire in his territory. What the hell was she up to? Stories of vampire killings were sure to draw more hunters into his territory, sooner rather than later.

"Something wrong?" Alex asked, taking his usual seat at the end of the bar.

"There's blood on your mouth. Been visiting Jean Marie again?"

Alex shrugged as he grabbed a napkin and wiped away the tell-tale stain. "What's got your tail in a twist?"

"Magdalena. She's as careless as Villagrande, leaving bodies everywhere. Before long, the wrong people will notice."

"You mean hunters," Alex said, and felt a wave of remorse for what he'd lost. He had loved hunting, the sense of excitement, the very real fear that each hunt could be his last as he tracked one of the Undead.

"Exactly. Too bad you're out of business."

Alex nodded in agreement. "I guess you'll have to be the one to take her down." He would have loved nothing more than to drive a stake into Magdalena's black heart. As a hunter, he would have had a good chance of success. As a fledgling vampire, he feared he was sorely outmatched, even though Costain had sired him. Dammit.

"Believe me, if I could find her, she'd be history. I don't suppose your old man would give it a shot."

"I don't think so." After Brandon had been killed and Daisy had been turned, his mother had made his old man promise he would never hunt another vampire. What the hell was he doing here, Alex thought as glanced around the club. He needed to call his parents and let them know what had happened, but he kept putting it off. It wouldn't be an easy tale to tell, he thought.

And it wouldn't be tonight.

But Fate had other plans. No sooner had he decided to wait a little longer to call his folks than his cell phone rang. With a shake of his head, he made his way to one of the empty rooms and closed the door. "Hi, Daisy, " he said with as much enthusiasm as he could muster. "What's up?"

"I'm not sure. I just had this feeling that I should call you. Is everything all right?"

"Oh, yeah, just great."

There was a long pause. And then she said, "What's wrong?"

"What's wrong?" He shook his head, not knowing whether to laugh or cry.

"Alex, you're scaring me. What's happened? Are you all right?"

He huffed a sigh of resignation, then dropped down on the bed and told her, as succinctly as possible, what had happened.

"How are you feeling?" she asked, when he'd finished.

"Like hell."

"Do you want me to come home?"

"Why? There's nothing you can do."

"Hey, I was a pretty good hunter in my time. And I still have my compass."

Daisy had an enchanted compass with a pointer that turned red when a vampire was in the vicinity. Alex chuckled softly. "Has it occurred to you that since *you're* now a vampire, it will always point toward you?"

"Oh," she said with a laugh. "I didn't think of that. Have you told the folks?"

"Not yet. It isn't the kind of news I want to give them over the phone."

"Aren't you home?" He heard the frown in her voice.

"No."

"Where are you?"

"In California. I'm staying with Costain."

"Really? Wow, talk about strange bedfellows. How's that working out?"

"Not as bad as you might think."

"I can tell Mom and Dad, if you'd like."

"No. I'll do it."

"All right. If you change your mind, or you need me, just call."

"Thanks, Daisy Mae."

"I love you," she said.

"Love you, too." Alex stared at his phone as the call ended, wondering how the hell she'd known something was wrong.

Erik drew Daisy back into his arms when the conversation was over. "How do you think he's really doing?"

She shook her head. "I'm not sure. It's hard to tell, over the phone. It has to be a difficult transition for him. He killed our kind for a living and now he's one of us." *One of us,* she thought. It hadn't been that long ago since she'd been a mortal woman—the notorious Blood Thief.

"I can't imagine Alex and Costain sharing the same space," Erik muttered. "There was never any love lost between them."

"Well, Rhys has no one to blame but himself. He turned Alex. The least he can do is look after him."

"True, enough," Erik murmured. "Now, what can *your* sire do for *you?*"

"Whatever he wants," Daisy said with a seductive grin. "I'm yours to command."

Rhys called the Council together the following night. Alex tagged along, since Costain hadn't given him any other choice. While Rhys and the others talked about the recent killings and the likelihood of hunters coming to town and what to do about it, Alex studied the vampires.

Rhys had told him Julius Romano was a California boy who had once been a drug dealer. Of medium height, he had close-set brown eyes and brown hair and looked like he'd been turned in his early twenties. A red-and-black snake tattoo ran the length of his left arm from shoulder to wrist.

The tall, angular vampire with wispy gray hair and blue eyes was Nicholas. He'd been an old man when he was turned, probably in his mid-seventies. Alex couldn't help wondering what his story was. In all his years as a hunter, he'd never encountered a vampire turned that late in life.

The handsome blood-sucker with slicked-back black hair, brown eyes, and a thin mustache was Rupert. The guy looked like that old movie star, Valentino.

Morris didn't look anything like a vampire, with his frizzy red hair and freckles, more like an insurance salesman.

"Hunters don't worry me," Romano was saying. "Not after Villagrande."

Rupert nodded. "Magdalena is more of a threat, at least as long as O'Donnell is in our territory."

"Alex stays," Rhys said.

"So, is there any evidence of hunters in town now?" Nicholas asked.

"Not that I know of, but keep your eyes and ears open. If you hear of anything, let me know." Costain's gaze moved over each of them. "I'm assuming it's Magdalena leaving the bodies in her wake, and not one of you."

As though pulled by the same string, Rupert, Nicholas, Morris and Julius all shook their heads vigorously.

Alex grinned. It was obvious the four of them were more afraid of Costain than Magdalena and the hunters combined. But then, who could blame them? Rhys was old and powerful—and totally ruthless, when necessary.

"You have anything to say, fledgling?" Costain asked.

"Not a thing."

"All right, then. Meeting adjourned."

Alex was surprised when Rhys lingered after the others had gone. "Something wrong?"

"I don't know. I hope not."

"What's that supposed to mean?"

"Did you notice anything unusual tonight?"

"Like what?"

"Like the fact that Rupert never looked at me directly."

Alex shrugged. "So?"

"So, maybe he has something to hide."

"Why don't you just read his mind and find out?"

"No way to do it without alerting him. If he's up to something, I don't want him to know I'm suspicious."

"What do you think he's up to?"

"I'm not sure. He's been with me a long time. Might be that he's thinking it's time for a coup."

Alex snorted. "No way. You could wipe the floor with him and not raise a sweat. Wait a minute! You don't think he's in league with Magdalena, do you?"

"If he is, you're the one in trouble. She wants you, not me."

"You sure about that?"

Rhys scrubbed a hand across his jaw. "No. No, I'm not sure at all."

After leaving the beach house, Alex and Rhys transported themselves to *La Mort Rouge.* It was late on a Monday night and there were only a handful of people in the place—and most of them were vampires.

Alex sat at the bar, a glass of blood-laced wine in his hand, his thoughts on Rylee. He wondered how she was getting along, if she ever thought of him. If she missed him as much as he missed her. No matter how often he told himself they were better off apart, he couldn't stop thinking about her. Wanting her. It didn't matter that he felt guilty for wanting another woman so soon after Paula's passing, didn't matter that he knew it was dangerous for Rylee to be with him.

He wanted her.

"What's the matter, *cherie?*" Babette asked, taking the stool beside him. "You look like you have lost your best friend."

"Maybe I have."

"Friends, they come and go," she said with a shrug. "Do you not find me attractive?"

"It isn't that."

"Ah." She placed her hand over his heart. "You are pining for someone. Someone special, I think."

"Yeah. I guess you could say that."

"Come with me," she coaxed. "I can make you forget her. At least for an hour or two."

Alex shook his head. "I'm not in the mood."

She brushed her hair away from her neck. "Perhaps you need a drink?"

His gaze moved to the pulse throbbing in the hollow of her throat. The flowery fragrance of her perfume didn't mask the tempting scent of her blood, nor did the slow, sensual music coming over the sound system mask the steady beat of her heart.

She tugged on his hand, winked at him when he stood and followed her into room number six.

Inside, she closed the door, then perched on the edge of the mattress, a come-hither smile curving her lips.

Alex stood with his back to the door. She was a pretty thing, with lots of curly black hair and the greenest eyes he'd ever seen. Her gown clung to her like as second skin, outlining every curve. "Why do you do this?" he asked, sitting beside her.

"Why not?" She shrugged one shoulder. "It is pleasant for me, as well." She ran her fingertips over his lips, down his chest, to his thigh. "Perhaps, after you drink, you will feel the need for a little exercise."

The woman was incorrigible, he thought, as he drew her into his embrace and brushed her hair out of the way. She smelled of honeysuckle and musk.

And blood. Blood to ease his thirst and satisfy the need roaring through him like a hungry, insatiable lion. He bent his head to her neck and tried not to hurt her as he bit into her tender flesh. Warmth spread through him as he closed his eyes and drank.

And drank.

Lost in the euphoria of feeding, he might have taken it all if Rhys hadn't slammed into the room and pulled him away.

"What the hell are you doing?" Costain snarled. "Are you trying to kill her?"

Alex stared at his sire, not comprehending, until he looked at Babette. She lay back on the bed, eyes closed, her lashes like ebony fans against her pale skin. "I...I didn't mean to," he stammered.

Pushing him aside, Rhys took the woman in his arms, bit into his wrist, and held it to her lips. "Drink, darlin'," he murmured. "Come on now. That's my girl."

"Is she going to be okay?" Alex asked anxiously.

"No thanks to you."

Alex backed out of the room. Horrified by what he'd almost done, he transported himself to Costain's lair. He could have killed her. The thought played and replayed in his mind.

Maybe he should have killed her, Alex thought bleakly, because if he took a life, Costain would take his—and that would put an end to his hellish existence.

It could have been Rylee.

The thought brought him up short and suddenly, ending his existence seemed like the best thing he could do for everyone concerned.

Maybe he would save Costain the trouble and go out to meet the sun. It wouldn't be a pleasant way to go, but it would be quickly over.

He glanced out the window.

Only an hour until dawn.

Chapter 16

Rhys swore under his breath as his fledgling's thoughts trickled into his mind. Damn fool kid. Maybe telling him to stay away from Rylee hadn't been the best idea he'd ever had. Alex had been happier when he was seeing the girl.

Maybe she was the answer. If the kid made sure to feed first, Rylee probably wouldn't be in much danger.

After making sure Babette was all right, Rhys sent her home, then transported himself to the penthouse.

He didn't give Alex a chance to say anything—simply grabbed him by the neck. "This is the last time I'm giving you a choice," he growled. "Life or death? It's up to you."

Alex struggled to free himself, but it was impossible. The hand at his throat was like iron, strong and unyielding.

"Don't be so hard on yourself. I know you're feeling guilty for what almost happened tonight, but it happens to all of us when we're new. Hell, it's partly my fault," Rhys allowed, releasing his hold. "I should have made sure you fed before we left for the meeting."

Alex rubbed a hand over his throat, thinking it was a good thing he didn't have to breathe. But people tended to look at you funny if you didn't.

"I've been thinking," Rhys went on. "I might have been wrong in telling you to stay away from Rylee."

Alex shook his head. "No. You were right. It could have been her tonight. If I'd hurt her…" He shook his head again. "I couldn't live with that."

"Listen to me. You were happy—well, happier—when you were spending time with her. I think maybe she's good for you. She makes you feel more human, for want of a better word. I think if you make sure to feed before you see her, you'll both be all right."

"You *think?*"

"If I'm wrong, I'll be there to stop you before you do anything that can't be undone."

Alex dropped into the nearest chair. Just the thought of seeing Rylee again made the world—and his future—suddenly seem brighter. And then his shoulders sagged. She knew what he was now and she was understandably afraid of him. He was probably the last person on earth she wanted to spend time with.

Rhys shrugged. "You won't know until you ask."

"Get out of my head," Alex muttered, but there was no heat in his words. If Costain wasn't constantly eavesdropping on his thoughts, Babette would have died tonight. "I'm gonna turn in. I'll think about what you said."

Rhys sank into the chair Alex had vacated. Bringing the kid across might have been a mistake, he mused, but only time would tell. In the meantime, maybe the love of a good woman would give his fledgling some peace of mind.

He grinned into the darkness. The love of a good woman had certainly had a positive effect on him, Rhys thought, as he reached for his phone and called his wife.

Rylee froze in the act of folding a load of laundry when someone knocked at the door. She told herself she needed to relax. It had been almost two weeks since she'd seen Alex. He hadn't called, hadn't tried to see her. And in all that time, nothing unusual or scary had happened—if you called it normal for a grown woman to lock herself in her house every night as soon as the sun went down.

When the knock came again, she made her way to the door and called, "Who is it?"

"It's me. Alex."

Alex! Her heart did a little leap of joy at the sound of his voice. And then she frowned. What was he doing here? He had assured her that she would never see him again.

Hoping Costain had been right when he said vampires couldn't enter a dwelling uninvited, she opened the door. "I'm surprised to see you," she said, folding her arms over her chest. "Is something wrong?"

"Everything. I know it might be hard for you to believe, but my life's no good without you. I'm asking you, begging you, to find it in your heart to spend a little time with me."

"I thought you said it was dangerous."

"It is. I know that. And yet being with you…I don't know how to explain it, Rylee, but it makes me feel human again, more in control. Costain thinks being with you might be good for me."

"Is that why you're here? Because he told you to come?"

"No! No. I've missed you every single night. You have no idea how much." He drank in the sight of her. She was even lovelier than he remembered. "I'm not asking for a lifetime commitment. Just let me come by once in a while and…and see you. Talk for a few minutes."

"I've missed you, too," she admitted. "Why did you run away the other night?"

"I hadn't…fed yet. And you were so close…I was afraid of losing control."

"What's changed?"

"I fed before I came here."

He'd fed. She knew what that meant—he had preyed on some poor, unsuspecting soul. She grimaced as images of Magdalena savaging his throat chased themselves across her mind. "Do you…?" She bit down on her lower lip. "You don't…?"

"If you're wondering if I kill those I drink from, the answer is no." So far, he thought, remembering his close call with Babette. He didn't know how he would ever face the poor girl again.

Rylee stared up at him. He looked so unhappy, so alone, like a little boy who had lost his way. And yet, he wasn't a little boy. He was a grown man, tall and broad-shouldered, with a firm jaw, chiseled cheekbones, beautiful, deep-brown eyes, and a smile that made her melt like chocolate left too long in the sun.

Taking a deep breath, she said, "Come in, Alex," and felt a peculiar tremor in the air as he crossed the threshold.

In the living room, she gestured for him to sit on the sofa before taking the chair across from him.

Alex glanced around the room, thinking it looked like her—warm and friendly. The walls were pale blue, the sofa and chair covered in a flowered print. Several portraits in white frames lined the mantel, a pair of large pictures depicting the ocean hung above the fireplace. He wondered if they were photos she had taken.

Shoving his hands in his pockets, he said, "Please don't be afraid of me, Rylee. I swear I won't hurt you, but if you get worried, all you have to do is tell me to leave and the same power that keeps vampires out of your house will compel me to go."

If she hadn't seen how the threshold affected Costain, she wouldn't have believed him. "How are you getting along, Alex? Truly? Is it getting any easier?"

"In some ways. There's no use wishing it hadn't happened because there's no going back. I'll be glad when Daisy gets home…"

"She's your sister, right?"

"Yeah. We've always been close, shared everything. Although I never thought we'd both end up like this. How about you? Everything okay?"

"Not really. I'm afraid to go out at night. It's hurting my business and making me stir-crazy."

"I guess that's my fault."

Leaning forward, she placed her hand on his knee. "No, it's that creature's fault. You can't blame yourself because she's crazy."

"If I hadn't killed her mate, none of this would have happened."

Rylee shrugged. "Split milk."

"You're awfully forgiving," he remarked, covering her hand with his. "Any other woman would probably hate me."

"I don't hate you."

"Rylee…"

She didn't know who moved first, but suddenly they were on the sofa, locked in each other's arms. She closed her eyes as Alex rained butterfly kisses on her cheeks, her temples, the tip of her nose, before settling on her lips in a long, slow kiss that spread through her like a brushfire.

He fell back on the cushions, carrying her with him, his hand stroking up and down her back as he kissed her again, and yet again. She knew a moment of trepidation when she felt the tension in him, the evidence of his desire.

He muttered an oath as he released her.

She sat up and he sat beside her, his head cradled in his hands.

"Are you okay?" she asked.

"Yeah. Just give me a minute."

She worried her lower lip between her teeth, wondering if she should put some space between them.

"For vampires, sometimes it's hard to separate hunger from desire," Alex said, his voice muffled. "I don't want to hurt you, or scare you."

"You didn't."

Lifting his head, he turned to face her. "It's late. I should probably go."

She stood when he did, then followed him to the door. "I'm glad you came by, Alex."

"Me, too. Is it okay if I kiss you goodnight?"

"More than okay."

He cupped her face in his palms, his gaze moving over her face before he kissed her lightly. "Would you mind if I came by again tomorrow night? Or is it too much, too soon?"

"I'd love the company."

Feeling as if he had just won the lottery, Alex kissed her again. "Sweet dreams, sweet Rylee." Whistling softly, he strolled down the brick path to the sidewalk.

Rylee stood in the doorway, her fingertips pressed to her lips, thinking the world suddenly seemed brighter.

She watched him until he disappeared into the darkness.

Alex paused when he reached the corner. Lifting his head, he opened his vampire senses, surprised that the power came to him so readily. So naturally. And there it was—Magdalena's scent, mingled with that of another female. Concentrating, he sent a mental call to Costain. A moment later, the Master of the City stood beside him.

"What's up, fledgling?"

"Do you smell that?"

Rhys inhaled. "Wonder why Magdalena didn't come herself?"

"Beats me. I say we follow whoever this is and see where she takes us."

"Lead the way."

Alex followed the scent around the corner to where a car had been parked. Rhys dropped down on one knee and ran his hand over the tire tracks. "We can try following these."

"You go on."

"What are you going to do?"

"I'm heading back to Rylee's."

"Magdalena wasn't there."

"I know. But that doesn't mean she won't show up."

"Watch yourself and don't take any chances. If you sense trouble, give me a holler."

"Count on it." A thought carried Alex back to Rylee's house. A light still burned downstairs. He stood at the end of the walkway, wondering if he should let her know the latest, then decided against it, thinking she'd sleep better if she didn't know one of Magdalena's henchmen had been prowling around her yard.

In the meantime, he would keep watch over her place until the sun came up. Costain had taught him how to cloak his presence and he did so now, then settled down on the front porch to pass the rest of the night.

Rhys swore softly when the trail he'd been following merged onto the freeway, the tire's scent mingling with those of thousands of others.

But he would recognize it if he found it again.

Chapter 17

Magdalena looked up when Sylvi entered her lair. "Where is she?"

"That vampire you tried to turn, he was with her."

Magdalena scowled at her. "Did he see you?"

Sylvi shook her head vigorously. "No. I ran away before he left the house. I'm sorry, mistress."

A low growl rose in Magdalena's throat. If not for the girl's incompetence, Eduardo's killer would be in her power now.

She had intended to turn O'Donnell. As his sire, he would have been hers to do with as she pleased. Where had she gone wrong? Once in her control, she had planned to force him to listen over and over again to how she had killed his pregnant wife and dined on her blood. She could have compelled him to do anything she wished—kill his friends and family, be her slave. And then some other vampire had carried him off, she thought irritably. And the woman, too. "You will go back tomorrow morning and bring her to me."

"Yes, mistress." Sylvi cowered in a corner of the sofa as Magdalena stalked past her, blew out a sigh of relief when the vampire disappeared into the night.

CHAPTER 18

In the last hour before dawn, Alex called Rhys at the club. "I can't stay out here any longer. Can you come and stay with Rylee until sundown?"

"Sure, if she's okay with me spending the day in her closet."

"I'll ask her. Hang on."

Transforming into mist, Alex slid under the front door, then resumed his own shape and padded up the stairs to Rylee's bedroom. Feeling like an intruder, he turned on the light, then shook her shoulder lightly. "Rylee, wake up."

She bolted upright with a start, eyes wide with fear—and then surprise when she saw him. "What are you doing here? What's wrong?"

"I caught Magdalena's scent when I left earlier tonight."

"She was here?"

"No, but someone associated with her was. Rhys went to see if he could find her. I thought I should stick around in case Magdalena showed up. After all, if it wasn't for me, you wouldn't be in this mess."

"You can't blame yourself for what she's doing."

"Well, I feel responsible just the same. The thing is, I can't protect you when the sun comes up. So…"

"So?"

"I asked Rhys to come and stay with you until sunset."

Rylee shook her head. "No. No, I don't want him here. He scares me."

"You'll be a lot safer with him than with me. And he can be awake during the day, if necessary."

Sitting up, Rylee smoothed a hand over her hair. "If you think having Rhys here is a good idea, then I guess it's okay." She blew out a sigh of resignation. "He can use the bed in the guest room."

"He'll probably rest in a closet."

"A closet!"

"He'll want a dark place. But don't worry, if anyone tries to get to you, he'll know." Alex cocked his head to the side. "He's here. You'll have to invite him in."

Throwing the covers aside, Rylee swung her legs over the edge of the bed, grabbed her robe, stepped into her slippers, and padded downstairs. This had to be a dream, she thought. Things like this just didn't happen in real life.

After tamping down her trepidation, she eased the front door open. For a moment, she just stood there. He looked just as intimidating as he had the first time she'd seen him. Inviting the Master of the City into her home seemed like a really bad idea, yet Alex trusted him.

And she trusted Alex.

The vampire stood patiently, one brow arched as he waited for her to say something.

Rylee took a deep breath, blew it out in a huff, and said, "Please come in, Mr. Costain."

Murmuring his thanks, he crossed the threshold, and she felt it again, that odd tremor in the air, only it was stronger and more pronounced this time. Was that because Costain was more powerful than Alex?

"I'll be going now," Alex said, taking Rylee's hand in his. "And don't worry. Rhys will protect you. He's older and stronger than Magdalena."

"Do the two always go together?" Rylee asked. "Age and strength?"

"Yes, which is why you're safer with him." Alex hesitated a moment, then kissed her on the cheek. "I'll be back as soon as the sun goes down."

"Be careful," she said, giving his hand a squeeze.

"You, too."

Rylee knew a moment of anxiety as she locked the door behind Alex. She was alone with Rhys now, at the mercy of an old and powerful vampire.

"Okay if I bed down in one of your closets?" Costain asked.

"Yes. Alex told me you might. Use the spare room upstairs at the end of the hall."

"Thanks. And don't worry. If Magdalena or any of her minions come around, I'll know it."

Before she could answer, he was gone.

Perplexed, Rylee stared at the place where he'd been standing. How was it possible for vampires to just vanish from sight like that? With a shake of her head, she climbed the stairs, crawled back into bed and pulled the covers over her head.

It was late morning when she woke up. Her first thought was for the house guest in the spare room. Unable to resist, she scuffed down the hallway and tiptoed inside. She paused in front of the walk-in closet. It held her winter coats, extra blankets, a couple of pillows.

And a vampire.

As quietly as she could, she eased one of the sliding glass doors open and peered inside. Costain lay stretched out on the floor, fully clothed, arms folded across his chest. He didn't seem to be breathing. Was that normal?

She took a hasty step back when he opened his eyes.

"Something wrong?"

"No. No. I was…I mean…"

"Just curious, were you?"

She bit down on her lip, her cheeks warm with embarrassment. "Satisfied?"

Too mortified to speak, she closed the door and ran out of the room, her cheeks growing hotter at the sound of his amused laughter.

After showering, Rylee headed downstairs. She fixed breakfast. Rinsed the dishes and put them in the dishwasher, then went into her office to check her email. But all she could think about was the vampire sleeping in her closet. And Alex. Where did he pass the day? She wished he was the one resting upstairs. She wasn't afraid of Alex, but Rhys Costain scared the living daylights out of her.

A glance at the calendar reminded her she had an appointment late this afternoon. After twenty minutes of indecision, she called Mrs. LeDuc to cancel it. The woman declined to reschedule.

Rylee set her phone on the desk and stared out the window, her brow furrowed. If this trouble with Magdalena didn't end soon, she was going to lose more clients than she could afford.

Time and again she glanced at the clock, willing the hours to pass. Finally, unable to concentrate on the work at hand, she padded into the living room and turned on the TV.

And wished she hadn't.

A reporter was on screen, standing in front of a blanket-shrouded corpse. "…body identified as Joseph Fleming was found this morning in front of his West Hollywood home by the mailman. Two wounds in his neck, identical to those found on the other bodies discovered recently, have led police to believe we have a serial killer on the loose in the city. More details as they become available. Jenny, back to you."

Rylee switched off the TV, then sat back, hands clasped in her lap. Serial killer, indeed. Was it Magdalena?

Too restless to sit still, too agitated to concentrate on anything else, Rylee threw herself into housework. She mopped the floors, dusted the furniture, and counted the hours until sundown.

Costain rose half an hour before twilight. He found Rylee in the living room, folding a load of bath towels.

Her eyes widened when she saw him and then she visibly relaxed.

"Didn't mean to startle you," he said.

She shrugged. "You didn't."

He decided to let the lie slip by, unremarked. "Anything I can do or say to put you at ease?"

"I can't think of a thing."

Rhys grinned at her candor. "Any questions you've got that you need answered? We have some time before Alex shows up. He'll have to…"

"I know," she said quickly, not wanting to hear him say *feed* or *hunt* out loud. She added a hand towel to the stack on the sofa. "Can I get you anything?" she asked nervously, then bit down on her lower lip, thinking the only thing she had that he needed was blood. And she wasn't willing to give him that.

His gaze moved to her throat and then he grinned at her. "No, thank you. I'll dine later. Mind if I sit down?"

"No, please do. I'll be right back," she said. "I'm just going to take these upstairs." And so saying, she grabbed the towels and made a hasty escape.

Rhys chuckled as he watched her go. No doubt about it, she was scared to death of him. Smart girl. She had good instincts.

Rhys had just opened the door for Alex when Rylee returned to the living room. Her relief at seeing O'Donnell was palpable.

After greeting Rylee, Alex looked at Rhys. "There's been another killing in the city. Body drained of blood. They're blaming it on a serial killer."

Costain muttered a vile oath. "Magdalena!"

"Who else?"

Rhys paced the floor for a few moments, his expression grim when he turned to face them. "Listen, you two, I've been thinking about this situation. I think Rylee should move into my place as long as Magdalena is a threat. My lair is a helluva lot more secure than this house. And Rylee will feel more at ease staying there with you than having me resting in her guest room." He glanced from one to the other. "What do you say?"

Alex looked at Rylee. "He makes a lot of sense. We can protect you better there than here."

She slid a dubious glance at Costain, then shook her head. "I don't know…"

"I won't be staying there," Rhys said, hoping to allay her fears. "I'll rest elsewhere."

Rylee looked at Alex. "If you think it's a good idea…"

"I do. Why don't you go upstairs and pack a few things?"

"All right."

"What's Magdalena up to?" Alex asked after Rylee left the room. "If it's me she wants, why is she leaving all these bodies in her wake? Doesn't she realize it's going to draw every hunter in the country? And they won't be after just you and me."

"I have no idea. It makes no sense at all. Hell, I'm not sure she's playing with a full deck. But at least we know she's still in the city."

"And that's good news why?"

"Always pays to know where your enemy is," Costain said with a rueful grin. "All we have to do now is find her."

CHAPTER 19

Rylee stood in the middle of the living room in Costain's penthouse, wondering what on earth she was doing in the lair of the Master of the City. Alex had driven her here in Costain's Jag and she'd had second thoughts all the way across town. She had to admit, the apartment was amazing, and after passing through two thick iron doors to get inside, she certainly felt protected, if not entirely safe.

"Rylee?"

She turned toward Alex, who stood beside the sofa, his arms crossed over his chest.

"You okay?" he asked.

"Not really."

"I guess I can understand that. I've turned your life upside down, haven't I?"

She didn't deny it, merely shrugged.

"Rhys is out hunting Magdalena. If anyone can find her, he will."

"And what if he can't? How long do I have to stay here?"

"Only as long as you want to. You're not a prisoner."

She smiled inwardly. If she had to have a warden, she was glad it was Alex and not Costain. And if this had indeed been a prison, she couldn't have asked for a more beautiful one. Dark blue-gray carpet that must have been two inches deep covered the floor. Twin sofas made of black leather faced each other in front of a white marble fireplace. She stared at the painting over the mantel, wondering if it was a genuine Botticelli.

"Where on earth did he get that?" Rylee exclaimed, gesturing at the life-size statue of a Madonna that stood in one corner. "It looks like it belongs in the Vatican."

"I think he stole it from a Catholic church a couple hundred years ago. But you ain't seen nothing yet," Alex said, picking up her suitcase, "until you've seen the bedroom."

Curious, Rylee followed him down a short hall, gasped when he opened the door.

"Holy cow," she murmured. "We've discovered Satan's boudoir." The room was gaudy beyond belief, all done in red and black. Heavy drapes covered the windows, no doubt to block the sun. The bed was the biggest she had ever seen, as was the TV that covered most of one wall, and the fireplace that occupied another. There were more paintings in this room. Rylee was no expert, but they all looked old enough to be originals. A curio cabinet held a number of figurines, all depicting mythical creatures.

"The bathroom's in there," Alex said, gesturing at a closed door to the right. He dropped her suitcase on the foot of the bed. "Seen enough?"

"More than enough," she muttered, thinking she wouldn't be surprised if staying in this room gave her nightmares. "Where will you sleep?"

He glanced from her to the bed and back again. "On the floor. Or in the closet."

Leaving the bedroom, Rylee noticed a closed door at the other end of the hall.

"That's Costain's office," Alex said as they made their way back to the living room.

Rylee sank down on one of the sofas and glanced around again. There was no sign of a kitchen, though she spied an office-sized refrigerator on the floor in one corner, alongside a large ice chest.

Following her gaze, Alex said, "I bought those earlier. The fridge is filled with sandwich makings and milk. There's soda, juice, and some fruit in the ice chest. If you let me know what else you want, I'll get it for you."

It would be like camping indoors, Rylee thought. All she needed was a propane stove and a plastic tub to wash her dishes.

"You haven't had dinner, have you?" Alex asked, when her stomach growled.

She shook her head.

"Do you feel like going out?"

"Do you think it's safe?"

He shifted from one foot to the other. "I doubt if she'd try anything in a crowded restaurant."

"What about getting there and back?"

"Do you trust me?" Alex asked, a mischievous glint in his eye.

She tilted her head to the side. "What do you mean?"

"I can get us there and back with little risk."

"How?"

"I'll just think us there."

Rylee frowned at him. "*Think* us there? How do you do that?"

"I don't know," he said with a disarming grin. "Are you game to give it a whirl?"

"What do I have to do?"

"Just hang on to me."

"I don't know." In the end, curiosity overcame her trepidation. "All right. Just let me change my clothes."

Being transported through time and space was an experience unlike anything she had ever felt before. Alex had put his arm around her waist, instructed her to lock her arms around his neck, and the next thing she knew, they were standing in the shadows beside an Italian restaurant in San Diego.

"Are you all right?" he asked.

"I will be, as soon as my stomach stops churning."

He grinned at her. "It takes some getting used to," he allowed as they walked around to the entrance. "If you don't like Italian, we can go somewhere else."

"No, it's my favorite."

The place was lovely, Rylee thought as she stepped inside. Classic Italian décor, pale walls adorned with oil paintings of vineyards and villas. They were seated immediately. She ordered a Caesar salad and ravioli. Alex ordered a bottle of red wine.

"Won't they think it's strange that you're not eating anything?" Rylee asked after the waitress left to turn in their order.

Alex shrugged. "Maybe, but it doesn't matter."

Wondering if her life would ever be the same again. Rylee nibbled on a bread stick, felt her cheeks grow warm when she noticed Alex watching her. "Do you miss eating?"

"Sometimes. Italian was my favorite, too."

"We should have gone somewhere else."

He shrugged. "It doesn't bother me." What bothered him was the scent of her hair, the fragrance of her skin, the constant temptation of her nearness.

Alex sat back when her dinner came, a glass of wine in his hand. They made small talk about the weather, the rising cost of gasoline, the latest movies, avoiding all mention of Magdalena and vampires.

Until they were back in Costain's lair and Alex turned on the news. And there, in living color, was a blanket-draped body surrounded by police while a reporter gave the grisly details.

"She's never going to stop, is she?" Rylee asked tremulously.

"I think she's baiting Rhys, hoping to make him give me up."

"Do you think that's what she wants?"

"Yeah. I think she's hoping to make a trade. Rhys agrees to turn me over to her and she agrees to leave the city."

"Would he do that?"

"I sure as hell hope not."

"So do I."

For a moment, silence stretched between them. They came together as if drawn by the same magnet.

Rylee closed her eyes as he wrapped her in his embrace, holding on as if he would never let go. She clung to him in return, as if her arms would keep him safe. She couldn't bear the thought of that vampire torturing him, destroying him—couldn't abide the thought of never seeing him again. The depths of her feelings shocked her. She scarcely knew him and yet he had suddenly become the most important thing in her life.

Alex held her closer as he rained kisses on her temples, her cheeks, the tip of her nose, the corners of her eyes, before settling on her lips. He was stunned by her passion. The attraction had always been there, but this…

It was as if someone had lit a fire between them. His hands skimmed her back, cupped her breast. They fell back onto the sofa, arms and legs entwined, mouths fused together.

Rylee moaned softly, both protest and plea as he caressed her. She wanted him to stop before it was too late.

She never wanted him to stop.

As the flames grew hotter, so did his urge to possess her, body and soul, to sink his fangs into the soft tender flesh of her neck and satisfy his thirst even as he longed to bury himself in her sweet flesh and satisfy his desire.

As though sensing the change in him, Rylee pulled away and scrambled to her feet, gasping for breath.

Alex stared at the floor, his breathing erratic. "Go to bed, Rylee," he growled. "And lock the door."

She wanted to run, but some innate instinct for survival told her that was the worst thing she could go. Murmuring, "Good night," she walked sedately to the bedroom and quickly bolted the heavy door behind her.

She stood there for several minutes, waiting for her heart to stop pounding, her breathing to return to normal. "Vampire," she whispered.

Sinking down on the mattress, she rocked back and forth. She had to remember that no matter how much she cared for Alex, no matter how attracted to him she might be, her life was in jeopardy every minute they were together.

⚜ ⚜ ⚜

Alex paced the floor, his hands clenching and unclenching. He needed to get out of here, needed to be outside, away from the temptation that was Rylee. But he couldn't go off and leave her alone. No matter how secure Costain's lair was supposed to be, he couldn't leave her alone, not with Magdalena prowling the city like some insatiable tiger.

Dammit!

He raked his fingers through his hair as he cursed his lack of self-control. He would never forget the stark horror in her eyes. The scent of her fear had permeated the air, crawled over his skin, reminding him that he was less than human now.

Nosferatu.

Undead.

A monster.

Tormented with regret, he drove his fist into the wall, felt a satisfying jolt of pain as his skin split, dripping dark-red blood on the floor. *Shit!*

"What the hell?" Costain's voice sounded behind him. "Do you know how hard it is to get blood out of that carpet?"

"No," Alex retorted. "But I'm sure you do."

"Smart ass." Tilting his head back, Rhys sniffed the air. "What happened?

Alex lifted one shoulder and let it fall.

Rhys grinned inwardly. There was really no need to ask. The scents of musk, fear, and desire hung heavy in the air, painting a clear picture of what had gone on. "You might need to slow things down just a bit," he suggested.

"Back off, Costain! It's none of your business."

"Excuse me if I disagree, *fledgling*. But this is *my* lair, not yours. To quote a certain TV father, 'I brought you into this world, and I can take you out.'"

Alex glared at him, and then shook his head. "You know what happened, dammit. Things got out of hand. I didn't mean to scare her, but...I don't know. Maybe it's not such a good idea for Rylee to stay here, at least not with me."

"Have you got a better idea?"

"You know I don't."

"Then you'll just have to control yourself, won't you?"

"You're no help at all, you know that?"

"Stop being so hard on yourself, kid. Everything gets easier, with time."

Time, Alex thought. If Magdalena had her way, he might not have a helluva lot left.

Chapter 20

Trying to be as inconspicuous as possible, Sylvi watched Magdalena pace the floor of her lair, heedless of the dead body sprawled in the corner.

"Where is he?" Magdalena shrieked. "Damn his soul, why can't I find him? I've looked everywhere!" Striding to the sofa, she slapped Sylvi across the face—once, twice, three times. "Are you sure he's *even* in Los Angeles?"

Sylvi cowered back against the sofa. "Yes. I watched his house day and night. I followed him to the airport and saw him buy his ticket."

"There are hunters in the city," Magdalena raged. "What if they find him first? And you," she hissed. "I don't know why I keep you around. You've been no help at all! And what about the girl? You were supposed to bring her to me!"

Sylvi flinched as the vampire struck her again. "I'm sorry, mistress," she whimpered. "The girl wasn't at her house. As for O'Donnell..." She shrugged. "I've asked everyone I know. They're all afraid to speak to me for fear of incurring Costain's wrath." The other vampires in the area weren't the only ones afraid of Costain., she thought. As terrified as she was of her mistress, she was more frightened of the Master of the City—which was one reason why she kept her mouth shut.

The second reason was more compelling, because she knew where to find Rhys Costain. And that was one vampire she wanted nothing to do with.

CHAPTER 21

Rylee shook her head, her expression mutinous. "Tell Rhys I don't want to go!"

"I know you don't," Alex said. "But I'm not leaving you here alone, and since I have to go, so do you."

Rylee sat back on the sofa, arms folded over her chest. She couldn't argue with both of them, but, after what had happened last night, she no longer felt entirely safe with Alex. She doubted if she would ever feel safe anywhere again.

"He'll be here in a minute," Alex said, "so put your shoes on."

She glared at him, then stomped into the bedroom and slammed the door.

Alex paced the floor, wondering if she would ever forgive him for last night. He knew he'd scared her. Hell, he'd scared himself because he'd wanted her so desperately. All of her. He wanted her warm and pliable in his arms, her hands caressing him. Wanted to taste her, not just her blood, but all of her. *Dammit!*

He sensed Costain's presence moments before the vampire materialized in the room. "Are you two ready?"

"Rylee's putting on her shoes.'

Grunting softly, Rhys strolled down the hall and pounded a fist on the bedroom door. "Let's move it along in there."

Mouth set in a tight line, Rylee flung the door open, no easy task considering it was solid oak.

Rhys grinned as he read her mind. "Hate me all you want," he said, striding into the living room. "You're going. The question is, who do you want to go with?"

She glanced from one vampire to the other, blew out a sigh of resignation, and muttered, "Who do you think?"

Alex didn't miss the way she shuddered when he slipped his arm around her waist, or her grimace when she laced her hands behind his neck.

When the world righted itself again, they were standing outside a small beach house with weathered siding.

Rhys opened the door with a wave of his hand.

Alex gestured for Rylee to precede him.

After being in Costain's penthouse, she had expected more of the same. But this place was devoid of furniture save for a pair of leather couches and two overstuffed leather chairs. Four men occupied the room—two on one sofa, two on the other. They all turned to stare at her with hungry eyes.

"She's mine," Alex said flatly.

"And under my protection," Rhys added. "Rylee, meet Julius, Rupert, Nicholas and Randolph."

The men nodded at her, each in turn.

"Rylee, sit down," Alex said.

She didn't argue. And even though she no longer trusted him, she was glad when he stood behind her chair, one had resting possessively on her shoulder.

Rhys, too, remained standing.

"So, why are we here?" Julius asked.

"There are two hunters in town," Rhys said. "Both experienced."

Nicholas frowned. "Are they hunting anyone in particular? Or will any head do?"

"I don't know. I'm more concerned about Magdalena's vendetta against Alex."

Julius dragged his hand across his jaw. "Still no idea where she is?"

Rhys shook his head. "I'm thinking I might just wander through the city. Perhaps she'll find me."

Nicholas leaned forward, eyes narrowed. "And then what?"

"I'm not sure. Maybe I'll offer to give her Alex if she'll get out of L.A."

Rylee stared at Costain, then glanced over her shoulder at Alex, wondering if the two of them had discussed such a trade, since Alex had mentioned the very same thing to her not long ago.

Costain glanced at Rupert. "You've been uncharacteristically silent tonight. Something on your mind?"

Rupert looked up, startled, then shook his head. "Whatever you want to do is fine with me. You know that."

"What if she agreed to your terms?" Julius asked, putting into words what they were all thinking. "What then?"

"I guess I'd meet with her," Rhys said with a wolfish grin. "After all, I can't take her head if I can't find her."

The meeting ended a short time later.

Rylee watched in amazement as Rupert, Nicholas, Randolph, and Julius simply shimmered out of sight.

"Take Rylee home," Costain said curtly "I'm going to the club." He disappeared without waiting for a reply.

"Are you ready to go?" Alex asked.

"I guess so."

"Rylee." Coming around the chair, he knelt in front of her. "Please don't be afraid of me," he said, when she flinched. "I'm sorry about last night. I know things got out of hand. I can't promise it won't happen again. I don't have a lot of control right now. But I'll keep my distance and when this is over..." He didn't want to think about that, because when this was over, he knew she'd never want to see him again.

Clasping her hands in her lap, she said, "I know it's not your fault. But it happened and you're right, seeing you like that..."

"I understand." He'd killed enough of them to know how vampires looked when they were about to lose control—fangs bared, eyes blazing red. "Come on, let's get out of here."

Rylee made an effort not to recoil when he reached for her. She told herself there was nothing to fear at the moment, and that, as long as she kept her distance, he would be able to control his hunger. But she didn't really believe it. Last night, every time she'd closed her eyes, she had seen his face, his eyes hell-red with hunger. She'd had horrible nightmares of being chased by ravening vampires, of blood and death, of being trapped in the dark with no way out and no one to help her. Dreamed of Alex rising over her, eyes glowing as he plunged his fangs into her throat while he ravaged her body.

When they reached Costain's lair, she pleaded a headache, went into the bedroom, and bolted the door.

Throwing herself on the bed, she cried until she had no tears left.

The sound of Rylee slamming the bolt home sounded like a death knell in Alex's ears and he cursed himself anew for shattering what little trust she'd had in him.

Dropping onto the sofa, he stared into the darkness, thinking he would have been better off if Rhys had just let him die.

He was so lost in feeling sorry for himself it took him a minute to realize his phone was ringing. Picking it up, he scowled when he saw who it was. "Daisy, what do you want?"

"Is that any way to talk to your only sister?"

"Sorry."

"Why are you so down in the dumps?"

"What kind of stupid question is that? Why do you think? Does the word *vampire* ring a bell?"

She blew out an audible sigh. "We're coming home."

"Not on my account, I hope."

"Why else? I'll see you tomorrow night. Where are you staying?"

"Costain's place."

"Still?"

"He doesn't think I'm ready to be on my own. And he's probably right," he muttered, thinking about last night. Maybe he *did* need a keeper.

"Well, cheer up, big brother. I'll see you soon."

"Yeah, yeah," he muttered.

But when he ended the call, he felt a lot better.

Rhys stood behind the bar at *La Mort Rouge,* all his senses alert. There was a hunter in the club. His gaze ran over the crowd, finally settling on an average-looking guy with cropped blond hair and a massive chest.

As though feeling Rhys' perusal, the man looked up and they stared at each other across the room.

The hunter mouthed the words, *You're a dead man,* as his left hand delved into the pocket of his over-sized jacket.

What was he hiding in there? Rhys wondered. A stake? Holy water? Or both? Not that it mattered. Baring his fangs, he grinned at the man.

Rhys closed up at four a.m. and then, instead of transporting himself to the lair he shared with Megan in Granite Hills, Rhys walked out the front door. He took his time locking up, and all the while his senses were tracking the hunter, who had apparently called for backup.

He strolled down the road, fully aware of the two men who trailed behind him. They smelled of mingled excitement and fear and he wondered if they were hunting him in particular or just looking for a quick kill.

La Mort Rouge was the only inhabitable building along this deserted stretch of old highway. He slowed as he approached the burned-out shell of an old gas station and motel. No doubt they would assume he took his rest there. If so, they were even dumber than they looked.

He paused at the office door, as if fumbling with the lock, grinned as they lunged toward him. He'd heard they were capable hunters but taking them out was all too easy. He quickly broke the neck of the first, slammed the second against the side of the building, one hand curled around his throat.

"Did someone send you after me?" Rhys hissed.

"Go to hell, you blood-sucking vampire."

"All in good time." His hand tightened around the hunter's throat. "If you want to see the sun rise, you'll keep a civil tongue in your head, and answer my question."

When the man remained mute, Rhys sank his fangs into his throat. The blood was clean but heavily laced with alcohol.

The hunter clawed at Rhys' hand. "No one," he gasped. "No one sent me." His eyes widened with horror when Rhys lifted his head, fangs still bared and dripping with blood.

"You wouldn't lie to me, would you?"

"No, I swear it…on the life of… of my daughter."

"What's her name?"

"Megan."

Rhys stifled a grin. The girl would never know it, but the coincidence of her name being the same as his wife's had just saved her father's life.

Easing his hold on the man's throat, he growled, "I'd advise you to get out of town and find another line of work. I might not be as forgiving if we meet again."

He vanished from the hunter's sight without giving him a chance to reply.

CHAPTER 22

Sylvi waited until Magdalena left to go hunting and then she called the vampire. He answered on the first ring.

"What?"

"She's scaring me," Sylvi said. "She really is crazy, you know. Losing Eduardo sent her over the edge. I'm not sure she even remembers why we're here. She's getting more and more violent. Rupert, I'm afraid for my life. If she finds out I know where to find Costain…" Her words trailed off as a sob rose in her throat. "She'll kill me."

Chapter 23

Rylee paced the living room floor. She was tired of reading. Tired of watching TV. Tired of having nothing to do. She thought of calling her parents, but after asking how they were, what would she say when they inquired how she was doing? *Hey, Mom and Dad, guess what? I'm a prisoner in a Hollywood penthouse. You wouldn't believe this place. It looks like Hell's waiting room. Oh, by the way, vampires are real, so keep your doors and windows locked.*

She grabbed a can of soda from the ice chest, kicked off her shoes, and plopped down on the sofa. She'd just taken a drink when there was a shimmer in the air and a young woman appeared.

Startled, Rylee almost choked as Coke spewed from her mouth.

"Oh. I'm so sorry! I didn't think anyone but Alex would be here. I thought he'd be awake by now."

Rylee stared at the stranger. "Who…who are you?"

"I'm Alex's sister. Daisy," she said, with a bright smile. "And you must be Rylee."

She nodded. So, this was Alex's vampire sister. She was young and quite pretty, with long, reddish-brown hair and deep green eyes.

Rylee glanced at the doorway that led to the hall when Alex appeared, a towel wrapped around his waist, his hair damp.

"Daisy, I thought you'd call first."

She shrugged. "You didn't answer your phone."

He glanced pointedly at the towel. "I was a little busy. I guess you two have met. If you'll excuse me, I'll get dressed."

Daisy perched on one of the chairs across from Rylee. "I'm so pleased to meet you," she said. "I would have come sooner, but Erik and I were out of town. I've been worried about Alex ever since…" She paused. "Sorry, I tend to ramble."

"I know about his wife," Rylee said.

"Oh, good. He's been so depressed. And then being turned on top of everything else…well, I was afraid he'd do something stupid. But you seem to be just what he needed."

"I'm not sure about that."

"Is his being a vampire a problem?"

Rylee stared at Daisy, not knowing whether to laugh or cry. "Of course it's problem. I thought he was going to kill me the other night."

Daisy's eyes grew wide. "Why? What happened?"

"It's none of your business," Alex said, striding into the room. "You know I can hear everything you two are saying, don't you?"

Daisy faked a look of surprise. "Really?"

Alex dropped into the other chair. "Listen, Daisy Mae, I know you're worried about me, but I've already got a babysitter in Costain and I sure as hell don't need another one."

"Is that right? I'm not sure a dozen babysitters could help an idiot like you."

Rylee sat back and folded her arms as a rush of preternatural power swept through the room.

"Well, well, home sweet home," Rhys muttered. "Can't you two take this argument somewhere else?"

Daisy stuck her tongue out at the Master of the City. "We're not arguing."

"No? Sure sounds like it to me. Where's Erik?"

"He's waiting for me at our place."

"Smart man," Rhys said dryly. "So, are you two finished?"

Alex shrugged.

"There's one less hunter in town," Costain remarked, his voice flat. He glanced from Alex to Daisy. "Watch your backs, both of you. I think I scared the second one off, but you never know about hunters.”

Alex and Daisy exchanged glances, then burst out laughing. When Rhys joined in, Rylee felt like she was at a party where everyone knew the punch line except her.

“Rhys, why don’t you and Alex go out for a while,” Daisy suggested. “I’d like to talk to Rylee. You know, woman-to-woman.”

“I’m not sure that’s a good idea,” Alex muttered.

Making a shooing motion with one hand, Daisy said, “I’m sure it is.”

“Come on, fledgling,” Rhys muttered. “We’re not wanted here.”

And that about summed it up, Alex thought glumly. Rylee didn’t want him.

When they were alone, Daisy leaned forward. “I came here to see if I could make Alex feel better about what’s happened, but I think maybe you’re more confused that he is. I don’t know what’s going on—or what’s gone on—between you and my brother, but Alex is a really great guy. I know he’s going through a rough patch right now, but give him some time. He’s been through hell these past few months. Losing Paula and the baby would have been bad enough, but having to deal with that and becoming a vampire is a heavy load to bear.” She paused a moment. “You said you were afraid he was going to kill you the other night. I’d love to hear what happened, if you feel like sharing.”

Rylee clasped her hands together. Strange as it seemed, she felt an odd kinship with Alex’s sister.

“We were making out on the sofa,” Rylee said, not meeting Daisy’s eyes. “Things were getting pretty hot and suddenly…I don’t know, something changed and I got scared. I pushed him away and stood up and he told me—growled at me—to go to bed. I’ve never been so scared.” She shuddered as images from her nightmares pushed to the forefront of her mind.

Daisy nodded slowly. "Desire and hunger are closely interwoven in vampires. Hunger sparks desire, desire arouses hunger. It's hard for new vampires to separate the two. Do you understand?"

"I can't say as I do."

"Well, I don't really understand it myself, but that's the way it is. All I know is, Alex would never deliberately hurt you."

"I'm not sure he can help himself. That's what frightens me."

"Of course it does."

"Do you…ah, like being what you are?"

"Yes and no. Mostly yes."

"Were you forced?"

"Not exactly. I was dying and I asked Erik to change me."

Rylee sat back, her brow furrowed. If it was life or death, would she make the same choice? She couldn't imagine such a life—never seeing the sun, unable to enjoy her favorite foods, having to hide what she was, always looking over her shoulder for fear some hunter would sneak up behind her and drive a stake into her heart. "Have you ever been sorry?"

"A little, at first. But now…how can I be sorry when it means never growing old, never being sick. To hopefully spend decades, maybe centuries, with the man I love?"

Rylee nodded thoughtfully. "What about the blood thing?"

"You probably won't believe this, but once you taste it, you won't want anything else."

"You're right. I don't believe it."

Daisy chuckled. "I wouldn't have believed it, either. Tell me, Rylee, how did you feel about Alex before Rhys changed him?"

Without hesitation, she said, "I thought he was wonderful, the nicest guy I'd ever met. Sweet and thoughtful."

"He's still the same man," Daisy said. "He just has an unusual lifestyle."

Rylee snorted softly. Unusual, indeed.

"Alex *is* a wonderful guy," Daisy said, squeezing Rylee's hand. "Kind, caring, generous, funny. I hope you'll give him another chance." Leaning back in her chair, she said, "They're back."

Moments later, Rhys and Alex shimmered into view.

"Well," Daisy said, rising. "Now that you two are here, I'm going home. It was nice meeting you, Rylee. I hope to see you again soon. You, too, brother." she said, giving Alex a hug. "Call you later."

"Hey, what about me?" Rhys asked, grinning. "Don't I get a hug?"

"You know we just tolerate you," Daisy said, laughing. "Night, all."

Rylee shook her head as Daisy disappeared from sight. How did they do that, anyway?

"All right," Rhys said. "I guess I'll head on home. Behave yourselves, you two."

Alex swore softly as Costain left the apartment. Damn his big mouth. A glance at Rylee's heated cheeks told him she hadn't appreciated his parting comment, either.

Feeling suddenly ill at ease and all too aware that they were alone, Alex shoved his hands in his back pockets and stared out the window. City lights glowed in the distance. The scream of a siren punctuated the quiet of the night.

"Your sister seems nice," Rylee remarked, disliking the taut silence between them.

"Yeah."

"She loves you."

Alex nodded, wondering what the devil Daisy had told her. "Is there any chance for us, Rylee?" he asked, still looking out the window. "You must know I'm in love with you."

She stared at his back, thinking those were the last words she had expected to hear. The last words she wanted to hear. She cared for him in spite of everything and didn't want to hurt him. But she didn't want to share her life with a vampire, either. Even if he and Rhys managed to get rid of Magdalena, there were always other vampires, other hunters, lurking in the shadows. If she stayed with Alex, she would never know another peaceful night. Every time he was late for a date or didn't call, she would wonder if he'd been killed.

When he turned to face her, his eyes were shadowed with pain. "Never mind answering," he said. "Your silence speaks volumes. I'll go stay in the bedroom until you're ready to turn in."

By the time she thought of something to say, she was alone.

Alex paced the bedroom floor. Rhys was going to have to find someone else to stay with Rylee at night. Maybe Erik and Daisy could take over for him, because he couldn't be this close to Rylee knowing she was afraid of him. He wasn't made of stone. He couldn't inhale her scent, remember the warmth of her in his arms, the taste of her kisses, and know he would never hold her again.

No way in hell.

Rylee stood in front of the living room window, staring out over the city. There were men and women out there, living normal lives, going to work, taking their children to school or to the park, helping them with their homework. Couples going out to dinner or the movies, falling in love. Teenagers huddled together over their phones. Even prisoners were better off. At least they got to go outside once in a while. She had been cooped up in here for over a week and had barely seen Alex in the last two days. He arrived as soon as the sun slid behind the horizon, made sure she was all right, then disappeared into the bedroom and stayed there—with the door closed—until she was ready to turn in.

She needed someone to talk to—needed to get out of this place, at least for an hour or two. She was almost out of food. And toilet paper.

Rylee watched the sun slip behind the horizon. Alex would be rising soon. Maybe tonight he would talk to her.

A few minutes later, there was a knock at the door. Rylee frowned, wondering who it could be.

"Hello? Rylee, are you in there?"

Daisy's voice. With a sigh of relief, Rylee unlocked the door.

"We're going to stay with you tonight," Daisy said, her voice overly cheerfully as she stepped inside, followed by a tall, good-looking man with black hair and ebony eyes. This is my husband, Erik. Erik, Rylee."

"Nice to meet you," he said, with an easy smile.

Rylee nodded, then asked, "Why did you knock on the door?"

Daisy shrugged. "You looked a little startled when I popped in the other night. I didn't want to frighten you."

"I'm getting used to it. Where's Alex?"

Sitting on the sofa next to her husband, Daisy took his hand in hers. "He isn't coming tonight."

Rylee blinked at them, surprised by the rush of disappointment that swept through her. "Is he all right?" she asked, dropping into one of the chairs.

Daisy glanced at Erik.

"You might as well tell her," he said, shrugging.

"Tell me what?"

"He's not coming here anymore," Daisy said. "We're going to keep you company at night, and Rhys will spend the days here, until Magdalena is no longer a threat."

CHAPTER 24

Rylee stared at Daisy. "Did he say why?" It was a foolish question. She knew why and it was all her fault. She'd hurt Alex's feelings and her silence had driven him away. She told herself it was for the best. They could never have a lasting relationship. And yet proof of the opposite was right before her eyes. Daisy and Erik sat side by side, holding hands like young lovers. And they would look like that forever, faces unlined by the years, bodies fit and strong...

Stop it! What was she thinking? It wasn't as if Daisy was mortal. She, too, was a vampire. Rylee shook her head. The only way to make it work with Alex was to become what he was, and no man on earth was worth that.

"So," Daisy said, "what would you like to do tonight? Watch TV? Play cards?"

"I need to go to the store."

Daisy frowned. "I don't think that's a good idea."

"I don't care!" Rylee slammed her hands on the arms of the chair. "I'll go mad if I don't get out of here! I need to see something besides these four walls. I need to see people, hear laughter, smell the fresh air."

Daisy looked at Erik. "What do you think?"

"I think we'd better clear it with Rhys."

"You're probably right."

Erik pulled a cell phone from his pocket. "Hey. It's Erik. Rylee wants to go shopping for something to eat." He listened a moment, then said, "I know. But I think she really needs to get out of here for a while." He listened again. "All right. See you in a few." Slipping his phone back into his pocket, he said, "Costain is going to take you."

Rylee swallowed hard, suddenly wishing she'd kept her mouth shut.

Rylee pushed her shopping cart down the aisle, all too aware of the vampire trailing behind her like some silent bodyguard. She didn't miss the fact that other shoppers avoided him, some even going so far as to turn around and go back the other way when they saw him.

Costain had told her to buy whatever she fancied, and she did. If he was going to keep her imprisoned, then she intended to eat well—of course, not having an oven was a handicap, but she bought the best of everything that she could fit in the ice chest and the small refrigerator—roast beef and Swiss cheese and croissants for sandwiches, apples and oranges and grapes to snack on, as well as half a gallon of milk and a couple of blueberry scones and muffins.

He threw her a sardonic look when she reached for a box of Count Chocula cereal.

Lastly, she tossed several bags of her favorite candy into the basket.

"Is that all?" Rhys asked when they reached the check-out line.

"Almost," she said, and plucked a bouquet of yellow roses from a display.

Reaching into his jeans, he pulled out a bankroll big enough to choke a horse, peeled off a hundred dollar bill, handed it to the cashier and told her to keep the change.

The cashier stared at him, speechless, as Rylee picked up the flowers, leaving Rhys to push the cart out to the Jag. She grinned inwardly when he sent her a sour look. No doubt he'd never pushed a shopping cart in his life, she thought, and he obviously didn't relish doing so now.

She waited in the car while he unloaded the groceries, grinned again as he slid—still glowering at her– behind the wheel of the Jag.

"I'm hungry," she said. "I'd like to get something to eat."

"I just bought enough to last you for a month. What more to you want?"

"I meant, I want to go out to dinner."

"Whatever her Royal Highness desires," he muttered irritably. "Pray tell, what is my lady in the mood for?"

"Steak and lobster."

With an aggrieved sigh, he drove to the nearest seafood restaurant where he pulled up in front of the Valet Parking sign. He handed Rylee out of the car and bowed her through the door. They were seated immediately.

Rylee ordered steak and the biggest lobster they had, Rhys ordered a bottle of the best red wine the house had to offer.

Sitting back, he regarded her through narrowed eyes. "You miss him, don't you?"

"Excuse me?"

"Don't play games with me, girl. You're in love with Alex and you miss him." He held up his hand when she started to deny it. "Don't."

"What if I am?" Rylee retorted. "What's it to you?"

"Nothing. It's the two of you who are unhappy."

"Better off unhappy than Undead."

He lifted one brow in wry amusement. "There are worse things than death."

"Like being a vampire?" she asked, ever so sweetly.

"Like being alone and unloved."

"I can't share my life with a vampire," Rylee said, her voice quiet and tinged with regret. "It might be fine for you. For Alex and Daisy. But I want a home and children. I want to travel and photograph the Wonders of the World. I want a man who can share my life. My *whole* life, not just half of it. Can you understand that?"

He nodded, his expression sober. It was hard to remember if he had ever wanted those things. If so, it had been centuries ago.

When her meal came, Rylee no longer felt like eating, but she forced herself to do so. She didn't want Rhys to know how unhappy she was, or how much she missed Alex. She ate every bite, then ordered dessert and choked it down.

It was a long, silent ride back to the penthouse.

Rylee looked around the apartment. "Where's Daisy?"

"I sent her and Erik home."

"Why?"

"They've got their own lives to live."

"And I've got mine."

"Well, right now, it's here. With me."

She stumbled backward and sank down on the sofa. "Do you even remember what it was like to be human?"

"Not really. "A wave of his hand and a fire sprang to life in the hearth. "But I know what it's like to be loved." He grinned at the look of disbelief in her eyes. "What? You don't think anyone could love me? Or is it that you don't think I'm capable of loving someone?"

"Both," she replied candidly.

"Well, you'd be wrong on both counts. I'm happily married to a wonderful woman."

"I don't believe it."

"Her name's Megan."

"And she's human?"

"Not anymore."

"I guess that was a silly question. Did you make her what you are?"

He dropped into the chair across from hers, legs stretched out in front of him. "I did, but only to save her life. She was hit by a car and in a coma with little hope of recovery. I told her parents what I was and that I thought turning her might save her life."

"And they agreed to let you do that?"

"They didn't want to lose their only child."

"What if they'd said no?"

"I would have done it anyway."

Rylee frowned. "What was her reaction when she realized what you'd done?"

"She wasn't particularly happy. For a while there, I thought I'd lost her. She wanted to go home and…" He shrugged. "I let her go. It was the hardest thing I've ever done."

"I guess she forgave you."

He nodded.

"And she has no regrets?"

"None that I'm aware of."

"Just because it worked out for you doesn't mean it will work for me and Alex."

"You'll never know if you don't try. Which is why he'll be looking after you from now on."

"But he doesn't want to."

"It doesn't matter. I sired him and he'll do what I say."

"You can't force me to stay with him!"

"Actually, I can. I'm a very old vampire. I have powers you can't begin to imagine."

"I don't believe you." She flinched when his gaze captured hers. Try as she might, she couldn't look away.

"Rylee, come to me."

An odd sensation engulfed Rylee as his voice wrapped around her. Soothing and yet compelling, his words pulled at her like velvet chains. She knew what he was doing and yet, helpless to resist, she stood and walked stiffly toward him.

"Sit on my lap, Rylee. Put your arms around me. And kiss me."

Try as she might, there was no way to refuse the power of his voice. Heart pounding, unable to deny him, she perched on his lap, slid her arms around his neck, and pressed her lips to his.

She didn't close her eyes and neither did he.

"Believe me now?" he asked.

She couldn't speak past the lump in her throat. The moment he released her from his thrall, she jumped off his lap and darted to the far side of the room.

Eyes wary, she stared at Costain, stunned by his power to manipulate her. And yet, as unsettling as it had been, she was even more troubled by the very real fear that Alex could do the same.

Chapter 25

Rylee woke in the morning, hoping that what had happened the night before had been nothing but a bad dream, that Costain hadn't been in the apartment, that he hadn't compelled her to do his bidding.

But when she peeked into the closet, it was Rhys sleeping on the floor.

She practically jumped out of her skin when he opened his eyes. With a startled cry, she turned and bolted out of the room.

Enough, Rylee thought furiously. She'd had enough. Magdalena or no Magdalena, she was going home. She rummaged in her purse, searching for her cell phone so she could call a cab. But her phone wasn't there. She frowned, trying to remember the last time she'd used it, but couldn't recall. Tossing her handbag on the sofa, she searched the apartment. Since there were only four rooms, it didn't take long.

Her phone was nowhere to be found.

Damn! Rhys had taken it. She was sure of it.

Well, she'd just have to walk. Tiptoeing into the bedroom, she grabbed her a change of clothes and padded into the living room to dress. If she couldn't call a cab, maybe she could hail one at curb side. If not, she could always take a bus.

Grabbing her handbag, Rylee marched resolutely to the door, turned the lock, and reached for the handle.

And nothing happened. The handle turned but the door remained closed.

Discouraged, she sank down on the sofa, wondering if this nightmare would ever end.

And as the hours crept by, she wondered if the *day* would ever end.

She was half-asleep when she felt a familiar shimmer in the air and Alex appeared.

"This wasn't my idea," he said.

"I know." Rylee glanced toward the bedroom. "Is Costain still here?"

"He left when I showed up." Alex shoved his hands in his back pockets. "I know you don't want me here, but it seems like we don't have any choice in the matter, so let's make the best of it, all right?"

Rylee nodded, unable to refute how happy she was to see him. She'd been lying to herself. And to Costain. No matter how she denied it, she had missed seeing Alex. She missed the sound of his voice, his smile. She missed being held in his arms, the way the world seemed better when she was with him. It made no sense. Alex was still a vampire. Nothing could change that. Just as she was beginning to think nothing would change the way she felt about him, either.

"Rylee?"

"Yes, we should make the best of it."

Alex stared at her, confused by the tone of her voice, the way she was looking at him, her beautiful sky-blue eyes sort of soft and dreamy. If he hadn't known better, he would have thought she'd changed her mind about him. But that was impossible. She had made her feelings about him and vampires perfectly clear.

"Alex?"

"Yeah?"

"I'd like to try again, if you want to."

He looked skeptical. "Really? I was at the restaurant the other night, when you were there with Rhys."

"I didn't see you."

"I didn't want to be seen. I heard what you said, though. You told him you didn't want to share your life with a vampire, that you wanted a home and children," he said bitterly. "That you wanted a man who could share your whole life, not just half of it."

"But…"

"Do you deny it?"

"No, but there was more to it than that."

"I didn't wait around to hear the rest."

"Maybe you should have," she retorted. "He said a lot of things that made sense."

"Yeah? Like what?"

"He said there were worse things than being a vampire, like being alone and unloved. And he said that…" She bit down on her lip and stared at the floor.

"Go on."

"He accused me of being in love with you."

"And what did you say?" Alex stared at her, feeling as if all the air had been sucked out of the room.

"I said even if I was, it was none of his business."

"Are you?" Hardly daring to hope, he took a step toward her as he waited for her answer.

"I think I might be," she admitted, her voice little more than a whisper. "I'm not sure. I've never been in love before." She looked up, her gaze searching his. "Can I ask you something?"

"Sure."

"Rhys compelled me to…to do something last night."

"Like what?"

Heat flooded her cheeks. "He…he made me sit on his lap and kiss him. He said he could make me stay with you whether I wanted to or not."

Alex swore under his breath. What the hell had Costain been thinking?

"Tell me the truth. Can you do that, too? Could you compel me to…to make love to you? To stay with you even if I didn't want to?"

"I guess I could." Seeing the look of horror in her eyes, he said, "But I would never do that, Rylee. Believe that if you believe nothing else. I'm not like Rhys." That was true now, he thought. But would it still be true if he survived as long as his sire? "Listen, do you want to get out of here?"

"What do you mean?"

"I can transport us to the east coast." He shrugged. "We could go dancing, take in a movie, anything you want."

"What about Magdalena?"

"I think we'd be safe enough for a few hours."

She hesitated only a moment. In the end, her desire to get out of Costain's penthouse outweighed her fear.

Rylee had experienced being transported before, but never so far. Her head was spinning, her stomach churning, when they the world righted itself.

"Are you all right?" Alex asked.

"I don't know." She glanced around. She had expected to be in a mall or restaurant row. Instead, they were on the sidewalk in a residential area. "Where are we?"

"Boston." Alex jerked his chin toward the house in front of them. "My folks live here."

"Oh." It was an older, two-story home, with a flower garden in the front and several trees on either side of the porch. Lights glowed in the windows. Brow furrowed, she glanced at Alex. What was he waiting for?

"Let's go."

"Aren't you going inside?

Alex shifted from one foot to the other. "They don't know about me yet." He wasn't sure why he'd come here. Maybe just to make sure they were all right. He heard their voices and the sound of the TV as clearly as if he'd been in the living room. His mother had fixed fried chicken for dinner and apple pie for dessert. His father was drinking a cup of coffee, his mother was brewing a pot of tea.

"Do they know about Daisy?"

"Yeah. Let's go." Slipping his arm around Rylee's waist, he transported them to the nearest nightclub.

It was a lovely place, the lighting low, the music soft. At the bar, Alex ordered a glass of wine and downed it like it was water.

Sitting beside him, Rylee sipped a café royal. Her heart ached for Alex. She didn't understand his reluctance to see his parents. If they knew about Daisy and accepted her, what was he afraid of? Why would it be different for him?

Alex pushed his glass aside, then gestured at the dance floor. "Shall we?"

"Sure."

Rylee sighed when he took her in his arms. She hadn't realized how much she'd missed being close to him until now. She closed her eyes, shutting out the other couples, shutting out the rest of the world. She was tired of fighting it. Right or wrong, this was where she wanted to be. Maybe not for always, but at least for now.

Chapter 26

"Another meeting?" Alex asked. "Why the hell do we need another one?"

"You'll see."

"I'll get Rylee."

"No. Just tell her we're leaving. We won't be gone long."

The members of the council were already at the beach house when they arrived.

"This is getting to be a habit, Costain," Julius groused. "Don't you have anything better to do?"

"I thought you'd like to know there's one less hunter in town."

"That's always good news," Randolph said.

"Is that all?" Nicholas asked. "I've got a date with a rather lovely older woman."

"We're almost done here." Rhys turned his laser-like gaze on Rupert. "There's just one more thing. Where's Magdalena?"

Rupert's head jerked up. "What?"

Costain regarded him through narrowed eyes, his voice silky soft with menace. "I think you know where to find her."

The other vampires all sat forward, eyes narrowed, as tension filled the room.

Rupert seemed to shrink in on himself. "You know I'd tell you if I did."

"Would you?"

Alex stared at Costain, who was probing Rupert's mind. He glanced at the other vampires. Were they aware of what was going on, or was he the only one who sensed it? "Who's Sylvi?" Rhys asked.

Rupert froze.

"Who is she?" Rhys asked again.

"Just a…a girl I met."

Rhys took a step forward, nostrils flaring. "I can smell her on you."

"It's the same scent we detected outside Rylee's house the other night," Alex said. "The same scent that was mingled with Magdalena's."

The tension in the room shot up a notch as Costain moved to stand in front of Rupert. "Where is Magdalena?"

Rupert shook his head, his eyes wild. "I don't know, I swear it!"

"Liar!"

"No. No! Sylvi never told me where the vampire's lair is, only that she's afraid for her life. She thinks Magdalena's out of her mind."

Rupert trembled visibly as Costain's eyes took on a faint, reddish glow.

Preternatural power flooded the room. Alex felt it vibrate through him like an electrical current. It seemed to go on forever, though, in reality, it was only a moment or two.

When it stopped, Rupert slumped back on the couch, as if all the energy had been sucked out of him.

Rhys turned away.

And in that moment, Rupert panicked and bolted for the door, endeavoring to turn into mist as he went.

But Rhys was too fast for him. He grabbed the other vampire and broke his neck with one quick twist.

Total silence filled the house.

"This meeting is over," Rhys said, his voice tight.

The three remaining vampires vanished in the blink of an eye.

"How did you know?" Alex asked.

"I smelled the same scent on him the last time we met. It was stronger tonight."

"Are you sure he wasn't telling the truth? Maybe he really didn't know where Magdalena's lair is located."

"It doesn't matter. I won't have anyone around me that I can't trust." Lifting Rupert over his shoulder, Rhys carried the body out the back door.

Curious, Alex followed him.

Rhys dumped the corpse on the ground, then broke off a piece of the picket fence and drove the sharp end into Rupert's heart. "The sun will take care of the body," he said. "As for Magdalena, I'll find her sooner or later. And when I do—"

Alex's eyes narrowed as images of Paula flashed through his mind. "And when you do," he interjected, his voice like flint. "Just remember she's mine."

CHAPTER 27

Alex had expected Rylee to be in bed, asleep, when he returned to the penthouse. Instead, he found her curled up on the sofa watching a movie.

She sat up when he materialized in the room. "Where did you go?"

"Rhys called another meeting." Reaching into his pants pocket, Alex pulled out a cell phone. "Rhys said to give this back to you."

"About time," she muttered, noticing that the battery was dead. "He calls a lot of meetings, doesn't he?"

"Lately, anyway."

"Why didn't he insist on my going this time?"

Taking the seat beside her, Alex slipped his arm around her shoulders. "Rhys had some urgent council business to take care of."

"Oh?"

"Just be glad you weren't there."

Rylee shivered. She didn't have to be psychic to know something terrible had happened at that meeting. She couldn't help being curious, even though she didn't really want to know. But whatever had transpired had been horrible, indeed. She could see it in Alex's eyes.

She snuggled against him. They were together now and that was all that mattered.

For the next two weeks, there were no new bodies drained of blood. Rylee checked the news every morning and every night. True, there were deaths—but they were the normal kind—a car accident, a house fire, a fall from a trail in Yosemite, an explosion at a factory. But no bodies drained of blood.

"Do you think she's left town?" Rylee asked Alex when she saw him that night.

"I sure as hell hope so."

"Maybe I can go home now."

"I'm not sure that's a good idea. Not until we know for sure that she's no longer a threat."

"I really *need* to go check on my house," she insisted. "Take my mail out of the box, empty my refrigerator. Water my plants."

Alex grunted softly. "I guess it wouldn't hurt to go for an hour or so. Grab your coat. It's cold outside."

Rylee paused inside the front door. It seemed like years had passed since she'd been here. A couple of magazines and weekly newspaper ads had been waiting in her mail box. A fine layer of dust covered the tables. Her plants were nearly dead. All the food in the refrigerator had gone bad.

Alex made himself at home on the sofa, thinking how right it seemed to sit there while Rylee bustled about the house, watering the plants, dusting the furniture, emptying the fridge.

"At least the food in the freezer is still good," she called.

A few minutes later she emerged from the kitchen carrying a huge bowl of vanilla ice cream.

"Is that your dinner?" he asked with a wry grin.

"I guess so. Want a bite?"

"What do you think?"

"Have you tried eating anything since…you know?"

"No." She frowned thoughtfully. "If you can drink wine, why can't you eat ice cream?"

"I just can't. Besides, I have no desire for it."

"None at all?"

"Not even a little."

"Oh, well," she said, with an impish grin. "More for me."

He watched her lick the spoon and felt a sudden desire to feel her tongue on his skin, her mouth on his. Leaning forward, he took the bowl and spoon from her hand and placed them on the coffee table, then licked a drop of vanilla from her lips.

"Sweet," he murmured, and he wasn't talking about ice cream.

Rylee looked at him, suddenly breathless as he slanted his mouth over hers. She moaned softly as she wrapped her arms around him, caught up, as always, in the magic of his kisses, the sense of belonging that swept over her. His hands skated up and down her spine, eliciting shivers of delight as he fell back on the sofa, drawing her down on top of him. She moaned with pleasure as his hands slipped under her sweater to caress her back.

"Rylee." He murmured her name, his voice thick with need and desire.

Fear doused the fire burning through her. What if he lost control again? What if this time he couldn't stop?

He took his mouth from hers. "Don't be afraid, love."

"I'm sorry."

He pressed his fingers against her lips. "Not to worry. I fed as soon as I got up."

She tried to feel relieved but couldn't help experiencing a moment of pity for the poor soul he had preyed on.

"I didn't hurt her," he said quietly. "We should go."

"Hang on a minute. I want to pack a few things."

"Alright."

Hurrying upstairs, Rylee pulled her old Samsonite from under the bed, then sorted through her closet and drawers, pulling out shirts and pants, socks and underwear. She added a pair of sneakers, then went into the bathroom for her hair brush and shampoo. She'd been using Costain's and while his were undoubtedly the best money could buy, she liked her own better.

Suitcase in hand, she hurried downstairs and dropped it by the door. Alex waited while she walked through the house, making sure all the lights were off.

He picked up her bag and followed her outside. After she locked the door, Alex warded the house against intruders, the way Rhys had taught him.

Rylee shivered as a wave of preternatural power whispered through the air. She looked up at him with a sense of awe. No longer human, he possessed the same supernatural powers as Rhys, though perhaps not yet as strong. But they would only grow stronger with time, she thought, remembering what Alex had told her.

"Ready?" Luggage in one hand, he slipped his other arm around her waist.

Holding tight to her purse, Rylee closed her eyes.

When she opened them again, they were back in Costain's apartment, and he was glaring at Alex.

"What the hell were you doing at Rylee's?" Rhys asked sharply. "I was about to come after you."

Alex dropped Rylee's bag on the floor. "She needed a few things."

Sensing the growing tension in the room, Rylee said, "I'm going to put this stuff away and take a bath. Good night."

"Night, Rylee," Alex said with a wink.

When they were alone, Rhys stared at Alex, his eyes narrowed. "Have you been eating ice cream?"

Alex burst out laughing, the first real laugh he'd had since being turned, and it felt damn good. For the first time, he thought maybe things could work out with Rylee. He had wanted her tonight and yet he'd been able to control his hunger and his desire. He felt strong, in control, no longer afraid of what he'd become.

He frowned when he felt Costain's power moving over him. It lifted the hair on his arms. "What are you doing?"

"I guess you could say I'm assessing your progress."

"What the hell does that mean?"

"Turning you might have been a mistake."

A little frisson of unease jolted through Alex. "What? Why?"

"I'd forgotten that you drank Erik's blood a while back. He was made by one of the ancients over three hundred years ago. You've been turned by me…"

Alex stared at his sire as a sudden feeling of dread engulfed him.

"Do you see why I'm having second thoughts?"

Alex nodded slowly. With the blood of two old ones running through him, he might one day be strong enough to challenge Rhys for control of the West Coast—and win.

"I can feel the power growing within you," Rhys said, his eyes going red. "Even quicker than I expected."

Hands clenched, Alex glared at his sire, felt his own eyes go red. "So, what the hell are you going to do about it? Destroy me the way you did Rupert?"

"Maybe. But not tonight," Rhys said. And then grinned. "I just wanted to see your reaction. I'm a pretty good judge of character. I saved your life, and while you may hate me for it, you're also grateful to still be alive. I don't trust very many people, O'Donnell, but I trust you. Besides, Daisy would never forgive me if I hurt you."

A tidal wave of relief washed through Alex, but before he could think of anything to say, Rhys was gone.

Chapter 28

The sun was climbing over the horizon when Sylvi arrived at Magdalena's lair. The vampire insisted she come at sunrise each day, do whatever cleaning up needed to be done, and then spend the rest of the day standing guard. For such a powerful vampire, her mistress seemed overly concerned with her safety.

Sylvi came to an abrupt halt when she entered the ten-digit security code and stepped inside. Unable to believe her eyes, she stared at the carnage in front of her. The floor was littered with bodies. Men, women and children of various ages stared up at her through lifeless eyes, their faces frozen in a rictus of terror, throats stained crimson. Blood splattered the walls, the furniture, squished beneath her feet as she closed the door behind her.

Covering her nose with one hand, she picked her way across the floor to the room where Magdalena took her rest. The vampire lay on her back in a shiny black coffin, her hands, mouth, and clothing coated with dried blood.

Choking back the bile rising in her throat, Sylvi backed out of the room and out of the house.

Outside, she vomited the contents of her stomach onto the dirt, then climbed into her car and drove away. She needed to find a place to hide before sundown.

Rhys swore as someone pounded on the club's front door. "What' the hell?" he muttered. "Can't you read?" The sign out front clearly said, *Closed.*

The pounding came again, louder and more insistent.

Swearing under his breath, he opened the door. "We open at ten."

"I can't wait that long. Please let me in."

His nostrils flared, his eyes narrowing as he caught the scent of blood and vampire. "Sylvi." Rupert's friend. What the hell was she doing here?

She glanced over her shoulder. "Please let me in."

Taking a step back, he gestured her inside. She had a lot of nerve, coming here, he thought. And then he frowned, wondering what, if anything, Rupert had told her about him

She stood in the middle of the darkened room, shivering violently. Waist-length hair the color of moonlight fell over her slim shoulders. Her eyes were blue-green, her skin pale and unblemished save for a dark purple bruise on one cheek.

Going behind the bar, Rhys filled a shot glass with malt whiskey and handed it to her. "You look like you could use this."

She didn't argue, just gulped it down.

"Wanna tell me what's going on?"

"Magdalena. She's gone completely mad. Her lair is filled with bodies. There's blood everywhere."

"So you *do* know where she is," he muttered.

"What?"

"Where's her lair?"

"I can't tell you that."

"Why the hell not?"

"She'll kill me."

"Yeah? What makes you think I won't?"

"Hide me, please."

"Only if you tell me where she rests."

"No." She shrugged one shoulder. "I can't. I swore an oath to protect her. I cannot break my word."

Rhys gazed deeply into her eyes. If she wouldn't tell him what he wanted to know, there were other ways of finding out, he thought. But for the first time since becoming a vampire, he couldn't penetrate another's mind. What the hell? The harder he tried, the more she resisted.

Sylvi smiled faintly.

Frustrated, he poured himself a drink and refilled the girl's glass. "Who are you?" he asked. "*What* are you?"

"Nobody." She perched on the nearest bar stool.

"You obviously know about vampires. Why can't I read your mind?"

"I don't know. Magdalena couldn't, either."

"You know she'll be able to track you when she wakes up."

"There's no blood bond between us. She doesn't drink from me."

"Why not?" he asked, intrigued. Vampires always drank from their human companions. Besides forming a bond, it was a means of exerting control.

"She took one taste and spit it out. She said I tasted bad."

Rhys stared at her in disbelief. Blood was blood, although some was sweeter and more satisfying than others.

"Go ahead," Sylvi invited, holding out her left arm. "See for yourself."

Taking hold of her wrist, he bit her lightly. He swallowed twice and then he gagged. "What the hell!" He studied her closely for a moment, myriad possibilities running through his mind. And then he swore softly. "You're an Elf." In all the centuries he'd lived, she was the first he'd met. They were a strange breed, each possessing different powers and abilities.

Sylvi nodded, a faint smile twitching her lips.

"What were you doing with Magdalena?"

"She found me when I was a child and saved my life. I didn't know what she was at the time."

"Why didn't you leave?"

"I owed her a life-debt. I swore an oath to stay with her and protect her, but after what I saw today…" She shivered violently. "I couldn't stay any longer."

"How did you find me?"

"A vampire told me about this place."

"A vampire by the name of Rupert?"

Her eyes widened. "You know him?"

"I knew him."

Sylvi gaped at Rhys. "He's...?"

"Yeah. There's a room upstairs. You can stay there today, if you like."

"Thank you. I'll be gone by nightfall."

He studied her a long moment, debating whether to let her go. He might not be able to read her mind, but he could ward the club so she couldn't leave. On the other hand, what was the point? Magdalena was probably long gone. "Where will you go?"

"As far away from Los Angeles as I can get."

"Well, good luck to you."

"And to you, Mr. Costain."

Rhys scrubbed his hand over his jaw as he watched her climb the narrow staircase to the second floor. So, Rupert had been telling the truth when he'd said he didn't know Magdalena's whereabouts, he thought bitterly, but he'd let his rage and his frustration get the best of him and in so doing, he'd destroyed an innocent man.

Closing his eyes, he opened the blood-link that bound him to Megan, then realized it was afternoon in Scotland and she would be at rest.

Pulling his phone from his pocket, he sent her a text. *Come home, love. I need you.*

Megan was in Edinburgh when she received her husband's text. She had sensed something was wrong for the last two days. After bidding her parents a hasty goodbye and arranging for them to bring her luggage home, she transported herself to the house she shared with Rhys.

She had barely set foot in the house when he emerged from the bedroom clad in nothing but a pair of black briefs.

Before she could ask what was wrong, he gathered her into his arms. For a long moment, he simply held her close. "I'm never letting you go away without me again," he murmured against the side of her neck. "It's been hell without you."

"I would have come home sooner," she said, stroking his back. "All you had to do was ask."

"I knew you were having a good time."

"I missed you, too." Taking his hand in hers, she said, "Come to bed with me, and I'll show you how much."

A wicked grin played over his lips as he followed her into their room. "One of us is overdressed," he murmured, and the next thing she knew, her clothes lay in a pile on the floor.

His gaze moved over her like a living flame as he took her hand and tugged her toward the bed. They fell on the mattress in a tangle of arms and legs.

"Too long," he murmured, as his hands and lips caressed her. "Too long."

Megan writhed beneath him, desperate to touch him and taste him. She moaned low in her throat as he pleasured her, cried out with need, her arms holding him close as he carried her over the edge.

Much later, sated and complete, she snuggled against him, her head nestled on his shoulder. "Do you want to tell me about it now?"

"No." His hand idly stroked her thigh. "Right now I don't want to think about anything but you."

Rylee worried her lower lip as she glanced at the time. Alex had gone hunting over an hour ago. Thoughts of Magdalena flitted through her mind. He had never been gone this long before. Had the vampire found him?

She paced the floor, too nervous to sit still, too upset to eat. Where was he?

And where was Rhys?

Magdalena stood in the middle of the living room, hands on her hips, nose wrinkled against the stink of the bodies that littered the floor. Where was that wretched girl and why hadn't she disposed of this mess?

She grimaced at the dried blood on her bodice. Why hadn't Sylvi undressed her while she rested? The stupid girl would never get the stains out now, she thought, and then paused with the sudden realization that Sylvi had probably left for good. Well, good riddance.

Scowling, she made her way into the bathroom, stepped out of her dress and tossed it on the floor. After a lengthy shower, she pulled on a black sweater and a pair of slacks. "Stupid, ungrateful chit," she muttered as she threw her belongings into a large suitcase and stalked out of the house.

A wave of her hand set the place on fire.

Still muttering obscenities under breath, she went in search of prey.

And a new lair.

Alex had just released his prey from his thrall when he smelled smoke. He followed the scent to an old, single-story house located in the hills above Hollywood. When he arrived, there was little remaining but ashes and the faint smell of death.

And vampire.

He swore under his breath. Magdalena had been this close and they hadn't been able to find her.

Now, perhaps they never would.

Chapter 29

Rylee breathed a sigh of relief when Alex materialized in the room. "Where have you been?"

"I hunted a little farther afield than usual," he said, taking her in his arms. "I was on my way back when I smelled smoke and decided to go and see what it was."

"Well, what was it?"

"Magdalena's lair."

Rylee stared at him. "She's dead?"

"No, more's the pity. She wasn't there. I followed her scent as far as I could, but then it vanished. There's no telling where she's gone."

Rylee's shoulders slumped as she muttered, "At this rate, I'll be staying in Costain's penthouse forever."

"Would that be so bad?" Alex asked. "Staying here with me?"

"No, it's not that. I just miss my own house. My own bed. Being able to come and go as I please."

"Yeah. I miss that, too." Dropping onto the sofa, he tugged on her hand and pulled her down beside him. "Have you had dinner?"

"I made a sandwich a while ago."

His gaze moved to the pulse throbbing in her throat. "Rylee, let me taste you."

"What?"

"Just one little taste."

"Why?"

"I can't explain it. I won't hurt you. I'm told it's pleasant."

"Pleasant!" she exclaimed. "Whoever told you that?"

"The women who frequent Costain's club like it. That's why they go there."

She stared at him. "You're telling me there are women who *ask* vampires to bite them?"

"Yeah."

She ran her fingertips along the side of her neck, trying to imagine what it would be like to feel his fangs at her throat. "Are you sure it won't hurt?"

"I'm sure."

"And you'll only take a little?"

"I promise."

Suddenly curious, she brushed her hair away from her neck and closed her eyes. "Remember, just a little."

Taking a firm hold on his self-control, Alex drew her into his arms and bit her, ever so gently. Her blood was warm and rich and sweet on his tongue. More satisfying than anything he'd ever known. The temptation to take a little more was almost over-powering, but he'd promised and so, reluctantly, he lifted his head.

Rylee blinked at him. "What did you do?"

"What do you mean?"

"You said you were going to bite me."

He frowned at her. "I did."

"But…it felt wonderful." She lifted her hand to her neck. The skin felt warm beneath her fingertips. "More than wonderful. And sort of…" She felt her cheeks grow hot.

"Sort of sensual?" he said, smiling.

She nodded. And then she frowned. "Did you ever bite any of those women?"

Alex rubbed his hand over his jaw, wondering if he should tell her the truth. But he wanted no lies between them. "A couple of times, while we were apart. But they weren't as sweet as you."

"You're just saying that."

"No, it's the truth."

She looked at him through narrowed eyes, then laughed. "This is the most bizarre conversation I've ever had. Will you bite me again?"

"As often as you like," he murmured huskily, and drew her gently into his embrace.

Rylee's days fell into a routine of sorts. As time passed, she found herself going to bed later, sleeping later. One night, she complained to Alex that she was bored and the next afternoon, she found a laptop sitting on a new desk.

It was like a gateway to the world. She spent the rest of the day setting it up, reading her email, watching ridiculous cat videos on YouTube, checking her Facebook and Twitter accounts. She contacted a few clients to explain an emergency had called her away.

After an early dinner, she returned to the computer.

She smiled at Alex when he appeared beside her. "This was so sweet of you. Where did you get it?"

"From *La Mort Rouge.*"

"Does Rhys know you took it?"

Alex shrugged. "Megan's come home and no one's seen him for a couple of days. He won't it, miss, though. He bought a new one a few weeks ago." He jerked his chin toward the screen. "Any chance I can woo you away from cat videos?"

Grinning, she shut down the laptop. "What did you have in mind?"

"A few hours away from here."

"I'd love some more ice cream."

Alex's gaze moved to her lips. "Buy chocolate this time."

He took her to a Cold Stone Creamery in Boston. Rylee looked over the menu and ordered a dark chocolate cone. Carrying it to one of the small tables, she sat down and took a taste.

"Good?" Alex asked.

"Very." She grinned at him. "Thinking about the vanilla you ate?"

"Are you talking about that drop I licked off your lips? I'd hardly call that eating."

"Would you like some chocolate?"

When he nodded, she lifted her spoon and smeared a bit of ice cream across her mouth, then leaned toward him.

Alex met her half-way, then slowly ran his tongue across her lips. "I could get used to this."

She grinned at him, then tilted her head to the side. "Why did we really come to Boston?"

"I need to see my folks," he said, with a sigh. "I chickened out when we were at the house the last time, but I need to let them know what's happened and that I'm all right." His gaze searched hers. "Will you go with me?"

"Well, sure, if you want me to."

Rylee finished her cone and tossed her napkin in the trash. "Why have you waited so long to see your mom and dad?" she asked as they left the shop.

"I needed to feel like I was in control. That's why I want you with me. I don't know how to explain it, except that being with you centers me, somehow, makes me feel more like my old self, less like some blood-thirsty monster."

"You're not a monster, Alex."

"No?"

"No."

"Then why do I want to taste you all the time?"

"*All* the time?"

"Pretty much."

She didn't know what to say to that. Oddly enough, it didn't frighten her.

His parents' house was only a few blocks from the mall. He paused on the porch and took several deep breaths. Then, holding tightly to Rylee's hand, he knocked on the door.

At the sound of footsteps, Rylee murmured, "They love you, Alex. It will be all right."

He nodded, his gaze fixed on the door.

"Alex!" His mother threw her arms around him. "Noah," she called over her shoulder, "it's Alex."

Releasing him, she said, "Come on in. I'm so glad to see you. It's been too long. And who's this lovely young lady?"

"Mom, this is my friend, Rylee. Rylee, my mother, Irene McDonnell. And this is my dad, Noah," he said as his father hurried into the room.

"So pleased to meet you, Rylee," Irene said. "Please, come in and make yourself at home. Can I get you anything? Coffee? Tea? Perhaps a piece of cake?" She smiled at Alex. "It's your favorite."

"Not right now, Mom." Alex sat on the sofa and pulled Rylee down beside him, his hand still holding hers.

"Rylee?"

"No, thank you, Mrs. O'Donnell. We just came from Cold Stone."

"Well, let me know if you change your mind," Irene said. Taking the chair beside her husband, she beamed at her son.

"We put the house up for sale last week," Noah said. "We've already had three offers on it. But that's not why you're here, is it?"

Alex's gaze slid away from his father's. "No. I found the vampire who…" He couldn't say the words. "Or rather, she found me."

Noah regarded Alex through narrowed eyes.

Irene gripped her husband's arm as if she knew what was coming.

"Go on," Noah said.

"Do I have to say it?" Alex asked, his voice raw.

"Oh, Alex," Irene murmured, and burst into tears.

Rising, Alex pulled Rylee to her feet.

"Don't go!" Irene dashed the tears from her eyes. "It…it doesn't matter."

"You're still our boy," Noah said, his voice gruff and thick with pain. "Just like Daisy's still our girl. Don't let this keep you away from us, son. You and your sister are all we've got left."

Rylee stepped back as Alex's parents both stood, put their arms around Alex, and held him tight.

"I knew something was wrong when you refused your Ma's devil's food cake," Noah said, blinking rapidly. "We love you, son. Nothing else matters."

Rylee smiled as she blinked back tears of her own.

"You're very quiet tonight," Rylee remarked. They had returned to the penthouse over an hour ago and in that time, he hadn't said more than a couple of words. Kicking off her shoes, she leaned back on the sofa. "I thought your visit went well."

"Yeah. I guess I'm just feeling a little homesick."

"I think that's normal, don't you?"

"I guess so, but it made me remember what it was like before Brandon died, before Daisy was turned. We had a good life. Now I look at my folks and the light's gone out of their eyes. I think about Paula…and the baby. No matter how I look at it, it's my fault they're dead."

"Oh, Alex." She scooted closer to him and clasped one of his hands in both of hers. "It's not your fault. You couldn't know what the repercussions would be when you killed Magdalena's lover. Nor is it your fault that Daisy became a vampire. Life happens. You can't control it. You just have to make the best of it."

"You're the best of it," he said, slipping his arm around her shoulders. "What you said is true, I guess. But none of it would have happened if my family had been in another line of work."

"Hindsight is a wonderful thing. If I hadn't been taking pictures on the beach the night we met…" She made a vague gesture with her hand. "Was it chance? Or Fate?"

"Whatever it was, I'm glad you were there." His gaze searched hers. "In spite of everything that's happened, I hope you are, too."

"I am," she said. "And I'll be even happier when this business with Magdalena is over."

That night, after Rylee had gone to bed, Alex paced the floor. He knew she was right, that what had happened to Paula and the baby wasn't his fault. That lay with Magdalena. And yet the guilt was still there. If he hadn't been a hunter…if he hadn't killed Tietjen…if he hadn't married Paula in the first place. That was what bothered him the most. Even knowing she hadn't loved him either didn't ease his guilt.

He blew out a sigh. They had been two lost souls seeking comfort.

Maybe they'd been doomed from the start.

<h1 style="text-align:center">Chapter 30</h1>

Another week passed with no new deaths and no indication that Magdalena was still in town. Sitting at the bar in *La Mort Rouge,* Alex wondered if that was a good sign, or if Magdalena was just biding her time, putting them all at ease before she struck again.

Rylee was itching to go home. Just that evening, she had brought the subject up again. Not that Alex could blame her. Even though he'd taken her out as often as he could—to dinner, to movies, dancing—he had never really relaxed, always looking over his shoulder, always worried that Magdalena was out there, like a snake in the grass, just waiting to strike.

He looked up as Rhys suddenly appeared behind the bar. "We haven't seen much of you since Megan got home," Alex remarked.

"Been making up for lost time. You doing okay?"

"Rylee wants to go home."

Rhys shrugged one shoulder. "It's her call."

"Have you heard anything about Magdalena? Has she left town?"

"Beats the hell out of me. If she's still here, no one's seen her."

"I can't believe she just up and left."

Rhys shrugged. "Maybe she's busy recruiting a new minion since her old one left. Or maybe she's found a lair somewhere else now that the old one burned down."

"She had a minion?"

"Yeah. An Elf."

Alex blinked at him. "An elf?"

"Sylvi."

Alex frowned. "Rupert's Sylvi?"

"One and the same. She came here the night after Magdalena's lair went up in smoke. Seems Magdalena went on a killing spree and left her lair littered with bodies. Apparently, it was the last straw for Sylvi and she split."

Alex plowed his fingers through his hair. An Elf. Shades of "The Hobbit." Maybe there were Orcs and Wizards, too. "Do you think I should let Rylee go home?"

"That's up to you. And her."

"Fat lot of help you are."

Rhys shrugged. "As long as she stays inside after dark, and doesn't open the door for strangers, she might be all right. Of course, if Magdalena mesmerizes some poor guy and sends him after Rylee, all bets are off."

Alex swore under his breath. Knowing the risks, how could he let her go back to her place?

"It's Rylee's life. Maybe you should let her decide what she wants to do. I'm guessing if she decides to leave, you'll be going with her."

"Damn right!"

"I'll contact the Council. Ask them to sniff around and see if they've heard anything about Magdalena's whereabouts. Maybe someone's seen her in the last few days."

Because Rylee was determined to go home, Alex called a company that installed security screen doors and protective bars on windows. Next, he mounted motion cameras inside and outside the house, as well as exterior lights that automatically came on when the sun went down.

Rylee frowned when she saw the additions two weeks later. "I feel like I'm living in a prison," she muttered.

"It's this or the penthouse," Alex said. "And if you're thinking of going back to work, remember you'll still be vulnerable during the day."

"I know, but if you'll be my bodyguard, I can still shoot night weddings, receptions, and birthday parties."

"Count on it." Since he was the one who had put her life in danger, it was the least he could do.

Rylee moved back into her house the next night. If she kept her curtains closed, she could ignore the bars and pretend everything was normal. Alex had agreed to stay with her. He moved some of his clothes into the guest room closet and parked the Jag in the garage next to her Mazda.

He accompanied her to the store later that night, and while she bought meat and produce, he bought several bottles of vintage wine.

In the days that followed, Rylee booked several night weddings and a couple of evening birthday parties. She spent her days editing digital photos and uploading proofs to the Internet, as well as working on the Summerville catalogue, and gradually her life fell back into a familiar pattern.

In many ways, it was almost like being married—except that Alex slept on the floor in the guest room closet. He sought his rest long after she had gone to bed, and rose an hour or so before sunset, which was something new. When she asked about the change in his resting habits, he said it had something to do with being sired by Rhys. She didn't quite understand it, but she knew Costain could be awake during the day. She wondered if it had more to do with the strength of one's preternatural power than how long they'd been a vampire.

Alex left to go hunting while she ate dinner, leaving them free to spend the rest of the evening together. It wasn't perfect, Rylee thought, and yet it worked for them.

She had just put the last of the dishes into the dishwasher when he came up behind her.

Sliding his arms around her waist, he nuzzled the side of her neck. "What's on the agenda for tonight?"

"I have a wedding at the Presbyterian Church in North Hollywood at seven, but I need to be there by six."

"You'd better get a move on then. It's almost that now."

"I'm ready. I just have to comb my hair, brush my teeth, and find my shoes."

Built of white brick, it was a lovely old church set amid a wide swath of green lawn and flanked by ancient oaks.

Alex dropped Rylee off at the side door before looking for a place to park the car. After locking the Jag, he dissolved into mist, drifted into the church, and then floated near the ceiling in the back. Rylee, he knew, was taking last-minute pictures of the bride.

The ceremony began at five after seven. Rylee stood behind a pillar—out of sight of most of the guests—where she could take photos, mostly unobserved.

There were more pictures after the ceremony, of course—with the bride and groom, her family, his family, *ad nauseum.* And still more photos at the reception that followed.

Alex materialized towards the end of the evening, just after the bride and groom departed, to help Rylee with the cameras. "How'd it go? Did you get all the pictures you needed?"

"And more," she said, following him out to the car.

"Great." He unlocked the passenger door and stowed her gear in the back seat. He'd just opened the driver's side door when Magdalena appeared beside him. In a blur of movement, he tossed the keys to Rylee, yelled, "Get out of here!" and lunged at Magdalena, his hands reaching for her throat.

Rylee clambered into the driver's seat, shoved the key in the ignition and stomped on the gas. Careening down the street, she ignored the speed limit and raced through red lights until she was a safe distance away, then pulled to the curb and looked for directions to *La Mort Rouge.* She was on the road again in less than a minute, hoping and praying that Rhys would be at the club.

She skidded to a halt in the parking lot, jerked the keys from the ignition, sprang out of the Jag and pounded on the door.

It was opened by a tall, stern-faced man who took one look at her frantic expression and let her in without a word.

She found Rhys sitting at the bar, playing cards with the bartender and a statuesque woman with curly brown hair.

He stood when he saw her. "What's happened?"

Breathless, she started to tell him about Magdalena.

But he was already gone.

Alex forgot Magdalena was a woman, forgot that she was older and supposedly stronger than he was. He stared at her as his fingers tightened around her throat, but all he saw was Paula sprawled across their bed, her eyes empty in death, her body awash in her own blood.

He let out a cry of rage when Magdalena raked her nails down his cheek and his neck, shrieking her hatred all the while. Fighting her was like fighting a wild animal, but, to his surprise, he knew he was winning. He might have been nothing but a puny mortal the first time she'd attacked him, but, thanks to Costain's ancient blood, he was almost her equal now.

She lifted her head, eyes blazing red, and then she sank her fangs deep into his shoulder and bit down. The pain was exquisite. Startled, he jerked away. She had no sooner vanished from sight that Rhys appeared beside him.

He had no sooner resumed his own shape when Rhys appeared. "Where is she?"

"Gone. Damn vampire! I think you scared her away. She took a bite out of me! Hurts like hell. I've got to go check on Rylee."

"She's okay. She's at the club."

Alex stared at his sire. He had expected Rylee to bolt for home.

"Are you sure you're all right?" Rhys examined Alex's shoulder. "I sensed something was wrong right before Rylee showed up. Damn, Magdalena took a chunk of meat out of you."

Alex probed the wound, which was about two inches wide and maybe three inches deep. "Shit. Will it heal?"

Rhys nodded. "You should be fine by tomorrow."

"I hope so," Alex muttered.

"I can give you a little of my blood, if you want. It'll speed things up."

When Alex hesitated, Rhys said, "It'll boost your strength, too."

"Fine."

With a wry grin, Rhys held out his arm. "Not too much now."

Alex scowled as he took hold of Costain's wrist and bit down. The blood was hot and thick and ancient and it burned through him like liquid fire. Hard to believe he had once found this repulsive. He would gladly have drained his sire dry.

"Enough!"

With a low growl, Alex lifted his head.

"Enough," Rhys said again, his voice filled with understanding. "Come on, Rylee's probably worried sick about you."

Rylee huddled in a booth in the back of the room. Never in all her life had she seen a place like this. She couldn't help gawking at the beautiful men and women who wandered through the club, smiling and flirting, or going into the numbered rooms that lined one wall. She could only imagine what transpired behind those closed doors. Not that she really cared. She was too worried about Alex. Was he all right? Had Rhys made it there in time to help? Or arrived too late? Why had she run away like a scared rabbit? And yet, it would have been foolish to stay. She had neither the strength nor the know-how to dispatch a vampire.

The bartender brought her another drink. Rylee hadn't asked for the first one, but she'd downed it in one swallow and been grateful to have it. Now, she sipped the second as she glanced at the front door again. And yet again. Where was he?

She felt his presence before he materialized in the booth beside her. "Alex!" She threw her arms around him, drew back when he winced. Her gaze ran over him, her eyes growing wide when she saw the dried blood on his cheek and neck, the hideous wound in his shoulder visible through the ragged tear in his shirt.

"I'm fine," he assured her. "I would have changed clothes first, but I wanted to make sure you were all right." He glanced at his shoulder. "Rhys said it'll heal up overnight."

"Is she…did you…?"

"No, dammit. She got away. Again."

Rylee couldn't sleep that night. Every time she closed her eyes, she saw the vampire, Magdalena, eyes red as hellfire. Had Rhys once been like that? A monster who killed without a qualm? Was Alex capable of such violence? Turning on her side, she clutched her pillow to her chest and wondered if this nightmare would ever end.

She swallowed hard when her bedroom door opened. *It's Alex,* she assured herself. With all the wards, cameras, and outside lights Alex had installed, surely no one else could get into the house.

"Rylee?" he called from the hallway. "Is it okay if I come in?"

"Please do." She sighed as he stretched out beside her.

He hesitated a moment, then wrapped her in his arms.

She snuggled closer, grateful for his nearness.

"It'll be all right," he murmured, lightly stroking her back. "I love you, Rylee. I won't let anything happen to you. And if anything happens to me…"

She covered his mouth with her hand. "Don't say that. Don't even think it."

He ran his tongue over her palm. She felt the heat of it in the core of her being. Removing her hand, he kissed her, long and slow.

Rylee clung to him as he deepened the kiss, wanting to be closer, closer. She slid her hands under his tee shirt, then trailed her fingertips up and down his back. His skin was cool, yet touching him ignited a flame deep within her and she pressed herself against him.

Alex groaned softly. She was soft and warm and he yearned to bury himself deep within her, to make her his in every way. He ran his tongue along the side of her neck, wishing he dared taste her, but he wasn't sure now was the time. Magdalena had given Rylee a hell of a scare. This probably wasn't the time to remind her that she had a vampire in her bed.

He stilled as her hands explored his chest, slid down, down, to his belly, only to stop when they reached the waistband of his sweatpants.

He covered her hand with his. "We'd better stop," he said, his voice thick with longing.

"What if I don't want to?"

"Rylee, you'd better be sure this is what you want, because once I make you mine, I'll never let you go."

Alex heard the change in her breathing, sensed her sudden apprehension as she realized what he was saying. Lifting her hand, he kissed her palm. "I love you, but I want you to be sure before things go too far."

Even though the room was dark, he saw the tears glistening in her eyes. "It's all right, love." When he started to rise, she clung to him.

"Please, stay with me," she whispered.

"Everything okay?" he asked, wiping away her tears with his fingertips.

"I guess so. Are you...are you mad at me?"

"Why would I be mad? I wouldn't blame you if you changed your mind about spending the rest of your life with me. It isn't a decision to be made lightly. We've really only known each other a short time and most of that hasn't been pleasant. I'm surprised you're still here."

"I don't want you to think I don't love you, but…"

"I understand, love. Go to sleep now. I'll keep the monsters at bay," he murmured, and then grinned into the darkness, thinking he was one of them.

Chapter 31

A lex woke with a frown. Since becoming a vampire, he had known immediately on waking where he was and what time it was. He usually roused an hour or so before sundown, which at this time of the year was around seven-thirty. But his interior clock told him it was a few minutes after five.

Sitting up, he checked the wound in his shoulder. The ragged hole was gone, leaving his skin smooth and unblemished. Was waking earlier the result of drinking from Costain last night?

He showered and dressed, then went in search of Rylee. He found her in her office, reading her Facebook page. Murmuring, "Hey, beautiful," he brushed a kiss across the top of her head.

Rylee smiled as she glanced over her shoulder, and then frowned. "Wow, you're up even earlier than you were the other day."

"Are you complaining?"

"Of course not."

He shrugged. "It's gotta be a perk from the blood Rhys gave me last night."

"Amazing." Who would have guessed that vampire blood could heal such a dreadful wound? What else could it do?

Alex frowned. "Are you doing all right?"

"As well as can be expected, I guess." And then, remembering what had almost happened last night, she felt a blush warm her cheeks. If Alex hadn't put the brakes on, they likely would have made love. In a way, she was disappointed that they hadn't. She knew somehow that he would be a wonderful lover. But once done, it couldn't be undone and would only lead to more complications in an already complicated relationship.

Alex hadn't meant to read her mind, but her thoughts were so strong, it was hard to resist. Nuzzling her neck, he whispered, "There's always tonight."

Mortified, Rylee stared up at him, her cheeks on fire.

He shrugged. "I just wanted you to know I'm willing if you've changed your mind."

"How…?" She swallowed hard. "How did you know what I was thinking?" she asked, and felt her cheeks grow even hotter.

"I…uh…" He cleared his throat. "The truth is, I can read your mind."

"That's impossible!" she exclaimed, even though she had proof that it wasn't. "How can you do that?" And then she frowned. There had been times when he'd answered questions she hadn't asked, when he'd seemed to know her thoughts before she expressed them.

"I always could. I try not to read your thoughts because I don't want to intrude, but sometimes they come through loud and clear and…" *Shit!* He cleared his throat again. "I'm sorry, Rylee."

"Sorry?" she sputtered. "You're sorry for violating my privacy?"

"I tried not to. I swear it. But, dammit, girl…" He made a vague gesture with his hand. And then he lifted her out of the chair and into his arms. "Hell, I'm not sorry," he said, and slanted his mouth over hers.

Rylee sighed as she felt herself being swept away by his kisses, the welcome invasion of his tongue, the press of his hard-muscled body against hers, the very real evidence of his desire.

She moaned in protest when he lifted his head.

"I love you, Rylee," he said, his voice low and intense. "And I want you more than you can imagine. But I'm an old-fashioned guy, and I want you to be mine, legally and lawfully wed, before we make love."

"Is that a marriage proposal, Mr. O'Donnell?"

"What would you say if it was?" he asked with a crooked grin.

"I'd say yes," she murmured, and new, in that moment, that for better or worse, she had given her heart to Alex and in so doing, had tied her future to his.

Feeling like he was on Cloud Nine, Alex called Rhys to tell him the good news.

"Married?" Rhys winked at Megan, who was sitting beside him on the sofa. "I'll be damned."

"Probably," Alex agreed. "I just wanted you to be the first to know."

Taking the phone from Rhys, Megan said, "Well, I think it's wonderful."

"Thanks. Although I think maybe I just caught her in a weak moment. I'm afraid if she stops to think about it, she might change her mind, and I wouldn't blame her."

"Well, there's no rush," Megan said. "When do I get to meet her?"

"How about tonight? Say, in an hour?"

"They're coming here?" Rylee exclaimed. "Tonight?" She glanced around the living room, glad she had dusted and picked up the place earlier in the day. She didn't have anything in the way of dessert to offer a guest, but then, with vampires, it really wasn't necessary.

"You got a problem with meeting Megan?"

"Yes…no…I don't know. I just wish you'd given me a little more time to get used to the idea." "Well," Alex said, grinning, "you've got about twenty minutes."

Rylee was a nervous wreck when the doorbell rang. She had been worried about meeting Daisy's sister, but that had gone all right.

Still, Megan was Rhys Costain's wife. Was she as scary as the Master of the City?

She pasted a smile on her face when Alex introduced her to Megan. Like Daisy, Costain's wife was lovely, radiant, with dark-red hair and sparkling brown eyes.

"I'm so happy to meet you," Megan said, smiling. "Rhys has told me so much about you."

Rylee glanced at Costain, wondering what he'd said. Nodding, she murmured, "Please, sit down."

It was interesting, watching Rhys. It was blatantly obvious from the way he looked at Megan, the way he held her hand in his, that he was madly, deeply, in love with her. His voice was softer when he spoke to her.

And Megan was just as in love with him.

It reminded Rylee of the way Daisy had looked at Erik, the way he had looked at her. What was there about vampire men, she wondered. She glanced at Alex. Like Rhys and Erik, he exuded strength and power and charisma. It was an intoxicating combination but a lot of men possessed the same attributes. And yet, there was something about the men in this room, something extraordinary. Was it just that they were vampires? Or was it more than that?

The evening flew by. Her guests tried to include her in the conversation, but time and again, she simply sat back and listened while Alex and Rhys reminisced about the past, before they were vampires. Megan, too, seemed fascinated. Costain's life was especially interesting. He'd had such a long life, seen so much of the world, so many changes in countries and kingdoms, so many inventions that she took for granted. Would Alex live as long? It was a sobering thought. He could live for two, three, four hundred years or more.

It was a thought that haunted her after Rhys and Megan left for home.

"What is it?" Alex asked. "Why so glum? Didn't you have a good time?"

"What? Oh, yes. Megan's very nice."

"Were you uncomfortable, having them here?"

"No. Rhys is a different man when he's with her, isn't he? Far less intimidating."

"Yeah. He said she changed his life. I guess it's true." Pulling Rylee into his arms, he said, "The love of a good woman changed my life, too. And I thank you for that. Now, are you going to tell me what's wrong?"

Tugging on his hand, she sat down on the sofa and snuggled against him when he put his arm around her. "I was just thinking about Rhys and how long he's lived."

"And?"

"I guess I just realized that you could live that long, too."

Alex frowned, and then he knew what was bothering her.

"Maybe we shouldn't get married," she said slowly. "It wouldn't be fair, expecting you to stay with me when I'm...when I'm old and you aren't. You'll feel responsible for me and probably grow to hate having to care for an old woman, and..."

"Rylee, hush. I'm not just in love with your looks, which are spectacular. I'm in love with *you*, with your sweetness and compassion, the way being with you makes me feel human. It has nothing to do with age. It's you. Your...your spirit."

She sighed, touched by his words. Yet a little voice inside insisted that the day would come when he would think of her as nothing but a burden.

Rylee woke with the same niggling worry on her mind. In the kitchen, she poured herself a cup of coffee, then sat at the table, her mind replaying everything that had happened since she met Alex—the good—and the bad.

And then she thought about Daisy and Megan and how happy they both seemed to be. If she had met them under other circumstances, she never would have guessed they were vampires. Neither one seemed to regret being changed. They both appeared to be perfectly content with living at night and dining on blood. Both were obviously head-over-heels in love with their husbands and apparently very happy with life in general.

What if she asked Alex to turn her? Would he be glad? Would she regret it once it was done? It wasn't like buying a pair of shoes and deciding they didn't fit. Once turned, there was no going back.

She mulled it over all day. Unable to think of anything else, she decided to do a little more online research on vampires. The number of web sites dedicated to the Undead still amazed her. She found information on how to detect one and how to destroy one, but the most intriguing was the mythology of how to become one. Most were ludicrous. According to myth, being bitten wasn't the only way to become a vampire. Other ways were to commit suicide, to be excommunicated from the church, dying without being baptized, having your parents curse you, having a cat or some other animal jump over your body before you were buried, being the off-spring of a human and a demon…the list went on and on.

Needing a break, she made a turkey and swiss cheese sandwich for lunch and carried it into the living room, along with a soda.

Did she want to give up eating? She loved bread and pasta and lemon meringue pie. She loved jogging on the beach in the morn-ing, watching the sun set. And children. She had always hoped to have five or six. All that would be lost if she let Alex change her. Was she willing to give up everything she knew and loved to be with him? To never have children and grandchildren? Maybe even great-grandchildren?

She considered what he called the perks—living for a very long time. Never being sick. Never growing old or wrinkled or having to worry about gaining weight. Being incredibly strong and able to do amazing things, like dissolving into mist or crossing great distances with little more than a thought.

Rylee was still sitting on the sofa—undecided—when Alex woke up two hours later.

"Hey," he said, "what's got you looking so serious?"

She shrugged. "Nothing."

"Nothing?"

"I was just wondering what it would be like to be what you are."

Alex stared at her, dumbfounded.

"Would you like me better if I was a…a vampire?"

"No. Why would you think that?" he asked, taking a place beside her.

She shrugged one shoulder. "I don't know. It just seems like a decision I'll have to make sooner or later if I stay with you."

"Dammit, Rylee, I would never ask you do that! I wouldn't wish this on my worst enemy."

"I'm confused. Megan and Daisy made it sound wonderful. Rhys certainly seems to love it."

Alex raked his fingers through his hair. What could he say to her? He hated what he was and yet, in a relatively short time, he'd grown to love the supernatural powers it gave him, the strength that coursed through him. Hell, he even loved the blood. How could he explain that in terms she would understand?

She regarded him through narrowed eyes. "So, do you hate what you are?"

"Yes. And no."

Rylee frowned, more confused than ever.

"Being a vampire is kind of like being addicted to a drug. From the outside, it looks horrible, disgusting. It's totally against human nature. And yet, once it's done…I don't know how to describe it."

"Would you be human again, if you could?"

"Honestly? I don't know. All I do know is that you should think it over carefully before you decide. It doesn't always turn out well."

"What do you mean?"

"Some people can't handle it and it makes them crazy. Some destroy themselves. Others go on killing sprees and have to be stopped."

"Like Magdalena?"

"Exactly. If Rhys finds her, he'll destroy her. All those killings have brought hunters to town. It makes it dangerous for the rest of us. Vampires tend to keep a low profile whenever possible for obvious reasons."

"You're right," she said, slowly. "There *is* a lot to think about."

"You haven't had dinner, have you?" he asked, when her stomach made a very unladylike sound.

"No."

"Do you feel like going out?"

"I guess so. If you think it's safe."

Rylee decided on a hamburger for dinner, and because she wanted to be surrounded by a lot of people, they went to the mall. Since it was Friday night, the place was more crowded than usual, which suited her just fine. Safety in numbers, she thought, as they made their way toward the escalator.

For the first time in days, she felt normal, at ease, just another cog in the wheel of life. It was good to hear laughter and see teenagers wandering around, most intent on their phones.

When they reached the food court, Alex wrinkled his nose as myriad smells assaulted him—Chinese and Mexican cuisine, onions, meat and condiments from the hamburger stand, popcorn and soda and hot dogs—all mingled with the scent of sweat and perfume and over all, the beating of a hundred hearts, the tantalizing scent of hot, fresh blood.

"Should we go somewhere else?" Rylee asked, seeing the look of revulsion on his face as they passed a pizza place.

"No," he said. "I'm fine. Just eat fast."

She ordered a cheeseburger, fries, and a strawberry shake.

Alex followed her to a table. He scanned the crowd while she ate, his thoughts troubled. Magdalena knew where Rylee lived. There was always a chance she had sent someone to follow them, though he hadn't detected the presence of any strangers when they left the house. But there were ways to disguise one's scent. Hunters used Scent-B-Gone. Perhaps vampires had something similar.

But he saw nothing suspicious.

To his relief, Rylee finished her meal in record time.

Alex had transported them to the Mall parking garage. Now, taking Rylee's hand, he looked for a quiet place where no one would notice their sudden departure.

The revenant appeared out of nowhere. Moving quicker than Alex would have thought possible, the creature flung a vial of holy water in his face, momentarily blinding him before lunging forward, stake in hand.

But Rylee was moving, too. Grabbing a nearby trash can, she threw it in front of the revenant, causing him to stumble and fall.

Grasping Alex's arm, she started running, heedless of the people who stopped to stare. What must they think? But she had no time to wonder.

She let out a shriek when she was suddenly airborne as Alex transported them back to the safety of her house.

Inside, she collapsed on the sofa, one hand pressed to her rapidly-beating heart. She gasped when Alex dropped down on the floor.

The left side of his face was blistered from his hairline to his jaw and halfway down the side of his neck.

"Alex. Oh, Alex, what can I do?"

"Nothing." He grimaced as he pressed a hand to his cheek.

"Will a cold cloth help?"

"I doubt it."

Needing something to do, Rylee went into the bathroom and wet a wash rag. This was all her fault, she thought as she hurried back to the living room and handed him the damp cloth.

Eyes closed, he pressed it to his cheek.

Not knowing what else to do, Rylee sat beside him. "Does it help?"

"Not much."

"It'll heal, won't it?"

Alex nodded, figuring if Costain's blood had healed Magdalena's bite and increased his own power, it should be strong enough to restore a little blistered skin.

He hoped.

Chapter 32

Magdalena laughed as she buried her fangs in the throat of a handsome young man. She might not have destroyed O'Donnell, but her revenant had hurt him, sure as hell, and that was almost as satisfying.

Thanks to Sylvi, she knew where O'Donnell's woman lived. She had no love for the Elf—the traitor—but the girl had possessed amazing talents and connections, only a few of which she'd been willing to share. *Damn her hide.*

But it didn't matter, Magdalena thought. All she had to do was find a way to flush the woman out and the hunter would follow. Of that, she had no doubt.

She tossed the lifeless body into a ditch, licked the last bit of blood from her lips, then sniffed the air in search of other prey.

CHAPTER 33

R hys swore as news of four more bodies appeared in his news feed. *Dammit!* This had to stop. The city was crawling with hunters. Morris had barely escaped being staked a few nights ago. Nicholas had had his own close encounter two nights before that, and Julius had killed one. Ordinarily, Rhys wasn't opposed to ridding the world of hunters, but at times like this, it only added fuel to the fire.

They had to find Magdalena and they had to do it now. Never before had he had so much trouble tracking down one of his own kind. She was as elusive as smoke in the wind.

He tried to think of a way to draw her out, but nothing came to mind. He had to give her credit—she had out-guessed and out-flanked him at every turn.

Muttering an oath, he poured himself a glass of wine heavily laced with blood donated by Jean Marie. If only Sylvi hadn't been so close-mouthed. In a way, he couldn't blame her. She was in fear for her life, and with good reason. Still, the Elf obviously didn't approve of Magdalena's incessant killing. If Sylvi would only help him, they might put an end to Magdalena's carnage once and for all.

Rylee had just finished an early dinner when Alex padded barefoot into the kitchen. "You look much better," she said, smiling.

He nodded as he lifted his hand to the side of his face. The pain and the blisters had disappeared while he was at rest. *Thank you, Rhys.*

"It's amazing." Rylee wiped her hands on a dishtowel, then ran her fingertips over his cheek. "Does it work on people, too?"

"Yeah."

"Maybe vampires should bottle their blood and sell it to hospitals."

"I don't think so. There are already enough people out there either trying to take our heads or stealing our blood and selling it on the Internet. Not for healing, though. A few ounces gives mortals a high unlike any other."

Frowning thoughtfully, Rylee said, "You'd think that someone who had an injury or a wound of some kind might have taken enough to get high and then noticed their injury was healed."

"I doubt if they'd put two and two together while they're high, and it's unlikely they'd make the connection when they came down. Although I imagine, sooner or later, someone will figure it out. And then we'll really be in trouble. Enough about vampires," he murmured.

Pulling Rylee into his arms, he rained kisses on her brow, her cheeks, the tip of her nose before settling on her lips.

Rylee clung to him, everything else forgotten as his mouth moved over hers, his tongue teasing hers in a mating dance as old as time.

Without releasing her, be backed into the living room and fell back on the sofa, carrying Rylee with him.

Feeling as contented as a cat, Rylee sighed as his hands caressed her. Soon, she thought, soon she would be his wife and they wouldn't have to stop at kisses.

She was lost in a sensual haze when Alex sat up, carrying her with him. "What's wrong?" she asked.

"I smell smoke!"

"What?" She blinked up at him, and then she smelled it, too.

"Stay here." Alex hurried toward the back of house. The down-stairs bedroom window was broken. Flames licked at the curtains, crawled along the carpet, snaked under the closet door.

When he returned to the living room, Rylee was calling the Fire Department. "Come on," he said, "we're getting out of here!"

"Wait! I need to find..."

"You don't need anything," he said. "Magdalena or one of her minions set the fire."

Eyes wide, Rylee stared at him, then dashed into the kitchen. She grabbed her purse, her cell phone, and her maternal grand-mother's antique cookbook before running back into the living room. She shut her eyes tightly as Alex wrapped her in his arms and whisked her away.

When Rylee opened her eyes, they were once again in Costain's penthouse. She stood there a moment, stunned, and then burst into tears as she realized she had likely just lost everything she owned—her clothes and the old family photographs that had been taken before she had a cell phone, her cameras, the china from her favorite aunt, all of her books, mementos from her childhood—like a CD signed by Tim McGraw. Her car was probably gone, as well. And Costain's Jag, which was worth more than the contents of her house and her Mazda combined.

Alex swore under his breath. Once again, Rylee had suffered because of him. If he had stayed out of her life, she wouldn't have been kidnapped and terrorized. Her house wouldn't be in flames. She wouldn't be forced to stay in Costain's penthouse again. He had brought her nothing but trouble since the night they met. And who knew what the future held? Nothing good, judging from past events.

Unable to think of anything to say to comfort her, Alex sat beside her and drew her gently into his arms. Now that Magdalena had tasted his blood again, she would have no trouble finding him. She had proved that tonight. The vampire must have known he was there. Had Magdalena hoped to incinerate him? Or grab him when he ran out of the house?

It was time to send Rylee away. As long as he kept his distance, Magdalena wouldn't be able to find her through him.

But Rylee was here now. He would hold her and love her and tomorrow night, he would send her away.

Rylee woke slowly. It took her a moment to realize where she was, and then it all came rushing back—the fire, their hasty return to the penthouse.

Alex had held her all night long. His kisses had been filled with love and tenderness, nothing more. He had rested at her side, whispering words of comfort when she woke from a nightmare, promising her that things would get better.

She was somewhat surprised to find him still lying beside her. In spite of all the bad things that had happened, there was no one she would rather be with.

Slipping out of bed, she wrapped one of Costain's robes around her and tiptoed into the living room, wondering if there was any need to be quiet when Alex was at rest. Were vampires aware of what was happening around them when lost in the dark sleep, or was it really like being dead?

Thrusting that morbid thought from her mind, Rylee called her next-door neighbor to find out if her car had been destroyed in the fire. She had been prepared for a 'yes' so she was happily surprised when Mr. Hawkins informed her that the fire department had saved the garage and both cars. Unfortunately, the rest of the house was a total loss. Mr. Hawkins also advised her that the cause of the fire was under investigation and she wouldn't be allowed to return for several days. Sighing, she thanked him and ended the call.

Feeling numb, Rylee wept for the loss of her home. Her maiden aunt had lived in the house for seventy years and bequeathed it to her only niece. It was just a small place on a quiet street in an L.A. suburb. Like the house itself, most of the things in it couldn't be replaced—the few childhood toys she hadn't been about to part with, the quilt her mother had made for her on her eighteenth birthday, a china teapot her father had brought her from Japan—things that had no real value, yet held memories she cherished.

After drying her eyes, she spent the next hour on the phone talking to insurance people. Luckily, her cameras and most of her personal belongings were covered and her policy included a replacement clause, so she could rebuild.

After a breakfast of tea and toast, she pulled a thumb drive from her purse, then sat at the small desk and inserted the drive into one of the USB ports. She scrolled through the files until she found the one that listed the contents of her house, as well as photos of her belongings, and emailed both to her insurance agent. Thankfully, the drive also held all of her business contacts, copies of invoices and other business-related information.

Feeling depressed all over again, she sat there for several minutes, just staring into space, trying to absorb everything that had happened. "Stop it," she muttered. "It's not the end of the world, even though it seems like it now. You're still alive. You're healthy. And Alex loves you."

Determined not to dwell on what she'd lost, she went to YouTube and scrolled though a couple of cat videos, hoping to take her mind off her troubles.

She had just shut down the computer when Alex padded into the office.

"What are you doing?" he asked, peering over her shoulder.

"Nothing really. I called my neighbor a little while ago," she said, trying not to cry. "The house is a total loss,"

The sight of the tears welling in her eyes tore at his heart. "I'm sorry, love. I feel like it's all my fault."

"It isn't. It's Magdalena's fault. How I hate that horrible woman!"

"That makes two of us." Alex took a deep breath. The timing for what he was about to say couldn't be worse, but Rylee's life was in danger. The fire last night had scared the hell out of him. He didn't want to think about what might have happened if he hadn't been there. He knew all too well what Magdalena was capable of. He still had nightmares of coming home and finding Paula murdered by her hand.

Resting one hip against the edge of the desk, he said, "We need to talk."

Feeling as though an acid pit was churning in her stomach, Rylee looked up at him. "What's wrong?"

Everything, he thought. "I can't keep you safe anymore. When Magdalena bit me, she swallowed some of my blood. She'll be able to track me wherever I go. And as long as you're with me…" He shrugged. "You're in danger. I can't keep you locked up here indefinitely. And while I'm pretty sure she wouldn't try to breach Costain's lair, I'm not willing to take that chance."

"What are you saying?"

"I had a long talk with Rhys last night. I want you to go stay at his other lair. I've never been there and Magdalena can't track him. You should be safe there until she's dead."

Or I am. His unspoken words hung in the air between them.

"But…"

"I'm not any happier about this than you are. But we're talking about your life, Rylee, and that's more important to me than anything else." He clenched his hands to keep from reaching for her. "I never should have entangled you in my life in the first place. I've brought you nothing but trouble."

"You brought me love," she said, her voice so quiet, only a vampire could have heard it. "That's worth everything else."

Almost, he changed his mind. But then he thought about Paula and the baby. He hadn't been able to save them, but he thanked the Good Lord that he'd been there to save Rylee. Had he not been at her house to spirit her away, she might have run out of the burning building and straight into Magdalena's clutches. And he couldn't let that happen. He had no doubt that Magdalena would kill Rylee without a qualm, or use her as bait to trap him. He had lost one woman to Magdalena's vengeance. He couldn't risk causing the death of another. Dammit! He hated feeling helpless. As a hunter, he'd had a good chance of destroying her, but he'd lost that edge when Rhys turned him. Though he had the blood of two ancient vampires in his veins, he wasn't sure he could defeat Magdalena on his own, and it wasn't a chance he was willing to take, not with Rylee's life hanging in the balance.

"I could go stay with my parents," she suggested.

"No. It's too easy to locate people these days. I can't take a chance on Magdalena finding your parents or hiring some detective to track you down. No one will find you at Costain's lair in Granite Hills."

She wanted to argue, but everything he'd said made sense. As long as they were together, her life was in jeopardy. "All right," she said, with a sigh of resignation.

Pulling her into his arms, he murmured, "I'm sorry for turning your life upside down yet again, love. And for the loss of your house."

Rylee clung to him, her heart breaking. How long? she wondered. How long until she could call her life her own again? Feeling the sting of tears in her eyes, she said, "I think I'll go lay down for a while."

"Okay." He hugged her close, reluctant to let her go. He'd said he was sorry, but it wouldn't bring back her home or the things she had lost, and yet he found himself saying it again.

Unable to speak past her tears, Rylee turned and hurried into the bedroom. After closing the door, she fell face down on the bed and cried until she was empty inside.

CHAPTER 34

Rylee had nothing to pack, didn't own anything but the clothes on her back. She stayed in the bedroom until Alex rapped on the door and told her it was time to go. Head high, she marched out of the bedroom, then came to an abrupt halt when she saw Rhys standing in front of the living room window.

"Where's Alex?"

"He asked me to take you. Magdalena can't track me."

"He couldn't even stay and tell me goodbye," she said, her voice bitter.

"Rylee, don't be too hard on him. He loves you. He's only thinking of your safety."

"Is he? He didn't say a word about… It doesn't matter."

"Give him some time. Alex has been through a hell of a lot lately. I'm surprised he's handling it as well as he is. He's afraid he can't protect you. And he might be right. As long as you're with him, you're in danger. And so is he."

Everything Rhys said was true, but it didn't ease the pain or erase her feeling of being abandoned. He could have stayed long enough to tell her goodbye, to assure her they'd be together again. That he loved her.

Keeping a tight rein on her emotions, she gathered her handbag and her grandmother's cookbook, stood stiff as a board when Costain put his arm around her.

Moments later, she was standing in the middle of the most beautiful room she had ever seen. Remembering Costain's penthouse boudoir, she had expected more of the same, but this room was exquisite—the walls a cool ivory, the carpets a deep mauve. A long, curved sofa, a pair of armchairs and a love seat faced a red brick fireplace. Paintings adorned the walls.

"Rylee," Megan said, coming forward to greet her. "Please make our home yours. The cupboards are stocked with food and drink. And chocolate."

Rylee forced a smile. "Thank you. I'm sorry to put you out of your house."

Megan waved it off. "No problem. If you need anything, or if you just get scared, we're just a call away. And if you get lonely, feel free to have someone come and stay with you."

"Thank you. Both of you."

Megan invited her to use whichever of the four bedrooms she preferred. "Just make yourself at home," she said with a smile. "Feel free to rearrange the furniture, if your like. We have Hulu and Netflix. There are computers in all the bedrooms."

"Thank you so much for letting me stay here," Rylee said, overcome with her generosity. "I hope I won't put you out for too long."

"Please, don't worry about it. Rhys has several other homes." Megan took Rylee's hands in hers. "I know you think this will never end, but don't give up hope and don't get discouraged. I've never known Rhys to fail at anything. He'll find Magdalena, sooner or later."

"I just hope it's sooner," Rylee muttered.

"We all do."

"One word of caution," Rhys said. "Try not to go out at night any more than you have to. Even though Magdalena can't track you here, I wouldn't put it past her to have spies out looking for you and Alex. Don't hesitate to call me if you need me. Day or night."

"I'm sorry to be such a bother."

"Forget it."

After Rhys and Megan took their leave, Rylee stood in the middle of the living room. She couldn't help wondering how much a place like this cost. Certainly in the hundreds of thousands of dollars.

Maybe a million or more. Curiosity sent her wandering through the house, which was even bigger than she'd imagined. Living room, dining room, kitchen, laundry room and two bathrooms filled the downstairs. There were three bedrooms and a master upstairs, each with its own bathroom and sitting room, each unique in color and reminiscent of a different time period—Roman in the master, Greek in one of the other bedrooms, Roaring 20s in the third and what looked like it had been pulled from the set of *Guardians of the Galaxy* in the fourth.

Wondering if Rhys or Megan had chosen the décor, she returned to the living room. Curling up in a corner of the love seat, she called home to tell her parents about the fire.

Alex was waiting at the penthouse when Rhys returned. "Is she all right?"

"Her feelings are pretty raw. Couldn't you have hung around long enough to tell her goodbye?"

"I was afraid if I saw her again, I wouldn't be able to let her go. Did I do the right thing?"

"You know you did."

"I hope so."

"She's better off at my place than here. With her gone, we can concentrate on trying to find Magdalena. I think from now on you and I will do a lot of hunting out in the open."

"Like sitting ducks?"

Rhys shrugged. "She might not bite, but then again… What the hell? I haven't fed tonight, and I know you haven't. What do you say?"

"Why not? I've got nothing better to do."

The weather suited Alex's mood perfectly—dark clouds shut out the moon and stars. Jagged bolts of lightning split the skies followed by rolling drumbeats of thunder. They had only gone a block or two when the clouds unleashed a torrent of rain.

"You picked a great night to go hunting," he muttered. His sire had left Megan every night for the last few nights to go hunting with him. He had a feeling Rhys tagged along not only in hopes of attracting Magdalena, but to make sure he didn't do anything stupid. Alex had to admit there had been times when he'd considered killing someone in hopes that Costain would retaliate and put him out of his misery.

"I see a perfect pair up ahead," Rhys said, jerking his chin toward two young women—one blonde, one brunette—who were making a dash for the shelter of a doorway. "Come on."

Alex watched with a small measure of envy as Costain quickly and effortlessly mesmerized the two females.

"Light or dark?" Rhys asked with a wry grin.

"I'll take the brunette," Alex said. The blonde reminded him too much of Rylee. He fed quickly, hating what he was doing, what he'd become, more than ever. Had he still been human, Rylee would be his.

After sending the women on their way, Rhys slapped him on the back. "The girl still loves you, you jackass. Once Magdalena is no longer a threat, you can go to Rylee, admit you've been a damn fool and beg for her forgiveness."

"Somehow I don't think it will be that easy."

"You think not? If she turns you down, I'll give you the Jag."

"You're on!"

Rylee immersed herself in keeping busy in the days that followed. She bought a new wardrobe—most of it online. Ordered several books from Amazon that she'd been wanting to read, as well as a new camera and equipment. Megan had invited her to use the computers and Rylee spent most of one day updating her web page and sending emails to clients with a brief—albeit phony—explanation for her absence. She took long baths in the sunken tub, immersed herself in the latest bestseller.

She had been tempted several times to call Alex, but never did. It still hurt that he hadn't taken the time to tell her goodbye. Coward. Sure, it would have been painful for both of them. Sure, he sent her away for her own good. But he'd said nothing about seeing her again.

She waited each evening, hoping for his call.

But it never came.

Three weeks after moving into Costain's place, she booked a flight into L.A., then hired an Uber to take her to see what was left of her house and pick up her car.

Rylee stood on the curb for several minutes, staring at the carnage. She had intended to poke through the wreckage to see if anything had survived the blaze, but it was obvious nothing was left. She wondered what Magdalena had used to start the fire. Thinking of Magdalena made her feel suddenly vulnerable and she hurried toward the garage.

As her neighbor had said, it was still standing. Other than being sprinkled with ashes, her Mazda was fine. The Jag was gone. No doubt Alex or Costain had picked it up.

For a moment, she was sorely tempted to drive by Costain's penthouse. But as much as she missed Alex, going to see him seemed unwise. Keeping her distance from him was the reason Alex had suggested they stop seeing each other in the first place.

But if their parting was only temporary, why didn't he call?

Rylee drove until dark, then spent the night in a motel. Lying in bed, she stared up at the ceiling. Since moving into Costain's house, she had managed to keep herself so busy during the day that she didn't have time to think about a handsome vampire with broad shoulders and beautiful, dark-brown eyes, or a smile that made her heart melt.

But at night in her lonely bed, there was no denying the longing of her heart. She ached for the touch of his hand, the sound of his voice husky with desire as he whispered her name, the magic of his kisses. He haunted her dreams and she was powerless to escape him. Nor did she want to. In dreams, he was hers—hers to hold and to love—the dreams so real, she sometimes woke in the morning expecting to find him lying there beside her.

She reached Costain's house in Granite Hills late the following afternoon. Feeling blue, she called home. Her mother answered the phone.

"How are you doing, hon?"

"I'm fine, Mom. Keeping busy."

"I wish you'd come home. There's no need for you to stay with friends until your house is rebuilt when your old room is ready and waiting."

"How are you and Dad?" she asked, hoping to change the subject.

A pause before her mother said, "There's something bothering you, and it's not the loss of your house."

Rylee smiled faintly at her mother's tone. She had never been able to hide her feelings from either one of her parents. "I met a man in Los Angeles."

"Go on," her mother coaxed.

"I fell in love with him, but..." Rylee blew out a sigh. "He had some issues that drove us apart."

"What kind of issues?" her father asked, and she wondered how long he'd been on the extension.

"You don't want to know."

Her father paused a moment and she knew he was stroking his mustache the way he always did when he was thinking. "Is he in trouble with the law?"

"No. No, nothing like that," Rylee assured him. If only it was something that mundane, she thought.

"You can tell us anything," her mother said. "You know that."

"Not this," Rylee said, and wondered if they would even believe her.

"If you change your mind, we're here to listen," her father said.

"I know, Dad. And I love you for it. Both of you. I'll call you again soon."

When the call ended, Rylee stared out the window. She'd found a contractor to build her new house and selected a floor plan from several he had emailed her. Since construction seemed to be in a slump, she'd gotten a good deal, plus his crew had been able to begin right away. She'd spoken to her insurance agent to make sure the money to rebuild was available.

Thinking of rebuilding reminded her of all she had lost. She blinked rapidly, determined not to cry. Things would get better, she assured herself.

How could they get any worse?

Rhys snorted softly as he watched Alex feed. The kid was hurting. It was apparent in the slump of his shoulders, the soul-deep misery in his eyes, the hopelessness in his voice. His lack of interest in hunting. Not that he was likely to starve to death, Rhys mused. The hunger would demand to be fed whether the kid wanted to feed or not.

They had prowled the streets every night for weeks now, but there had been no sign of Magdalena, save for the bodies that had turned up with clockwise precision and then suddenly stopped. They had encountered hunters on several occasions. Rhys had been forced to kill one, but Magdalena remained elusive.

Alex had checked the hunter site on the Dark Web, hoping for info on her whereabouts, but to no avail.

Was she trying to lull them into a false sense of security, Rhys wondered, because he was pretty sure she hadn't given up her quest for vengeance.

He glanced at Alex. The kid was still feeding. Muttering an oath, he grabbed Alex by the shoulder and pulled him away from the woman. "What the hell are you trying to do? Kill her?"

Alex stared at him blankly. "No, I..." He shrugged. "I guess I wasn't paying attention."

"I guess not." A thought sent the woman on her way. "You were thinking about Rylee again, weren't you?"

"Yeah."

Damn, the kid had it bad. "Why don't you go see her?"

"Are you nuts?"

"Maybe so, but I'm sick of that hang-dog expression. Why don't you call her and ask her to meet you somewhere? I'll tag along to keep an eye out for Magdalena. If I do the mist thing, she'll never know I'm there. And if she shows up, we'll have her. If she doesn't, at least you'll get to spend a little time with Rylee."

Hands shoved into his pockets, Alex strolled down the street after Rhys, sorely tempted to take him up on his offer. The thought of seeing Rylee again warred with his fear of putting her in danger yet again. Of course, there was some doubt that she would agree to meet him after the way he'd left her. But maybe she would, even if it was only to tell him to go to hell. At least he would see her, hear her voice, inhale the warm, womanly fragrance that was hers alone and hers alone.

"I'll think about it," he said when they returned to the penthouse.

But there was nothing to think about. He had to see her again, even if it was for the last time.

CHAPTER 35

Rylee stared at her phone. She read the text and then read it again. Short and sweet, it simply said, *I miss you. Please meet me tonight at nine at Ristorante Sarto. If you agree, Rhys will pick you up.*

Should she? Or shouldn't she? What did he want? Rylee started to write 'no', but it showed up as 'yes.' Taking a deep breath, she hit Send. She regretted it immediately, then told herself that meeting him might be a good thing. It would give her a chance to ask why he'd never called after sending her away. She ignored the little voice that reminded her she could have called him. But he had sent her away—for her own good, that was true. But he should have called. Or at least said good-bye.

Rylee started getting ready at seven. She showered and washed her hair, applied her makeup with care, put on one of the new dresses she had ordered on line—a slinky black number bought on a whim. She stepped into a pair of black heels, grabbed her handbag and her keys, and went into the living room to wait. Glancing around, she had to admit she would miss this place when her new house was ready.

Rhys showed up at five minutes to nine. He whistled softly when he saw her. "You'll break the kid's heart," he muttered as he slipped his arm around her waist.

As soon as they arrived at the pier, Rylee had second thoughts. What was she doing here? She turned around to tell Rhys she'd changed her mind, but he was nowhere to be seen.

And then Alex appeared beside her. "You look beautiful." He glanced around, then said, "Let's go inside." It was a week night and the crowd was light. He asked for a booth in the back and slid onto the bench across from Rylee. "Thank you for coming."

"What do you want, Alex?" she asked, her voice frigid.

"I wanted to apologize for the abrupt way I left you. I was afraid if I told you goodbye, I wouldn't be able to let you go."

She made a soft sound that was neither positive or negative. "You never called. Not even once."

"I know. I should have. But I checked on you every chance I got to make sure you were okay. As for calling…" He blew out a sigh. "I guess it was selfish of me, but I knew if I heard your voice, it would be that much harder to stay away."

Rylee folded her hands in her lap when the waitress came to take their order. Alex asked for a glass of wine. Rylee ordered a small antipasto salad, garlic bread, and a soda.

He waited until the waitress left to turn in their order before saying, "I love you, Rylee. You know I only sent you away because being with me is dangerous. Believe me, it was the hardest thing I've ever done."

"Then why are you here now?" she asked, her voice still cool. "Is Magdalena dead?"

"Not yet. I'm here because Rhys said he was tired of my 'hang-dog' expression."

A faint grin played across her lips and was gone. "Is he still around?"

"I'm sure he's somewhere nearby."

Rylee stared at him, eyes narrowed. "He's hoping she'll show up tonight, isn't he? I'm just bait."

"No. No!" But even as he denied it, he wondered if that had been Costain's motive all along. "Other than being your taxi, he's here for back-up in case Magdalena followed me. I'm not sure I'm strong enough to defeat her on my own."

Alex fell silent as the waitress arrived with their order, irritated by the interruption. When they were alone, he leaned forward. "It's been weeks since there's been any sign of her. No more grisly deaths. Rhys thinks she left town." He sipped his wine while he watched her sample the salad.

Rylee kept her gaze downcast while she ate. What should she do? Nothing had changed. He was still a vampire. Magdalena was still a threat and like he'd said, as long as they were together, her life was in danger.

And so was his.

And yet...she missed him dreadfully. One way or another, she had to decide if she wanted to spend her life with or without him. And tonight was as good a time as any. Yes, there were risks, but living was a risk. People died in accidents every day. Shootings and gang violence were commonplace in most cities. Sickness claimed countless others. Tomorrow wasn't guaranteed to anyone.

Lost in thought, she finished her dinner, though she scarcely tasted a bite of it.

Alex kept quiet. He didn't have to read her mind to know that their future together was on the line. He paid the check and they left the restaurant.

A chill breeze ruffled Rylee's hair as they made their way down to the shore.

When Rylee paused to remove her high heels, Alex took them from her and slid them into the pockets of his jacket

They walked along in silence for a time before he stopped and took her hand in his. "What are you thinking, Rylee?"

"Don't you know?"

"I try not to read your mind if I can help it. I realize our whole relationship has been a little rocky but..."

She snorted softly. "Rocky?"

"All right, rough as hell. I wouldn't blame you if you never wanted to see me again, but...can we pick up where we left off when this business with Magdalena is over?"

Rylee huffed a sigh that seemed to come from the soles of her feet.

Alex balled his hands into fists, waiting for her to send him away for good.

"I love you, Alex," she said. "I don't know how. I don't know why. I have no idea how I'll explain you to my parents. They don't believe in Bigfoot, the Loch Ness monster, or extraterrestrials. I don't know how they'll handle having a vampire in the family."

Stunned, he stared at her for a breathless moment before sweeping her into his arms. He twirled her around and around before claiming her lips with his in a long, slow kiss. "I love you, Rylee! You'll never know how much."

"I love you, too," she said, laughing and crying at the same time because the world suddenly seemed bright again. "But what *am* I going to tell my parents? *How* am I going to tell them?"

"We can keep it a secret. At least for a while."

"They'll want to meet you. Mom will expect you for dinner. They'll wonder why they never see you during the day." She bit down on her lower lip. "Rather than trying to come up with one lie after another, I think we should just tell them the truth and get it over with."

"It's your call, love. I'm not sure it's a good idea, but however you want to handle it is fine with me."

"I wanted to call you weeks ago," she confessed. "I missed you so much."

"Why didn't you?"

"I guess my feelings were hurt. You didn't say goodbye and when you didn't call, I thought you didn't care." She smiled up at him. "I'd like to get married at Christmastime, if that's all right with you."

"Better than all right." It was the first of August, Alex thought. Hopefully, the Magdalena problem would be resolved by then. Reaching into his pocket, he withdrew a small, silver box and handed it to her. "I bought this a few days before things got out of hand. I hope you like it."

Speechless, Rylee stared at it for a moment before lifting the lid. Inside, nestled on a bed of black velvet, was the most beautiful diamond engagement ring she had ever seen.

"We can change it if you don't like it."

"I love it!" she exclaimed as she slipped it on her finger. "And I love you! Let's tell my folks tonight," she said, tugging on his hand. "Before I lose my nerve."

It took less than a minute for Alex to transport them from the beach to the house where Rylee's parents lived. She stood on the sidewalk for several moments, thinking this was going to be even harder than she'd thought.

"We can do it another night," Alex said, squeezing her hand. "There's no hurry." He had debated the wisdom of coming here, hoped he wasn't making a mistake. But no one had seen or heard from Magdalena in a month or more. Rhys was convinced she'd left town and Alex was inclined to agree. Hopefully, she would never learn he'd been here.

"I have to warn you, my Dad's a little gruff. He scared away more than one of my boyfriends when I was in high school. I'm not sure which will upset him more, learning that I'm going to marry someone he's never met or that that someone is a vampire."

"Rylee, I'm not sure springing all this at once is a good idea."

"Me, either. But the sooner we tell them, the better. Besides, it will give my Dad plenty of time to get used to the idea before the wedding."

"If that's what you want, love, let's get it over with," he muttered dubiously "But I've got a bad feeling about this."

Rylee took a deep breath as she opened the front door. "Hey, Mom? Dad?"

"In the kitchen, dear," her mother called.

Of course, Rylee thought with a grin. *Major decisions were always made in the kitchen.*

Her parents sat side-by-side at the rectangular table. Her father cradled a cup of coffee in his hands. The dinner dishes were stacked in the sink.

"Mom, Dad, this is Alex O'Donnell. Alex, my father, Brian, and my mother, Margaret."

Shaking her father's hand, Alex said, "I'm pleased to meet you, Mr. Wagner. Mrs. Wagner."

Brian Wagner nodded, his expression vaguely hostile. He was a tall man, solidly built, with black hair graying at the temples and dark brown eyes.

Rylee took the seat across from her mother and tugged Alex down beside her.

"How long have you known our daughter?" Brian asked.

"A few months. We met at the beach."

Margaret Wagner smiled. "Rylee *does* love the ocean."

"Yes." Rylee looked a lot like her mother, Alex thought, except Mrs. Wagner's golden hair was shorter and streaked with silver, her eyes a darker shade of blue.

"Can I get you anything, Alex?" Margaret asked. "A slice of cake? Coffee?"

"No, thank you, we just had dinner."

Rylee took a deep breath. "Alex and I are getting married."

"Married!" her mother exclaimed.

"After only a few months?" Her father's eyes narrowed suspiciously. "You're not...?"

"No!" Rylee said quickly.

"Then what's the rush?"

"Dad, it's not until Christmas."

"That's still pretty sudden," Mr. Wagner remarked. "What do you do for a living, Mr. O'Donnell?"

Shit! He should have seen that coming, Alex thought. "I'm between jobs at the moment, but I have enough money to provide Rylee with a home and anything else she wants."

"Uh-huh."

"Dad, there's something else you and Mom need to know."

"What is it, I'm afraid to ask?" her father said.

"Alex is…" Rylee looked at her parents, unable to say the word.

"Alex is what?" Margaret asked.

"He's…he's thinking of moving to…to Arizona, that's why we're rushing the wedding," Rylee said.

"You're moving?" Brian asked, a note of disapproval in his voice.

"It's not for certain," Rylee said quickly, then drew a deep breath. She was a terrible liar.

Looking crestfallen at the news, her mother said, "I guess we'd better start making wedding plans as soon as possible."

"I know, Mom, but not tonight. I…I have a late meeting. We'll get together another time."

Brian and Margaret exchanged glances.

Suddenly needing to get out of there, Rylee stood, grabbed Alex's hand and tugged him to his feet. "I'll call you tomorrow."

"But Rylee…"

"We'll come over again soon, Mom, I promise," she said, and practically ran out the door.

"Lose your nerve?" Alex asked as they strolled down the street.

"I just couldn't say it."

"Like I said before, there's no need. They never have to know."

"Maybe you're right."

"Come on, I'll take you back to the pier. You can call Uber from there and get a ride back to Granite Hills."

She was getting used to being transported, Rylee thought when she opened her eyes. Her stomach wasn't churning, nor did she feel disoriented. Standing next to Alex, she called Uber. "They'll be here in a few minutes. Will I see you tomorrow?"

"I'll get in touch with you as soon as I wake up."

"All right. I wish we could spend more than a few stolen moments together. Isn't there some place we can go where Magdalena can't find us?"

"I don't know. Costain's beach house might work. Or maybe a hotel in another state." He glanced over his shoulder as her ride pulled up at the curb. "I love you," he murmured as he drew her into his arms.

Rylee's eyelids fluttered down as his mouth slanted over hers. Right or wrong, she had made her choice. All she had to do now was convince her parents she's wasn't making the biggest mistake of her life.

"I love you," Alex murmured. "Dream of me."

"Always." She smiled as he caressed her cheek.

"Good night, love." He waited until she was safely inside the car before transporting himself back to the penthouse. Rylee loved him, he thought, and all was right with the world.

CHAPTER 36

Magdalena strolled down the street, thinking she would soon return to Los Angeles. Weeks ago, she had realized that the numerous bodies she'd left in her wake had drawn more hunters to the area than she would have possible. With that in mind, she had decided to visit Portland for a while, another city with a large homeless population, which made for easy pickings on the street.

She had destroyed the only other vampire in the city, and now hunted to her heart's content. Few of the derelicts or transients were ever missed and she'd made an effort not to savage the bodies.

There had been a brief run-in with three hunters the night before. It had been a close call. She had been reminiscing about Eddie and the night he proposed when the attack came. She had been wounded in the fight but had managed to dispatch all three of the men.

Her thoughts turned to O'Donnell. His woman had left him and he was hiding out in Costain's penthouse. She wasn't fool enough to try to take O'Donnell at Costain's lair, which was known to be impregnable, nor crazy enough to confront him at *La Mort Rouge*.

Magdalena paused to stare at the lights of the city. She was growing bored with this endless game of cat-and-mouse. Soon, she thought, soon she would return to Los Angeles and fulfill her vow to avenge Eduardo. O'Donnell would plead for death a thousand times before she granted it to him. Still, there was no hurry. She had all the time in the world, she thought, smiling.

But he didn't.

CHAPTER 37

"I tried to get out of it," Rylee said, pacing the floor. "But I promised Mom we'd come by tonight for coffee and cake. She's been wanting to have you over for the last week and she just wouldn't take no for an answer.

Alex groaned. This was not going to end well.

"She's expecting us at six-thirty. You'll come, won't you?"

He hesitated a moment, then said, "Sure, love. I'll meet you there."

Rylee was a nervous wreck when she arrived at her parents. She paid the Uber driver, then stood on the curb, wondering how she would explain why Alex didn't eat or drink. Maybe she should call him and tell him not to come.

She found her mother in the dining room, putting the last of the good silver on the table.

"Wow, don't you look lovely," Margaret said, giving her a hug.

"What's all this?" Rylee asked, gesturing at the table.

"For dinner, of course. You didn't think I'd let you eat off paper plates, did you?"

"But...I thought we were just having coffee and cake?"

"Didn't you get my text? I decided to have dinner instead."

Rylee stared at her Mom, then pulled her phone out of her pocket. Sure enough, there was a text from her mother. How had she missed it? She glanced at the dining room table. The good china. The good silver. Her grandmother's crystal glassware. Mom's favorite tablecloth and matching napkins. Candles. Margaret had gone all out. "Where's Dad?"

"Working overtime, but he'll be here soon. Come on in the kitchen while I check the roast."

Rylee was about to call Alex and warn him when the doorbell rang. "I'll get it," she said. Hurrying into the living room, she opened the door. Alex looked fantastic in a pair of black slacks and a white, pullover sweater. He held a bouquet of pink carnations.

He grinned at the worried look on her face. "Still think this is a good idea?"

"Don't start. We've already got a problem. Mom fixed dinner."

"Just tell her we've already eaten."

"I'm not sure that will work."

"It's worth a try. Don't worry about it." He gave her a quick kiss, then followed her into the kitchen.

"Hi, Alex," Margaret said cheerfully. "I'm so glad you could come. "

"Thank you for inviting me, Mrs. Wagner. These are for you," he said, handing her the bouquet.

"That's so sweet of you," Margaret exclaimed. "I hope you're hungry."

Alex looked at Rylee, his gaze lingering on her throat. "Always."

Rylee and her mother had gone into the kitchen to do whatever last minute things had to be done, so that Alex was alone in the living room when Rylee's father got home.

He stood when Mr. Wagner entered the room.

For stretched seconds, the two men simply stared at each other, then her father excused himself to wash up before dinner.

It was going to be a fun evening, Alex thought, with a rueful shake of his head. It was obvious Rylee's old man didn't like him one bit. Why, he had no idea, unless it was just some kind of protective instinct all fathers had where their daughters were concerned. Or maybe he was one of those people who instinctively sensed danger when in the presence of vampires. Either way, it didn't bode well for the evening.

Margaret called them to dinner a few minutes later.

While her father blessed the food, Rylee slid a quick glance at Alex, who sat with his arms folded and his head bowed. She noticed he had managed to angle his chair away from the mirror over the sideboard.

Her nerves were on edge when her mother passed the platter of roast beef to Alex, who passed it on to Rylee without taking any.

"Don't you like roast?" Margaret asked.

"We already ate, Mom," Rylee said quickly. "But I've got room for a bite or two. It's been a long time since I had dinner at home." She glanced at Alex. "You don't know what you're missing."

They made small talk during dinner—the weather, the price of gas, the upcoming election.

"Looks good," Alex said, when Margaret dished up devil's food cake and vanilla ice cream for dessert. "But I'm afraid I'll have to pass. I'm diabetic."

Rylee grinned behind her hand.

"So, Alex, tell me about yourself," her father said. "Do you have family in the city?"

"No, sir. They live in Boston."

"Do you have siblings?" Margaret asked.

"Yes, a brother and a sister, although my brother passed away not long ago."

"Oh, I'm so sorry. I hope I'm not bringing up unhappy memories."

"Not at all."

"You said you were between jobs, as I recall," Mr. Wagner remarked. "What do you do when you *are* working?"

"I was a bounty hunter," Alex said flatly.

Wagner's eyes narrowed. "Were you good at it?"

"I took down my share."

"Did you bring them in alive?"

The question caught Alex off-guard. *Shit!*

"Well?"

"What do you think?" Alex asked, irritated by the man's tone and attitude.

"I think you're hiding something," her father said. "I've been a detective for over twenty years and a beat cop before that. I know when someone's skirting the truth."

Alex shrugged. "I'm sure I don't know what you mean."

Bristling, her father said, "I'm sure you do. If I ran your name though the department database, what would I find?"

"Not a thing."

"Uh-huh. Rylee, what do you know about this guy besides his name?"

"Dad…" She looked helplessly at her mother.

"Brian, that's enough." Margaret folded her napkin and placed it on the table. "Would anyone like some coffee?"

"That's not nearly enough, Meg. Rylee's our daughter. Our only child. I'm not going to let her marry some guy I don't know a damn thing about." Her father pushed away from the table. "Excuse me, I've got a few phone calls to make."

"Dad! Don't you dare!"

"I knew it!" He whirled around, a knowing gleam in his eye. "What is it? What's he hiding."

"I don't have a record," Alex said, his voice tight with anger. "I'm not a pimp or a drug lord. I don't rob little old ladies and I've never been arrested. Look all you want. You won't find a damn thing!"

"You insolent pup. Get out of my house."

Unable to help himself, Alex vanished from the room.

Margaret stared at the place where Alex had been seated, her eyes wide, her face pale.

"What the hell!" Brian stared at his daughter. "What just happened here? Where did he go? How the hell did he do that?"

Pushing away from the table, Rylee blurted, "It's easy, Dad. He's a vampire." Stunned silence followed her declaration. For a moment, she stood frozen, one hand clapped over her mouth, and then she hurried toward the front door.

"What?" her father roared. "Rylee, come back here!"

She ran out of the house and down the block, then paused on the corner, her gaze darting left and right. Where was Alex? Had he left her there? She ducked behind a bush when she heard her father call her name, breathed a sigh of relief when Alex emerged from the shadows.

"Good thing you don't need your parents' permission," he said dryly. "Let's get out of here."

He transported the two of them to a movie theater a few blocks away.

She was used to being whisked through time and space, Rylee thought when she opened her eyes. Her stomach wasn't churning, nor did she feel disoriented. Standing next to Alex, she called for a ride. "They'll be here in a few minutes. Will I see you tomorrow?"

"I'll get in touch as soon as I wake up."

"All right. I wish we could spend more than a few stolen moments together. Isn't there some place we can go where Magdalena can't find us?"

"I don't know. Costain's beach house might work. Or maybe a hotel in another city." Alex glanced over his shoulder as her ride pulled up to the curb. "I love you," he murmured as he drew her into his arms.

Rylee's eyelids fluttered down as his mouth slanted over hers. Right or wrong, she had made her choice. All she had to do now was convince her parents she's wasn't making the biggest mistake of her life.

"I love you," Alex murmured. "Dream of me."

"Always." She smiled as he caressed her cheek.

"Good night, love." He waited until she was safely inside the car before transporting himself back to the penthouse. Rylee loved him, he thought, and all was right with the world.

❧   ❧   ❧

Rylee had just walked in the door when her phone rang. She stared at the number, debating whether to answer it or not, but there was no point in putting it off. She took a deep breath, exhaled slowly, sat on the sofa, and said, "Hi, Dad."

"Are you out of your mind? Bringing that creature into our home?"

"Is Mom there?" she asked, kicking off her shoes. "Is she all right?"

"I doubt if your mother will ever be all right again. What the hell were you thinking?"

"I love him."

"Love," her father sneered. "He's a vampire."

"He wasn't always one."

"You can't marry him," her father said flatly. "I forbid it."

"I don't need your permission or your approval," Rylee said. "But I'd very much like both."

"It's never going to happen. Good Lord, don't you read the papers? Until a month or so ago, the police in Los Angeles were finding bodies drained of blood on the city streets. Dozens of bodies. I've seen a few of them with my own eyes and I can tell you it's not a pretty sight. Dammit, Rylee, for all you know, he's the one responsible."

"He's not like that!"

"How can you be so sure?"

"I just know," she said, and realized how lame that sounded. How childish.

"If you marry him, you're no longer my daughter."

"Brian!" Her mother's voice came over the extension. "You don't mean that!"

"I *do* mean it." There was a loud click as he hung up.

Rylee stared into the distance, unable to believe her ears. She had always been so close to her father, confided in him, looked up to him.

"Rylee, however did you meet a … a vampire?" her mother asked quietly.

"He wasn't a vampire when I met him, Mom. Just a guy."

"He's the man you mentioned before, isn't he? The one you met in L.A.?"

"Yes." As succinctly as possible, Rylee related how she had met Alex, how she'd tried to stay away from him. She neglected to mention Magdalena and Rhys. "What am I going to do about Dad?"

"I don't know, dear. I only hope you know what you're doing. Just remember, I love you, no matter what."

"I love you, too. Night, Mom."

Rylee fell back on the sofa, her thoughts troubled. How was she supposed to choose between the father she adored and the man she loved?

Rhys materialized beside Alex shortly after he reached the penthouse. "The course of true love never runs smooth," he remarked with a wry grin.

"Fat lot of help you are. Her folks are never going to accept me."

Rhys shrugged. "There are ways to arrange that. A suggestion planted here, a memory planted there."

"Forget it. I'm not going to mess with their minds."

"It's the easiest solution all the way around. If you don't tell Rylee about it, she'll never know."

Alex huffed a sigh, afraid that Costain was probably right.

CHAPTER 38

Alex rose, smiling, only to have it turn to a frown when he wondered if Rylee's parents had called her last night and talked her out of marrying him. He'd heard her tell his parents he was a vampire after he left the house.

He showered and dressed, then grabbed his phone.

She answered on the second ring, a smile in her voice. "Hi!"

"You sound a lot more cheerful than I thought you would. Have you talked to your Dad since last night?"

"Yes. He's…upset." An understatement, she thought.

"I'm not surprised."

"My mom thinks he'll come around." She decided not to mention her father's ultimatum.

"And if he doesn't?"

Rylee blew out a sigh, the hurt still fresh. "I don't want to talk about it."

Alex paused a moment, tempted to read her mind to discover what she was holding back, but decided against it. Changing the subject, he said, "So, what are your plans for the day? Or the night?"

"I'm just finishing up a shoot near Monterey and then I'm flying down to L.A. I have a meeting with Mr. Sommerville at eight and I can't put him off any longer. I need his business."

"Can't you do it over the phone?"

"Not this time. I should be done around nine."

"How about if I meet you afterwards, say at *La Mort Rouge?*"

"Do you think it's safe?"

"A hell of a lot safer than you running around alone in Monterey," he muttered. "I think we'll be all right. No one's seen or heard from Magdalena in months. No dead bodies in the city. Besides, it would be suicide for her to go anywhere near Rhys or his place."

Rylee hesitated a moment, then said, "Okay. I should be there around ten, ten-thirty."

"We can meet somewhere else, if you like."

"No, the club's fine." He was right, she thought. Magdalena would be a fool to confront them on Costain's turf.

"See you soon." Alex shoved his phone in his back pocket. He had plenty of time to hunt before Rylee arrived.

Rhys looked askance when Alex materialized inside the club. "What are you doing here? I thought you'd be curled up in my lair with the future Mrs. O'Donnell."

"Very funny. You know it's not safe for me go there. She's meeting me here later."

"Ah."

"Where do you think Magdalena's gone?"

"Beats the hell out of me. She's not in town. I'm sure of that."

"How do you know?"

"Intuition?"

"Why would she leave?"

Rhys shrugged. "Maybe things got too hot. I've never seen so many hunters in one town at the same time in my life. And that covers a lot of years."

"Well, I hope she stays gone."

"Don't count on it. No need for her to be in a hurry, you know. Barring accidents, she's got centuries to avenge her mate."

Centuries. Damn, Alex thought. He had never really considered that possibility. Sure, he knew vampires lived a long time, but he had never applied it to himself. What would he be like in a hundred years? Two? Three? What would the world be like? And then he frowned. Rylee might live another sixty years. Maybe seventy if she was lucky. It wasn't nearly long enough. He couldn't imagine his life without her.

He shook the gloomy thought from his mind when the door opened and Rylee stepped inside, bringing the scent of the night and the fragrance that was hers and hers alone.

She smiled when she saw him.

"Hey," he said. "I missed you."

"I missed you, too."

"Can I get you a drink?" Rhys asked.

"Not right now, thanks."

Rhys waved the bartender over. "If they change their mind, give them anything they want. It's on the house. Nice to see you again, Rylee. Room number six is free if you two want to be alone."

Alex glanced at Rylee. "What do you say?"

She took a quick look around, then nodded. It made her uncomfortable, knowing there were vampires in the club, but she'd have to get used to that, she thought. After all, Alex had a sister and a brother-in-law who were vampires. And then there was Rhys. And Megan.

Room number six looked just as she had imagined, Rylee thought when Alex opened the door for her. It was clean and neat, the furnishings simple but expensive, with a king-sized bed, a small mahogany table, muted lighting, and a bathroom. Nothing but the necessities.

"Have you heard anymore from your folks?" Alex asked, closing the door.

"The secret's out of the bag now. Disappearing from the living room like that left no doubt about what you are," Rylee said, and then she grinned. "Maybe I should have said you were a magician." Sobering, she said, "My father said he would disown me if I married you."

Shit "I don't want to come between you and your parents, love. Maybe you should think it over."

"That's all I've done since we met. I love my Dad, but I can't let him make my decisions for me. I'm not a little girl anymore."

"I'll say." Grinning, he sat beside her and drew her into his arms. "I love you, Rylee. I will always love you. But if you change your mind, I'll understand. I never want to cause you pain or unhappiness."

"I love you, too. My Dad will come around one of these days. Probably."

"And if he doesn't?"

"It's not all bad. My mother still loves me, no matter what." Cupping his face in her palms, she kissed him. "Everything will work out," she murmured. "You'll see."

"How long are you going to be in town?"

"I'm leaving in the morning."

Alex fell back on the bed and pulled her down on top of him. His gaze searched hers as his tongue swept across her lower lip and then he kissed her, long and slow and deep, again and again, until he was on fire for her. He groaned softly as his hunger sparked to life, ignited by her nearness and his desire for her. "Rylee?"

She heard the question in his voice, the need, and knew what he wanted. Murmuring assent, she lifted her hair away from her neck. His bite was ever so gentle, the heat of it pulsing through her in warm, sensual waves of pleasure.

It took every ounce of Alex's self-control to let her go. Easing her onto the mattress, he sat up. "Come on, let's go find an all-night movie or something. You're far too tempting and this bed is way too handy."

Laughing softly, she sat up and ran a hand over her hair. For the first time, she was sure that everything really *would* work out.

Summer gave way to fall and there were signs of Halloween everywhere—pumpkins and scarecrows, witches and fairies. And vampires, of course. As usual, along with decorations for All Hallow's Eve, there were copious decorations for Thanksgiving and Christmas in the stores, as well.

Rylee was swamped with job offers, which made the days pass quickly, but that was okay, because she lived for the nights and the hours she spent with Alex. For once, his being a vampire was a plus, since he could transport them anyplace they wanted to go—usually to hotels in other states, where she ordered room service for dinner and they spent the night watching movies and talking. The more time she spent with Alex, the more she loved him.

Her father remained cold and unrelenting. He refused to speak to her on the phone. Her mother assured her that, sooner or later, he would come around, but Rylee was beginning to doubt it.

The building contractor called in early November saying he wanted to meet her for a walk-through at the house the following morning. After agreeing on a time, she called Rhys.

"Hey, girl, what can I do for you?"

"I need a favor."

With Rhys acting as her bodyguard, Rylee met the contractor at the appointed time. The house was going to be perfect, she thought. With Magdalena in mind, she had taken the third little pig's advice and built her house of reinforced brick and concrete. Best of all, the builder was right on schedule and expected the house to be ready for occupancy near the end of the month.

"It's a nice place," Costain remarked after transporting then back to Granite Hills.

"Yes. I just hope I get to live in it before I'm old and gray."

Rhys chuckled. "Magdalena's bound to make a move sooner or later."

"I'm hoping for sooner. I feel like my whole life is on hold. Anyway, thanks for going with me."

"My pleasure," he said with a wink. "Hang in there, Rylee. You'll have your happy ending yet."

"I understand you're in a hurry to move into your new house," Alex said when she told him the news that night. "But it's not a good idea and you know it." They were curled up on the sofa in a hotel in Salt Lake City.

"I know. But I'm getting tired of traveling to a different place every night. And I'm sure Rhys would like to have his house back."

"I doubt that. They've taken up residence in some cozy hacienda he owns in Mexico."

"Mexico!" She started to say that was a long way to travel to *La Mort Rouge* and back but then she remembered that distance meant nothing to vampires. "How many houses does he have, anyway?"

"I think he's got three or four in the states, the one in Mexico, and another somewhere in Italy."

"Must be nice," she murmured and then, as Alex wrapped his arms around her, she forgot all about Costain and everything else.

In the nights that followed, Rylee took a cab to a different, designated place in the city and Alex met her there. Rylee made a game of deciding where they would go for the night. She gave each state a number and put the numbers in a bowl. Whichever state she drew was where they spent the evening. Alex picked the hotels. Although it would have been nicer if he could have come to the house in Granite Hills, it didn't really matter where they were, so long as they were together.

But always, no matter where they were, the threat of Magdalena was never far from her mind.

Chapter 39

"Guess what?" Rylee exclaimed as they settled onto the sofa in a New York City hotel room. "My house is almost finished! They installed the carpets and drapes this morning. All I need now are towels and dishes and bedding and furniture." And a wedding dress, she thought with a smile.

"Rylee…"

"I know, I know. It isn't safe for me to move in. But can't we at least go take a look at it?"

Alex grinned. She looked so eager, so excited, how could he refuse?

The following night, Rylee took a cab to a restaurant. She met Alex in the parking lot and he transported the two of them to her new house.

It was beautiful, she thought as they walked up the flagstone path. Fresh white paint covered the exterior, the trim was sage green, the front door a dark-red. She pictured how it would look once the lawn was in and there were flowers growing near the porch.

Feeling a sense of coming home, Rylee unlocked the door and stepped inside. Never before had she owned a brand new house, she mused as she switched on the light in the entry way. Glancing over her shoulder, she said, "Come in, Alex," and felt again that peculiar shimmer in the air as he crossed the threshold.

"Nice," he said, glancing around. The carpets and drapers were a light beige, the walls a slightly darker shade.

"I can't wait to go shopping for furniture. The sofa will go there," Rylee said, gesturing at the wall to the left. "Maybe a love seat and chair there. And a coffee table, of course." She hurried down the hallway to the master bedroom, which had a built-in fireplace and a large, walk-in closet.

Alex trailed behind her. There were two bedrooms on either side of a wide hallway. One room, which he assumed would be her office, had built-in shelves of various sizes. A window offered a view of the backyard.

He paused in the doorway of the master bedroom, one shoulder propped against the jamb, while she looked around, obviously pleased.

"Do you think we could go shopping?" she asked.

"If you make it quick."

Fortunately, she had a good idea of what she wanted and no trouble finding it. After arranging to have the furniture delivered, Alex transported them back to a café in San Francisco, stood beside her on the curb while they waited for her ride.

"I hate leaving you every night," he murmured. "Damn Magdalena. I wish she'd make her move and get it over with."

After Rylee was safely on her way to Granite Hills, Alex returned to Costain's building. He stood on the sidewalk, hands shoved in his pockets. It was too early to go to bed but not too late to hunt.

Leaving the apartment behind, he strolled down the sidewalk. Luck was with him and he found his prey in an alley lighting up a joint. He fed quickly and sent the young man on his way.

Alex stood there a moment then decided to take a walk around the block before returning to the penthouse. It seemed safe enough. There hadn't been any bodies drained of blood in months and as far as he knew, most—if not all—of the hunters had left town.

The streets were deserted, the night dark and quiet. Gray clouds hung low in the sky, promising rain before morning.

Alex didn't know what alerted him, but he whirled around in time to see a hunter creeping up behind him, stake in hand. Alex wasn't sure who was more surprised, and for a moment, neither of them moved. The guy was huge, with massive shoulders and legs like tree trunks. Hatred gleamed in his close-set eyes.

After the space of a heartbeat, the hunter lunged forward.

The guy was big, but he was slow. Alex swore as he ducked out of the way, then darted to the side. The hunter turned and charged at him again, one hand grabbing hold of Alex's coattail.

Alex quickly slid out of his jacket, then shot forward. Grabbing the Hulk by the neck, he called on every ounce of preternatural power he possessed and broke the man's neck with one, savage twist.

Rhys was beside him before the body hit the ground. "What the hell? I thought they'd all left town."

"Apparently one stayed behind."

"Apparently. You okay?"

"Yeah." Alex jerked his chin toward the body sprawled on the sidewalk. "What about him?"

"The cops will pick him up sooner or later," Rhys said with a shrug. "Let's get out of here."

Alex turned and headed back toward the penthouse.

Rhys fell into step beside him. "You and Rylee getting along all right?"

"So far, so good. Her new house is ready and she's anxious to move in. I'm getting tired of asking this, but have you heard anything about Magdalena?"

"Not a damn thing."

"You don't suppose some hunter took her head, do you?"

"I doubt it. I was on my way to a council meeting. Why don't you come along?"

Alex shrugged. He had nothing better to do, though he couldn't help wondering if Rhys had business with the council, or if he just met with them from time to time to weigh their loyalty. He didn't think any of them had the guts or the ability to defeat Rhys in battle, but there was always a chance. Few vampires liked being kept in subjugation to another, but there was safety in numbers and in being under the protection of a master vampire as old and powerful as Costain.

"As you probably know," Rhys said, taking his customary chair, "there's been no sign of Magdalena for months, which is troubling on several levels. Have any of you heard anything at all?"

"I think I might have seen her up in Portland last week," Julius said. "If it *was* her, she's going through the homeless population like a hungry wolf through a herd of sheep."

"And you waited until *now* to tell me! What the hell's the matter with you?"

Julius shrugged. "I..."

"Haul your ass back to Portland and keep an eye on her. And you'd better let me know damn quick if she heads back this way. What the hell are you waiting for? Get going."

Looking grateful to still be alive, Julius vanished from the room.

"Any other news?" Costain asked, his gaze settling on each member in turn.

One by one, the vampires shook their heads.

"You doing okay, Morris?"

The red-headed vampire shrugged. "I'm getting the hang of it."

"Come see me if you need help."

Morris nodded.

Rhys glanced around the room. "If there's nothing else, let's call it a night."

"Portland," Alex mused when the others had gone. "How long do you think she'll stay there?"

"For a while, I imagine," Rhys said with a grin. "Prowling among the homeless is like having smorgasbord every night. Come on, let's go home."

Chapter 40

In the week that followed, Rylee's days were hectic at best. When she finished her work for the day, she shopped—mostly online. She had never realized how many mundane things she used every day until they was gone—pot holders and dish soap, dryer sheets and hangers, a toaster and a can opener, hand soap, a shelf for the bathroom, toiletries—the list went on and on. Not to mention the need for new holiday decorations, indoors and out. The Amazon guy was at the door in Granite Hills practically every day. She was going to have quite a bit of baggage to haul to L.A when she finally moved into her new house.

But it was the hours she spent with Alex that she lived for. Each night, in one hotel or another, they snuggled together, getting to know each other better, talking about their future, sharing stories of their past.

They were on the sofa in an Arizona hotel now, with a fire burning in the hearth and the lights turned low.

Gazing at the flames, Rylee told him about her childhood and how she had hated taking piano lessons. "I wish now that I'd stay with it," she said, with a sigh. "Even though I had no real talent for it."

"It's never too late to learn," Alex said. Then, with a smile, he told her about the night he'd gone hunting with Daisy, and how she had broken into a vampire's lair and found the vampire stepping out of the shower and reaching for a towel. He grinned with the memory. "I don't know who was more surprised, the hunted or the hunter."

"I always wanted a brother or a sister," Rylee said wistfully. "Not so much when I was a little girl. It was fun being an only child then. My parents spoiled me something awful. But it would be nice to have siblings now that I'm older. Do you want children?" she asked, and then, remembering his loss, she wished she could call the words back. But it was too late.

Alex tensed beside her.

"I'm sorry," she said, "I didn't mean to bring up bad memories."

He sat up, hands clenched on his thighs.

"Alex?"

"Vampires can't reproduce," he said flatly. "I can't father a child."

At a loss for words, Rylee blinked at him.

"I should have told you sooner, but..." He shrugged. "With everything else going on, I never thought about it."

She never had, either. Somehow, she had just assumed that since he'd fathered one child, he could have another. It had never occurred to her that vampires couldn't have kids.

"Say something," he said, his voice tight.

"I don't know what to say."

"But it matters, doesn't it?" *Dammit, why hadn't he seen this coming?*

"It doesn't change the way I feel about you."

"But?"

"A lot of people can't have children, not just vampires."

"Rylee, be honest with me. Does this change anything between us?" He wouldn't blame her if she called off the wedding. She was young, in the prime of life. What right did he have to deprive her of the chance to raise a family?

"I won't deny that I want children," she said slowly, thoughtfully. "But there are a lot of babies out there who need homes. And there's always artificial insemination. Or maybe a miracle."

"The only miracle I believe in is you."

She smiled, touched by his words. "You haven't been a vampire very long," she mused. "Besides, maybe you can still father a child. You know, like some men are still fertile for a little while after a vasectomy."

"Don't count on it."

"I'm not, but we'll never know until we try."

Alex slipped his arm around her shoulders, his brow furrowed. What if she was right? What if there *was* a chance?

Rylee slid her hand under his shirt and ran her fingernails lightly up and down his chest. "You know, the longer we wait, the less likely it is to happen."

"Are you propositioning me, Miss Wagner?"

Surprising them both, she murmured, "It certainly sounds that way, Mr. O'Donnell."

"Hey, I'm ready now if you are."

"What happened to being married first?"

"I'm sure there's a minister or two in town," he said, then drew away, his gaze searching hers. "Are you serious about this?"

Rylee nodded. "I think we should just elope. I don't have any close friends in L.A. And my father isn't in any mood to walk me down the aisle." She shrugged. "I don't see any reason to spend a lot of money on a wedding, do you?"

"I don't need anybody there but the bride." "I'll cancel the arrangements in the morning."

"Are you sure?"

"Yes, very."

Pulling her into his arms, he crushed her close. "Just name the day and I'll be there."

They moved the date of the wedding up to the first of December. Rylee called her mother to let her know there'd been a change in plans. She had expected an argument, but none was forthcoming.

After making a few phone calls, Rylee found a non-denominational church that was available on that night. The guest list was short—Rhys and Megan, Daisy and Erik, Alex's parents and Rylee's mother, plus Debbie Strong and Connie Holden, two of Rylee's good friends from college.

In the morning, Rylee shopped online for a wedding dress. After checking several web sites, she found exactly what she wanted—a white satin gown with a square neck adorned with crystals, long, fitted sleeves, and a slim skirt. It was perfect. Knowing it was risky, she called a cab and went to the store to try it on, just in case it needed alterations.

Which it did.

She was smiling when she left the shop. In addition to the gown, she'd bought a sheer white nightgown and peignoir, a pair of lacy bikini panties and a matching bra. All she needed now were shoes.

Giddy with anticipation, she called a cab and headed back to Costain's house.

She paid the driver, then hurried up the porch steps, only to pause when she saw an envelope taped to the front door. Frowning, she slipped it into her jacket pocket, unlocked the door, and stepped inside.

Dropping the packages on the sofa, Rylee opened the envelope and withdrew a single sheet of paper. She felt the blood drain from her face as she read the message once and then again. Five short words in bold black letters.

I KNOW WHERE YOU LIVE

With a wordless cry, she sank down on the sofa.

Magdalena had found her.

Alex stirred as Rylee's cry penetrated the dark sleep. Bolting upright, he reached out to her with his mind. Then, sensing her distress, he pulled on his pants and a shirt and materialized at her side. "What's wrong?"

She thrust a sheet of paper into his hands.

He read it, then crumpled the note and tossed it into the fireplace.

"You shouldn't be here," she said dully.

"I don't think it matters now. She knows where you are." He shook his head in exasperation. "How the devil did she find you?"

"What difference does it make?"

"None, I guess." But it bothered him just the same. He'd taken every precaution he could think of. Where had he failed?

"What if she burns this place down, too?"

"That's the least of my worries." Dammit! They'd been so careful. Thank goodness Magdalena hadn't been able to breach Costain's wards or she would have been inside, waiting.

Rylee leaned into Alex, needing his strength. She felt weak for being so frightened and yet who wouldn't be afraid when they were being stalked by a vengeful vampire? "What are we going to do?"

"Remember when I took you out to dinner awhile back and you thought Costain was using you as bait?"

She nodded.

"Maybe he was. I think he was hoping to draw Magdalena out, and right now I believe that's our best chance of catching her."

Rylee looked up at him, wide-eyed. "I think so, too." Scared or not, it was time to end this. She was tired of being forced to stay inside, angry because she had a brand new house and she couldn't even live in it, tired of always looking over her shoulder, wondering if Magdalena or one of her minions was lurking in the shadows. Enough was enough!

"We'll go back to the restaurant on the pier tomorrow night," Alex said, thinking out loud. "If she shows up, we'll lure her down to the beach. I'll ask Rhys to come along. In his mist form, she won't be able to sense his presence. If she takes the bait, we'll have her once and for all."

He hoped.

Alex decided to spend the night with Rylee. Now that Magdalena knew where Rylee was, there was no way he was going to leave her alone. And if the vampire showed up, he could transport Rylee to safety, if necessary.

He called his sire after Rylee went to bed and they agreed to meet at the pier at nine the next night.

Rylee was a nervous wreck as she dressed the following evening. Doubts plagued her. Maybe this *wasn't* such a good idea. Maybe Rhys and Alex couldn't defeat Magdalena. Maybe the vampire would be the victor and Alex and Rhys would pay the price. There was no way to guarantee the outcome, Rylee thought. No way to guarantee that she, herself, would escape unscathed.

Of course Alex, being Alex, he knew what she was thinking.

"We don't have to go through with this, love. I'll call Rhys and –."

"No! It's never going to get any easier." But even as she insisted they go that night, she couldn't help hoping Magdalena wouldn't show up.

Alex asked for a table by the window. Rylee ordered shrimp that she knew she wouldn't eat, he ordered a glass of Pinot Noir.

Rylee glanced around. "Can you tell where Rhys is?"

"No."

Rylee bit down on her lower lip. They had driven to the beach in the Jag. She didn't ask why, but she suspected it was so she would have a way to get home if Rhys or Alex couldn't take her. When they arrived at the pier, Rhys stayed outside.

She picked at her dinner when it arrived, thinking how silly it had been to order a meal when she had no appetite. Her stomach was in knots, she flinched at every sound.

Rylee felt a rush of unease when Alex turned his head to the side and then frowned as if someone had just given him bad news. He nodded once, his gaze darting around the room, then out the window.

"What is it?" she asked anxiously. "What's going on?"

"Magdalena's here."

"She is?" Her voice emerged in a terrified squeak.

"Finish your dinner."

Rylee shook her head, knowing she would never be able to swallow past the lump in her throat.

"All right." Alex signaled for the check and signed the receipt. "When we get outside, we're going to walk to the end of the pier and take the stairs down to the beach. Rhys will be right behind us. It's pretty windy tonight. That should keep most people indoors. You stay close to me and when I tell you to, you run like hell back to the car and get out of here as fast as you can. Don't go back to Granite Hills. Find a hotel and stay there until you hear from me."

Rylee nodded, wishing she could stay in the relative safety of the restaurant and let Alex and Rhys confront the vampire. But if she did that, Magdalena would surely suspect a trap. Or worse, storm the restaurant and kill everyone in the place.

Reaching into his jacket pocket, Alex withdrew a sharp wooden stake and offered it to her. "Just in case."

Rylee hesitated a moment before taking it.

Reaching into another pocket, Alex said, "And this," and handed her a small bottle of what looked like ordinary water.

She didn't have to ask what it was or what it did. She had already seen the effects of holy water on preternatural flesh. As they left the restaurant, she tucked the bottle into her handbag and hid the stake inside her coat.

A chill breeze ruffled Rylee's hair as they walked to the end of the pier and down the short flight of stairs toward the shore. But it wasn't the cold that had her shivering, it was the thought of facing Magdalena again.

As casually as she could, she glanced around, but there was no sign of the vampire. No sign of Rhys, either. As Alex had predicted, they were alone on the beach save for one old man fishing from the shore near the restaurant. A thick gray haze added to the chill and made it difficult to see more than a few yards ahead.

They had left the pier far behind when Rylee felt an odd sensation crawl along her skin. Before she could remark on it, Magdalena appeared out of nowhere. With a shrill scream, the vampire hurtled toward Alex.

It happened so fast, Rylee barely had time to register what was happening. She stared, transfixed, as the two vampires battled one another, let out a startled cry when Rhys appeared beside her. "Do something!" she exclaimed.

"This is his fight. I'm just here as backup. Come on," Rhys said, taking her by the arm, "Change of plans, I'm taking you to the penthouse. You'll be safe there."

"You're leaving him? What if he needs you?"

"I'll be back before he knows I'm gone."

Tempted as she was, Rylee shook her head. "I'm staying." Twisting out of Costain's grasp, she dropped the stake onto the sand. Reaching into her handbag, she withdrew the bottle of holy water, and tossed her purse aside.

Rhys grinned wryly. The girl had grit, he mused. He'd give her high marks for that.

Rylee watched in open-mouthed fascination as the battle raged on. And on. Claws and fangs ripped through preternatural flesh yet the wounds healed before her eyes. Dark-red blood stained their hands, their faces, sprayed over the sand at their feet, yet the fight went on.

Rylee frowned. With their preternatural strength, it occurred to her that neither was likely to tire. Injuries didn't slow them down, which meant the battle might last for hours if neither inflicted a fatal wound.

The thought had no sooner crossed her mind than Magdalena's nails tore a deep gash across Alex's stomach. Dark red blood oozed from the wound.

Rhys took a step forward but Rylee's attention was focused on Magdalena. Without thinking of her own safety, she uncapped the bottle, darted forward, and hurled the contents in Magdalena's face.

The vampire let out a hideous shriek as the liquid splashed over her cheeks and trickled down her neck and chest. Enraged, fangs bared, she lunged toward Rylee, who scrambled backward, only to trip over a large pierce of driftwood.

Rhys darted after the vampire, only to be shoved out of the way by Alex, who hissed, "She's mine!" as his hand closed over Magdalena's shoulder. In a blur of movement, he scooped up the stake Rylee had dropped, and drove it into Magdalena's back.

The vampire let out a high-pitched wail of pain and outrage as the wood pierced the center of her heart. Eyes wild with disbelief, she stood there a moment and then spiraled slowly to the ground and lay still.

Rylee felt her stomach churn as the body slowly disintegrated until nothing remained but ashes, and then they, too, were gone, swept out to sea by the outcoming tide.

Gagging, Rylee dropped to her knees and turned her head to the side as nausea roiled through her.

Alex knelt beside her. "Are you all right?"

Rylee nodded, though she wasn't sure she would ever be all right again. And then she remembered that he had been horribly wounded. Hardly daring to look, she risked a glance at him. The gash was still bleeding, still deep. Why hadn't it healed like the rest of his injuries?

"Go home, Rylee," he said, his voice tight and laced with pain. "You'll be safe there now."

"No!"

"Go…home."

She shook her head, determined to stay, until Rhys took hold of her arm and lifted her to her feet.

"You can't do anything here," Costain said. "Go home and wait. I'll take care of Alex."

She stared at him, mutinous. "You'll call me if…?"

He nodded.

Rylee blinked back her tears as she watched Rhys cradle Alex in his arms and disappear from sight.

Heavy-hearted, she found her handbag, then plodded down the beach toward the pier. Sliding behind the wheel of the Jag, she wondered if she would ever see Alex again.

"Stay with me, kid," Rhys said.

Alex groaned as Rhys laid him on a smooth stretch of sand.

Rhys swore softly. He had hoped to get back to the penthouse, but there wasn't time. Blood continued to leak from the ragged wound, which should have healed over by now.

"Help is on the way," Rhys promised. After biting into his wrist, he held it to Alex's mouth. "Drink."

"Where's…Rylee?"

"She's fine. You need to drink. Now."

Alex closed his eyes, sighed as he swallowed his sire's ancient blood. It moved through him like liquid fire, burning away the pain. It was like nothing else in all the world, and yet, he wished it was Rylee's blood coursing through his veins, chasing away the cold.

"Rylee." He whispered her name as he fell into oblivion.

Rhys stared at the wound. There was no change. "Shit!" Lifting Alex into his arms, he transported them to the penthouse, then sent a message to Daisy. *I need you.*

Daisy knew a moment of panic when she read Costain's message.

"What is it?" Erik asked. "What's wrong?"

"I don't know. Rhys needs me."

"That can't be good," Erik muttered. "I'll come with –."

But she was already gone.

Daisy materialized in Costain's penthouse. The scent of fresh blood drew her toward the bedroom. She paused in the doorway to stare at Alex, who lay as still as death on the bed. A blood-stained sheet covered him from the waist down. "What's happened?"

"I have no idea. I was hoping you could tell me."

"How should I know?"

"Magdalena found us. They fought. She ripped a hole in his stomach. If he was human, he'd be dead now." Rhys lifted the sheet. "As you can see, it's not healing. I've never seen anything like it before. I mean, it's deep, but not that deep. My blood should have healed him."

She wrinkled her nose as she moved closer to the bed. "*Dragedrepe*," she murmured. "No wonder he hasn't healed."

Rhys shook his head. "I don't smell anything."

"It's an ancient Norwegian poison. The name means dragon slayer."

"Poison! What the hell?"

"It's very rare. Most vampires can't detect it, but I've seen it used by hunters. Magdalena must have dipped her hands in it."

"The other wounds healed. Why not this one?"

"Cuts and scratches and bites are just surface wounds. The poison has to penetrate deeper than that."

Rhys stared at the bloody sheet, his brow furrowed. "Is there an antidote?"

"Yes, but I don't know where you can find it, unless you know an Elf."

"An Elf?" *What the hell?*

"It's Elf magic."

Sylvi. "Stay here. I'll be back as soon as I can."

"Where are you –?"

But she was talking to empty space.

Rylee paced the floor. She had stopped at the first motel she'd seen. There was no way she was going home to L.A. Not now. She wanted to be close by in case…well, in case they needed her. Unable to rest, unable to think of anything but Alex, she paced back and forth. Why hadn't the wound in his belly healed? The others had. Was he all right? Was he…she refused to even think the word.

She paced for another five minutes, then grabbed her phone and called him.

It rang several times and then a woman answered.

"Who is this?" Rylee asked.

"It's Daisy. Rylee, is that you?"

"Yes. How's Alex?"

"Not good, I'm afraid."

"I need to be there."

"Where are you?" After listening to Rylee's directions, she said, "I'm on my way."

Rylee had barely ended the call when Daisy knocked on the door.

CHAPTER 41

A horrified gasp escaped Rylee's lips when she saw Alex. His face was beyond pale. He wasn't breathing. The sheet that covered him was wet with blood. She prayed that he was only resting and not…

She shook her head. He couldn't be dead. She would feel it if he was. But it was still dark outside. Why wasn't he awake?

"Where's Rhys?" she asked. "Shouldn't he be here?"

"He's gone off to find an Elf."

"An…an Elf?"

"We need an antidote."

"An antidote? From an Elf?" Rylee stared at Alex's sister. Vampires were one thing, but Elves? Was she dreaming?

With a nod, Daisy quickly explained what had happened.

"What if Rhys doesn't get back in time?"

"He will," Daisy said adamantly. "He has to."

Rylee blinked back tears as she sat on the edge of the bed. Closing her eyes, she took Alex's hand in hers. "Don't leave me," she murmured. "Please, don't leave me."

Minutes that seemed like hours crawled by. Daisy lifted the sheet that covered him to check the wound. Bile stung Rylee's throat as she glanced at the hideous gash in his belly. Blood—thick and so dark it was almost black—continued to seep from the ugly wound. The skin around the edges looked like it was rotting.

He was going to die, Rylee thought, and there was nothing any-one could do to stop it. She stilled when his hand squeezed hers. *Blood.* Her head jerked up when she heard his voice in her mind, as clearly as if he had spoken aloud. And then she heard it again. *Need. Blood.*

Did he mean hers? "Daisy?"

"What?"

"I heard his voice. In my head. Saying he needs blood."

"He means yours," Daisy said.

"But…you're a vampire. Wouldn't yours be better?"

"No. We rarely drink from each other."

"Alex drinks from Rhys."

"That's different."

"Why? Because Rhys is his sire?"

"And because he's a master vampire. But in this case, I think the mortal kind might work better."

Rylee glanced at her arm, then held it out to Daisy.

Smiling faintly, Daisy bit into Rylee's wrist, just deep enough to draw blood. "Hold it to his mouth. Alex will do the rest."

Rylee did as bidden, trying not to be sick as she watched her blood drip onto his lips. One drop, two, and he reached for her arm, his mouth fastening onto her wrist as though he would never let go. Feeling a sudden panic, she looked at Daisy. "You won't let him take too much?"

"No."

It was the oddest sensation, having him drink from her arm. True, he had taken her blood before, but it had seemed sort of romantic when he nibbled on her neck, filling her with a sensual pleasure. There was nothing the least bit romantic about this. She was not lover now, but prey.

Just when she thought he would never stop, he released his grip on her arm. Hoping for a miracle, she glanced at the wound in his abdomen, but it looked no better than before.

Where was Rhys? What was taking him so long?

Costain knocked on the door of an apartment in the Village. The Elf hadn't been kidding when she said she wanted to get as far away from Los Angeles as she could, he mused.

"Sylvi! I know you're in there." He pounded on the door again. "Dammit, open this door or I'll break the damn thing down!"

He heard the sound of cautious footsteps, the turn of a lock, and the door opened.

"What do you want?" she asked. "Do you know what time it is?"

"I need your help."

Yawning behind her hand, she gestured for him to enter.

"My friend is dying," Rhys said curtly. "Your former mistress attacked him tonight. Apparently, she had some kind of poison coating her hands."

"*Dragedrepe.* She's used it before."

"What's the antidote?"

She hesitated a moment and he knew she was thinking of refusing to answer.

Rhys summoned his power until it filled the room. "You owe me a favor, remember?"

"I remember. How long ago was he hurt?"

"Twenty, thirty minutes. Does it matter?"

"Yes. You still have time, but not much. You need the blood of a friend, the blood of an enemy, and the tears of a loved one."

Rylee guessed she was getting used to vampires coming and going when she didn't even blink when Rhys appeared in the room with a young woman in tow. He didn't waste time with introductions except to say, "This is Sylvi."

"I need a glass," the woman said.

Daisy didn't ask why, just left to get one. She looked at Rhys askance when she returned and offered it to the woman.

"The blood of a friend," Sylvi said, looking at Rhys. "I assume that's you?"

"Yeah." He bit deep into his wrist and held it over the glass.

"That's enough," Sylvi said, when the glass was about a third full. "The blood of an enemy?" She glanced at Daisy and Rylee.

Rhys cursed volubly. "How much do you need?"

"Not much."

"I'll be right back."

Rylee glanced at Daisy. "Where's he going?"

"I have no idea."

He returned a few moments later, a blood-stained stake in his hand.

Sylvi shuddered. "Is that…?"

"The stake that destroyed Magdalena. Daisy, get me some water."

She quickly did as bidden, then watched as Rhys dipped the bloody end of the stake into the water, which quickly turned dark-red.

"That might do," Sylvi said, and poured the contents into the other glass. "Tears of a loved one?"

"Mine," Rylee said. It took little effort to summon her tears. Blinking rapidly, she added them to the mix.

Sylvi murmured a few words in a foreign language and as she did so, the bloody water hissed and boiled and turned black. When it settled, she lifted Alex's head and held the glass to his lips.

"Drink!" Rhys commanded.

Alex took a swallow, grimaced, and then gulped it down.

"What now? How will we know if it worked?" Rylee asked, then let out a cry of mingled joy and relief when Alex opened his eyes.

"Rylee?"

"I'm here!" Laughing and crying, she threw her arms around him.

"We're even now, Costain," Sylvi said. "Take me home."

"Thank you!" Daisy exclaimed. "If there's ever anything I can do…"

"Not necessary," Sylvi said. "I want nothing more to do with vampires."

Grinning, Rhys wrapped one arm around her waist and they vanished from the room.

"What happened?" Alex frowned when he saw the bloody sheet that covered him.

Rylee's gaze searched his. "Don't you remember?"

"I remember staking Magdalena…" He took a deep, shuddering sigh. It was over. Paula and the baby had been avenged at last. "After that…" He shook his head. "I don't remember a thing."

"She had some kind of poison on her hands," Rylee explained. "It kept you from healing and then you passed out, or whatever vampires do. Rhys went after an Elf, hoping she'd know the antidote. Lucky that she did."

"It tasted vile," Alex said, grimacing. "But it did the trick. What the hell was in it?"

"Some blood and the tears of a loved one."

Lifting his hand, he wiped a single tear from her cheek. "They must have been yours. And the blood?"

"Some was Costain's. And some was Magdalena's."

"A friend and an enemy." Alex glanced at Daisy. "We've seen this before, haven't we?"

"Yes." She shuddered with the memory Years ago, during a hunt, they had found a vampire dying from the same poison. They hadn't known about the antidote back then. Alex had staked the vampire to put him out of his misery.

Alex grunted softy as he swung his legs over the edge of the bed. "Good thing you were here, Daisy Mae. They never would have known about the antidote without you."

"It was a close call," Daisy said, throwing her arms around him. "We almost lost you."

"Naw, he's too mean to die," Rhys said, materializing in the room. "Now that all the excitement's over, I'm going home. I've spent enough time away from my woman."

"I guess I'll go, too," Daisy said, sending Alex a knowing wink. "Keep in touch."

Moments later, Rhys and Daisy were gone.

"Alone at last," Alex murmured.

Rylee nodded, her mind whirling. So much had happened so fast, she didn't know what to think, what to feel. Vampires and Elf magic. Life and death.

"Rylee?"

"Hmm?"

"I seem to be asking this all the time, but…"

She pressed her fingers to his lips, and then kissed him. "Yes," she said, "In spite of vengeful vampires and never knowing what bizarre things might happen from one day to the next, I still want to marry you. But right now, you need to take a shower."

A week later, Rylee stood in front of the mirror in the bride's dressing room, her heart pounding with nervous excitement. She was getting married! She had asked Daisy to be her maid of honor; Alex had asked Rhys to be best man.

"You look beautiful, dear," her mother said as she straightened Rylee's veil. "Like an angel."

"Thanks, Mom."

"Are you sure about this? It's not too late to change your mind. Maybe take a little more time to think it over."

"I'm sure." Rylee squeezed her mother's hand. "I know you're worried about me and you don't approve, but I love you for being here." It hurt that her father still refused to speak to her, that he wouldn't bend enough to walk her down the aisle. "Alex is so good to me, Mom. I know you don't trust him, but he's kind and sweet and he's not at all the way you think he is. He's not a killer. He's never hurt me. I know in my heart that this was meant to be."

Blinking back her tears, Margaret took her daughter in her arms and hugged her close. "I'll always be on your side," she said. "If you ever need me, or need anything, I'll be there."

"I know," Rylee said, smiling through tears of her own.

A knock at the door, and Daisy's voice asking if they were ready.

"We are," Rylee said resolutely.

Because her father had disowned her, Rylee had asked her mother to walk her down the aisle. Now, as they followed Daisy toward the altar, Rylee had eyes only for Alex. Never had he looked so handsome. Or so deliciously sexy.

Her heart skipped a beat when he winked at her.

Standing beside Alex, Rhys also looked quite resplendent in an Armani tux.

When they reached the altar, the minister asked, "Who giveth this woman to this man?"

Her voice thick with emotion, Margaret Wagner said, "I do," as she placed Rylee's hand in Alex's.

"We are gathered here this evening to join this man and this woman in holy matrimony. Marriage is a sacred covenant, not to be entered into lightly. Alexander O'Donnell, do you take Rylee Wagner to be your lawfully wedded wife? Will you love her, cherish her, and keep yourself only for her as long as you both shall live?"

"I will."

"Rylee Wagner, do you take Alexander O'Donnell to be your lawfully wedded husband? Will you love him, cherish him, and keep yourself only for him as long as you both shall live?"

"I will."

"I understand you wish to exchange rings," the minister said. "The circle is an ancient representation of eternity. As such, wedding rings are a symbol of a love that has no end. Alex?"

Taking the wedding band from his pocket, Alex murmured, "I will love you forever and ever," as he slipped the ring on her finger.

"And I will love you all the days of my life and throughout eternity," Rylee said, blinking away tears of joy as she slipped a heavy gold band into place.

"By the power vested in me, I now pronounce you, Rylee and Alexander, husband and wife, legally and lawfully joined together. Alexander, you may kiss your bride."

As if she were made of glass, Alex carefully lifted Rylee's veil. Murmuring, "Always and forever," he drew his wife into his arms and kissed her.

Rylee hated for that kiss to end, but their guests swarmed around them, offering hugs and congratulations.

She had met Alex's parents briefly before the wedding. Both had welcomed her to the family. They hugged her now, insisting they come for a visit as soon as possible.

Rylee had decided against a formal reception, since half the guests couldn't eat or drink anything other than wine. Instead, they dropped in at the best nightclub in town where Rhys toasted the bride and groom with a cabernet that cost three hundred and fifty dollars a bottle.

"Where are you going for your honeymoon?" Connie asked.

"We haven't decided yet," Rylee said. "Tonight we're just going home."

"I wish you every happiness," Debbie said. Leaning forward, she whispered, "Girl, you are *so* lucky. Alex is gorgeous. If you ever get tired of him, give me a call."

"No way," Rylee said. "He's all mine. Forever."

Later, after Connie and Debbie had left for home, Rhys handed Alex an envelope. "I'm not good at buying wedding gifts," he said, "so I'm giving you the Jag, even though I won the bet."

"I don't know what to say. You love that car."

"Not to worry, Alex," Megan said. "He's already bought himself a shiny new red one."

Alex grinned as he slipped the envelope into his coat pocket. "I'll take good care of it."

"See that you do," Rhys said. "It's parked outside."

"Erik and I didn't know what to buy you, either," Daisy said, "so we bought you an all-expense paid trip to Barrow, Alaska."

"It's dark there from November to January," Erik said with a grin. "Lots of long winter nights. Don't forget to send us a postcard if you can find the time."

"Your mom and I are just giving you cash," Noah O'Donnell said. "Spend it wisely, son."

Rylee blinked back a tear as Alex's mother hugged her.

"If you ever need anything," Mrs. O'Donnell whispered, "anything at all, please let me know. You've made our happy when I was afraid he'd never smile again."

When Irene turned away to speak to Daisy, Rylee looked for Alex. He was standing a short distance away, talking to her mother. Curious, she drifted in that direction, hoping to overhear what they were saying.

Pretending to be watching Erik and Daisy on the dance floor, she eavesdropped on the conversation.

"Welcome to the family, Alex," her mother was saying. "I can't say that I approve of this marriage, but I can see that you love my daughter and she loves you. Be kind to one another."

"I'll take good care of her, Mrs. Wagner. I promise."

Not long after that, Alex and Rylee slipped out the side door.

"I can't believe Rhys gave you his car," Rylee said as they drove to her new home. "What bet was he talking about?"

"When I sent you away, I was afraid you'd never forgive me. Rhys was sure I could win you back if I admitted I'd been a damn fool and begged for your forgiveness. I told him I didn't think it would be that easy and he said if you turned me down, he'd give me the Jag."

"And he gave it to you, even though he won? He must really like you."

"Yeah, I guess."

Rylee felt as if a million butterflies had taken wing in the pit of her stomach when Alex carried her across the threshold and into their bedroom.

"Welcome home, Mrs. O'Donnell," he said.

She glanced around as he set her on her feet. A bottle of wine and two crystal goblets waited on the table beside the bed. Vases filled with flowers were on every available surface. Hundreds of fragrant rose petals were spread across the quilt. "Did you do all this?"

He nodded.

"When did you have time?"

"While you were at the church getting dressed. Mom helped me."

"I love you, my husband," she said, slipping her arms around his waist.

"I love you more, my wife," he said, his voice husky. "So much more than you'll ever know. I'll try to make you happy."

"You already make me happy." She smiled up at him as she slid his jacket over his shoulders and tossed it on the chair in the corner. "Don't you think it's time we tried out our new bed?"

"Past time, I would say." Removing her veil, he laid on top of his jacket.

Gazing into each other's eyes, they took turns undressing each other down to their underwear.

Rylee felt her cheeks grow hot when she saw the evidence of his desire. She had never been intimate with a man, and although she had come close a few times in college, she had always backed away. She frowned, feeling suddenly jealous of Alex's first wife, and how wrong was that?

Drawing her close, Alex murmured, "I've never loved anyone else the way I love you. You are and always will be the love of my life and the wife of my heart."

His words brought tears to her eyes but when he lifted her into his arms and laid her gently on the mattress, everything that had happened before this night ceased to matter. He loved her, of that she had no doubt, and she loved him, body and soul.

"I asked Rhys about a baby," Alex whispered as he caressed her. "He said he'd never heard of that happening, but that anything is possible."

Rylee's eyelids fluttered down as he rained featherlight kisses over her face, breasts, and belly. "I believe in miracles," she whispered. How could she not, when this incredible man loved her?

She gasped as his clever hands aroused her to fever pitch.

And then, as Alex rose over her, there was no more time for thought, only sensation after sensation as he carried her away to a world where there was room only for two.

Epilogue

18 Years Later

Rylee stood naked in front of the bathroom mirror, turning this way and that. Thanks to drinking a little of Alex's blood every year, no one would ever guess she was over forty years old. The lines on her face were faint, her body still firm and slim.

The last eighteen years of her life had been wonderful. To the astonishment of everyone in the family, she had given birth to a healthy little girl. Not only was Miranda a miracle baby, her birth had performed a miracle on Rylee's father, who had swallowed his pride and apologized for his past behavior, all so he could hold his first, and likely only, grandchild.

Miranda had grown up to be a strong, independent young woman. She had graduated from high school a few months ago and gone off to college in New York City.

Rylee and Alex had told their daughter the truth about her father when she was old enough to understand and keep his secret.

Rylee had been a stay-at-home mom until Miranda was old enough for kindergarten, and then she had returned to her love of photography. In the intervening years, she had become quite well-known, and had even won a few local and national awards.

Tonight, she was going to pursue an adventure of another kind.

She glanced over her shoulder as Alex came up behind her. He wore only a pair of black briefs and a smile.

Slipping his arms around her waist, he nuzzled her neck. "Are you ready?"

She looked at her reflection in the mirror. Was she?

"You don't have to do this, love."

She turned in his arms, her gaze moving over his face. He looked exactly the same as he had the night they'd met. And while she didn't look to be in her forties, she didn't look like she was in her twenties, either. "I want to."

"You're sure? There's no going back."

"You've never done this before," she remarked thoughtfully. "Are you sure you know how?"

"Not really. That's why I alerted Rhys. He'll be here in a heartbeat if I need him."

Rylee had grown quite fond of the Master of the West Coast vampires. It was comforting to know he was on call should anything go wrong. "Let's do it."

Hand-in-hand, they kissed their way into the bedroom. Rylee grinned as she looked around. While she'd been bathing, Alex had filled the room with flowers. Candles provided a soft, warm glow. He had turned down the covers on the bed and sprinkled the sheets with rose petals. It reminded her of their wedding night.

"Any questions before we begin?" he asked, gathering her into his arms.

"Will it hurt?"

"Not at all."

She blew out a sigh, kissed his cheek, then stretched out on the mattress.

Alex removed his briefs, then drew her into his arms again.

Feeling giddy and a little anxious, she ran her hands over him, loving the way her touch aroused him, the low growl that rumbled low in his throat as they kissed and caressed. They had been married for years, yet every time they made love was as wonderful and exciting as the first time.

When she was on fire for him, he buried himself deep within her, carrying her over the edge to completion. She cried his name as wave after wave of pleasure coursed through her.

And then, while she was still caught up in the aftermath of their love-making, he bit her. But tonight was not like any other night. Tonight, as he had so often yearned to do when he'd been a new vampire, he drank to his heart's content, drank until she was at the point of death. He knew a moment of panic as her heartbeat grew faint and the color faded from her cheeks. Had he taken too much? Biting into his wrist, he fed her his blood.

Relief washed through him as the color returned to her cheeks, her breathing slowed, her body relaxed.

Everything's okay, fledgling. Costain's voice sounded in his mind. *Well done.*

Alex slipped an arm around Rylee's shoulders, pulled the sheet over the two of them and drew her close to his side. When she woke tomorrow night, she would be a new vampire. She would see the world as if for the first time. And he would be there to share it with her.

Time no longer had any meaning, he thought as he brushed a kiss across her cheek.

Tomorrow night, they would begin a new life together. But best of all, she would be his now and forevermore.

~ finis ~

About the Author

Amanda Ashley started writing for the fun of it. Her first book, a historical romance written as Madeline Baker, was published in 1985. Since then, she has published numerous historical and paranormal romances and novellas, many of which have appeared on various bestseller lists, including the *New York Times* Bestseller List and *USA Today*.

Amanda makes her home in Southern California, where she and her husband share their house with a Pomeranian named Lady, a cat named Kitty, and a tortoise named Buddy.

For more information on her books, please visit her websites at
www.amandaashley.net
and
www.madelinebaker.net
Email: darkwritr@aol.com

About the Publisher

This book is published on behalf of the author by the Ethan Ellenberg Literary Agency.
https://ethanellenberg.com
Email: agent@ethanellenberg.com